NO ONE CAN TELL A TRUE CRIME STORY QUITE LIKE A REAL-LIFE DETECTIVE

JOHN DILLMANN spent eighteen years with the New Orleans Police Department and was involved in over five hundred homicide investigations. He has been awarded the New Orleans Medal of Merit for bravery an unprecedented five times, and now heads a private investigating firm.

PRAISE FOR JOHN DILLMANN'S *UNHOLY MATRIMONY:*

"A HAYMAKER OF A STORY—BOILING WITH GREED, PERVERSION AND INHUMANITY . . . THE READER WILL BE RIVETED TO EACH PAGE." —*Kirkus*

"BRINGS NEW MEANING TO THE PHRASE 'IN COLD BLOOD' . . . The simple prose and straightforward reporting lend *Unholy Matrimony* a miasma of horror that a more emotional narration could never supply." —*Cosmopolitan*

"A SUSPENSEFUL TALE . . . THE TRIAL PROVIDES AN UNEXPECTED SHOCKER."
—*Publishers Weekly*

D1024027

Berkley Books by John Dillmann

**UNHOLY MATRIMONY: A True Story
of Murder and Obsession**

**THE FRENCH QUARTER KILLERS: The Story
of the Protected Witness Murders**

THE FRENCH QUARTER KILLERS

THE STORY OF THE PROTECTED WITNESS MURDERS

JOHN DILLMANN

B
BERKLEY BOOKS, NEW YORK

This Berkley book contains the complete
text of the original hardcover edition.
It has been completely reset in a typeface
designed for easy reading and was printed
from new film.

THE FRENCH QUARTER KILLERS

A Berkley Book/published by arrangement with
Macmillan Publishing Company

PRINTING HISTORY
Macmillan edition published 1987
Berkley edition/August 1989

ISBN: 0-425-11685-9

A BERKLEY BOOK ® TM 757,375
Berkley Books are published by The Berkley Publishing Group,
200 Madison Avenue, New York, NY 10016.
The name "BERKLEY" and the "B" logo
are trademarks belonging to Berkley Publishing Corporation.

PRINTED IN THE UNITED STATES OF AMERICA

10 9 8 7 6 5 4 3 2 1

*TO
my family—
Diane, Todd,
and Amy*

Acknowledgments

I want to thank Judy Hoffman, Don and Linda Guillot, Kim Blackledge, Bill Myers, Dick Short, Karon Dillmann, Charles Ced, Betty Duke, Harold Walzer, Jr., Fred, Bea, Ryan, Kelly, and Ricky Dantagnan, Paul Emmet, Linda and Joe Lewandoski, Emmett Thompson, Sam Gebbia, Eddie Clogher, Joe and Judy Miceli, Romain Pellerin, Delores and Al Rohli, Rachel and Joy Leonard, Mike and Mae Robichaux and staff, John P. Dillmann, Jr., and Beverly Dillmann, Lea, Ethan, and Micah Lewis, Joe Mancuso, Bill Elder, Nick Noriea, Henry Morris, Ned Chase, Dominick Anfuso, Mike Trunk, Tracy Brigden, Clyde Taylor, John and Anita Reeves, Leonard and Bess McBrayer, Johnnie Sue and James Blackledge, Jim and Donna Cherrier, all my neighbors in Evangeline Oak Estates, John Dillmann, Sr., and Germaine, Alred Rohli, Bill and Jackie Sharp, Nancy and Don Norton, Austin Anderson, Ola Graney, Beverly and Adam Schaff, Christine Wright, Catherine Lala, Dawn, Tony, and Rachel Piazza, Pat Allen, and especially all my good friends in the NOPD.

THE FRENCH QUARTER KILLERS

CHAPTER
–1–

Room 215 of the Howard Johnson's Motor Lodge bristled with brass. I made my way through the law enforcement big shots milling around in the cramped quarters, and a few moments later saw two dead bodies on the floor. The murder victims didn't surprise me—the police radio dispatcher had sent me to the motel at 4200 Old Gentilly Highway to conduct a double homicide investigation—but the presence of so many high-level officials did. At a murder scene, homicide detectives usually find four uniformed cops—two preserving the crime site, two for crowd control—and no one else.

But everybody who was anybody had stuffed themselves into Room 215, and I tried unsuccessfully to imagine whose murder would attract such a throng. It was 7:30 P.M., July 20, 1976, and the individuals I saw there didn't make appearances at such scenes even during working hours.

Time and place didn't matter to this conclave, a Who's Who of New Orleans criminal justice: District Attorney Harry Connick, Assistant District Attorney Tim Cerniglia, Chief of Detectives Henry Morris, Captain Anthony Polito, Captain Robert Mutz, and Homicide Commander Lieutenant Thomas Duffy.

And that was just for starters. There were six uniform

1

officers, plus their sergeant; two crime lab technicians; three other homicide detectives—Emmett Thompson, Sam Gebbia, Eddie Clogher—who'd be working under my direction; three district attorney's investigators; and three hippie types I didn't recognize—they turned out to be Drug Enforcement Administration (DEA) agents.

Two dozen police personnel in all, most of them in Room 215 (typical motel size for two double beds), plus the two bodies lying face down in pools of blood at the foot of the bed nearest the sliding glass doors that led to the motel's swimming pool. Dozens of motel guests rubbernecked from the pool area, shoulder to shoulder with reporters and TV camera crews, but the distractions they generated could be overcome by drawing the drapes. Instead, it was the mass of police inside the room, barking instructions into walkie-talkies (Chief Morris seemed to be ordering every detective in New Orleans to Howard Johnson's), bumping into one another, and wearing worried, grave expressions, that prevented an organized investigation. I had to clear out the crowd and get to work finding and preserving evidence before it got trampled in this high-ranking stampede.

But how do you tell District Attorney Harry Connick to leave? Or Henry Morris, second in command to the superintendent of police himself? I was only twenty-nine years old and had been a homicide detective just five years, but even a twenty-year veteran wouldn't feel comfortable telling his bosses to get out.

"What's going on?" I asked Tom Duffy, my commander at Homicide.

"You just stepped into a bucket of shit," Duffy said matter-of-factly. Irish ancestry was written all over the face of this husky cop, who worked his way up through the ranks.

"Why all the brass?"

"The victims were witnesses in a big drug case—a really big one—and that case is flushed down the toilet now. Everyone's crappin' his pants scared he'll take the heat, not only for losing the case but for losing the two witnesses. The victims were supposed to be protected."

"By whom?"

"I don't know. And judging from the diversity of the crowd here, I'm not sure anyone else is certain right now either. But you can bet somebody's ass will wind up in a sling." Duffy laughed bitterly. "Great protection, huh," he said, waving a hand toward the two dead bodies.

"Lieutenant," I said, "we need to move everybody out of here so we can conduct a scene investigation."

"I'll take care of it," Duffy said. "Have you detailed someone to the hospital?"

An ambulance had rushed a wounded third victim to Charity Hospital in downtown New Orleans, two blocks from the Superdome. "I sent Eddie Clogher," I said. It was the *only* thing I'd been able to do since arriving.

"Don't talk to the media," Duffy told me before he gently but persuasively started clearing out the room. Some of the officials didn't want to leave. They left the impression that these murders were too important to be handled by Homicide.

"You can call on any backup you need," Duffy said before leaving. "Use the day watch if necessary. When you wrap up the crime scene, come straight to my office and we'll try to straighten out this mess."

"The scene's going to take hours."

"Fine. Let 'em sweat it out."

It took no special expertise to recognize these murders as executions, professional hits. I knew what happened almost as clearly as if I'd been there. The door's chain lock had not been ripped out of its facing, nor were there other signs, such as damage caused by a foot or shoulder, to indicate forcible entry. The assailant or assailants probably charged in quickly —why else didn't the victims flee through the sliding doors to the swimming pool?—with guns leveled, forced the victims to lie on the floor, covered their heads with pillows to muffle sounds, and fired several bullets into the left temple of each.

There were three pools of blood marking the execution spots, one each under the head of the two victims laid out in front of me, and a third from the man rushed to Charity Hospital. How he had survived, if he had, I couldn't imagine.

I dug my fingers into the blood, felt about, and located and retrieved two small-caliber bullets, which I turned over to the crime lab technician on the scene. He marked them for identification before carefully placing them in a manila envelope. I asked this same man to cut out large portions of the carpet. From these we found two more bullets and seven fragments, potentially critical evidence if we could match it ballistically to a gun.

Looking at grisly murder scenes never makes me queasy. It never did, for some reason. What bothers me more is the terrible smell of a partially decomposed corpse, and the homey, rather ordinary, places where sudden death occurs. This room, for example. Howard Johnson's usually conjures up images of ice cream, a young couple honeymooning, a family on vacation; but this evening an assassin's bullets blew away remembrances of the fun times and left two guests dead on the floor.

The victims were black, ages thirty and twenty-one: Eddie Smith and Paulette Royal. I had learned their names from identification found in the room. The wounded man was Samuel Williams, age twenty-one.

Easy as the murder might be to reconstruct, it promised to be difficult if not impossible to solve. Contract killings, a category the HoJo murders most likely fit, usually go unresolved, especially if the hit men are professionals. I believed they probably were in this case since the victims had been protected witnesses in a major drug case. Over the past sixty years or so in Chicago, for example, hundreds of mob-related hits have resulted in only a handful of convictions. The best contract killer has no ties to the victim, and no motive other than the money he receives from a third party. Such an individual is a virtual phantom.

Getting down to business, I directed the crime lab technician to photograph both the bodies and murder room from numerous angles; conducted an initial, cursory check for obvious items of evidence (a half-empty water glass, for instance, that we dusted for fingerprints); measured the entire room, including distances between various objects, particularly the bodies; examined along with the coroner the corpses themselves, discovering that each victim had been shot several times (this completed, the bodies were transported to the morgue); and called in a criminalist to take blood, hair, and fiber samples while at the same time the lab technician dusted the entire room for fingerprints. When finally left alone, the drapes long ago pulled shut to protect from outside eyes, I conducted a thorough search of the room.

I found a gun right away, a .32-caliber revolver with a two-inch barrel, jammed underneath clothing in one of the dresser drawers. I called the lab technician back to photograph the weapon. It also needed to be dusted for fingerprints, test-fired in a ballistics check, and traced through the National Crime Information Center to, I hoped, an owner.

I didn't believe I'd found the murder weapon. The gun probably belonged to one of the victims, which could open up a whole new can of worms. "A bucket of shit" as Tom Duffy had called it.

What were these victims doing with a gun? The little I knew indicated they possessed protected-witness status. Were they supposed to protect themselves? I'd never heard of such a thing.

And if they weren't protecting themselves, who in such final and dramatic fashion had failed to do the job? I began to understand why so many law enforcement brass believed they couldn't afford to stay away from these murders.

The gun worried me, not a positive diversion as I launched a murder investigation. I doubted if two protected witnesses in a big drug case were individuals of simon-pure character, people the public wanted toting a gun. I figured the victim who owned the pistol either felt the need for protection or decided to combine his activities as a witness with some freelance crime.

Checks of the closet, dresser drawers, and suitcases uncovered only women's clothing. One of the murder victims, and the individual at Charity Hospital—still alive? —were men. Odd, I thought, while burrowing like a mole through every inch of the room, but the extraordinary significance of only women's clothing remained lost to me.

I had to force myself to stay in that room wielding the figurative fine-tooth comb. I knew the case might already have been solved, that at this very moment other officers could be making arrests. While I ransacked the room I wondered what Eddie Clogher had learned from the wounded Samuel Williams at Charity Hospital? Williams could have named the killers, complete with descriptions and addresses.

Everything had to be checked, examined, and catalogued, if deemed important. A phone number scribbled on a book of matches could lead to the killer. A photo found among belongings might actually capture the image of the murderer —I've seen this occur several times; not so unusual, I suppose, since most homicide victims are killed by someone they know.

I worked alone in the sealed room, eerily blazing with lights—I'd turned every bulb in the place on high—until 10:30 P.M. Satisfied I hadn't missed anything, I called Eddie Clogher at Charity Hospital.

"What's happening, Clodge?" I asked. "Is this guy gonna make it?"

"Make it?" Clogher asked and laughed. "He's trying to walk out of the hospital."

"With a bullet through the head?"

"He must carry a pocketful of rabbits' feet. The bullet went in under his left ear and traveled down, into the jaw, where it's lodged now. If it had gone up into the brain, as the killer intended, his ass would be on the end of a pitchfork."

"Does he know who shot him?"

"Three men. He says one of them was a sissy." (Street talk for a gay man.)

"Does Williams have names?"

"No. He gave descriptions, but I don't know how good they are. Other than the sissy, I'd say we're looking for two tough, black, cold-blooded killers."

"Why don't you like the descriptions?"

"Williams is a country kid. From Alexandria." The geographical center of Louisiana, about two hundred miles northwest of New Orleans on the Red River. "I don't think he's ever ventured away from home until now. Lady Luck may have guided that bullet away from his brain, but she sure dealt a dead man's hand by hooking him up with Eddie Smith and Paulette Royal. They met him in Alexandria and asked if he wanted to party in New Orleans for a couple of days. The next thing he knew, people were trying to kill him."

"What were Smith and Royal doing in Alexandria?"

"I don't know."

"How did the hit come down?"

"Williams was asleep. He heard a loud crash and all of a sudden three men were in the room, two of them with guns. He was yanked out of bed and forced to lie on the floor next to Smith and Royal. Williams figured it was a robbery. The next thing he knew they were all getting domed. Three shots. A pause. Three shots. Pause. Then a single shot into his head. He played dead, and the killers probably believed him, but I'd guess the gun jammed, and that's why he took only one. He waited twenty minutes, then staggered into the pool area for help."

"What time did the killings take place?"

"A little before six P.M."

"You say Williams wants to go back to Alexandria?"

"Can't leave soon enough."

"What does the doctor say?"

"That he'll be all right."

"Well, don't let him go, Clodge. Bring him down to headquarters if necessary and we'll hold him as a material witness. And put a guard on him, will you? Twenty-four hours a day. We've already had witnesses killed. How would it look if the witness to the death of the witnesses got killed?"

It sounded like a joke, but it wasn't amusing to us, and especially not to the victims.

Nor to the police brass who congregated in Tom Duffy's office waiting for me. They radioed several times, asking me to report in, but I ignored the messages, believing once I got involved with superiors the investigation would bog down in a muddy marsh of conflicting strategies. Too many chiefs, not enough Indians. Besides, I reasoned, they really didn't want me to leave a fresh murder scene investigation. There'd be time for talk later, this was a *motel,* after all, most of the witnesses would be gone in the morning.

I went to the office of the motel's manager, Trout Felker. He was a nervous man and very concerned about the kind of publicity his establishment would get from all this, though he would have been heartened to know that some of the most powerful people in New Orleans wanted things kept as quiet as possible.

"Mr. Felker," I said, "I need photostat copies of every registration card filled out this week."

"That's quite a job, Detective Dillmann."

"We've got a double murder."

"Do you think the killers might be staying here?" Felker didn't like that thought at all.

"I don't think you have to worry," I said.

"Well, I suppose if you really need those records."

"I do." And I did. People in the motel were potential witnesses. Someone might have seen the killers on their way to Room 215, or casing the motel beforehand, or exiting a car in the parking lot. A witness not realizing the importance of what he saw could leave for another city or state before we interviewed him.

"Detective Dillmann," Felker said, "when can we get in that room and clean it up?"

I blinked. Was he worried about how soon he could rent it out? "Not for a few days at least," I said. I didn't add that it all depended on quickly solving the case, an unlikely occurrence because of the nature of the crime. "For now," I added, "I've sealed both the hall door and the sliding doors.

You can't get in. Even the governor couldn't.'' I thought this saved Felker additional stress. He'd have a conniption if he saw how badly we'd ripped the place apart.

"Mr. Felker," I said, "I realize copying all those cards will take time. But I'd like to see the card for Room two-fifteen right away, please."

Motels usually ask guests for the model and license number of their car. I knew the victims had driven from Alexandria, and I wanted to check out the automobile. It was listed on the card all right—a 1960 blue Chevrolet, Louisiana license plate 743B286—but something else I saw set my head spinning. I let out a little whistle, shook myself, and looked again.

"You okay?" Felker asked.

"Fine."

I stared at the registration card and thought Duffy's words hadn't conveyed the half of it. The room had been paid for with a credit card issued to the Orleans Parish District Attorney's Office—Harry Connick's office!

So the witnesses were under Harry Connick's protection. The ambitious, high-profile, first-term prosecutor in his mid-forties occasionally got mentioned for higher office— the governorship, perhaps, and after that, who could tell? Citizens of New Orleans liked his no-nonsense, law-and-order approach to criminal justice. Slim, five feet ten inches, with silver-gray hair, an excellent speaker, married to a judge, his son a gifted concert pianist, Connick appeared to have everything going for him. But if he'd let two witnesses under his protection get killed, he would be wasting his time and money even if he ran for dogcatcher.

I liked Connick. An honest man who spoke his mind. Unlike many prosecutors, he didn't require an airtight, can't-lose, the-defendant-served-up-on-a-platter case before he agreed to go to trial. Many prosecutors want sure winners, which often isn't possible. They keep track of their win/loss record as carefully as Vince Lombardi of the Green Bay Packers once did, trumpeting that percentages measure performance; they shy away from cases where the defense attorney is no pushover, or where the outcome isn't preordained, or where conviction depends on their ability to present complicated facts to a jury in a simple, easily understood manner.

In the most positive meaning of the phrase, Connick was a southern gentleman, intelligent and cultured, soft-spoken. He reminded observers of the district attorney's office of an enthusiastic, though not a noisy, cheerleader. He'd go from employee to employee, talking about the alarming increase of crime, and urge them to do their part to make New Orleans a better place to live.

The word dignified comes to mind with Connick. A gracious man in the old New Orleans tradition, he'd stop on his way to a fire at his own house to retrieve a lady's dropped handkerchief.

I found the 1960 Chevrolet in the motel parking lot, searched the car without finding anything, and arranged to have it towed to the city pound. It was a typically steamy July New Orleans night, 95 degrees, 85 percent humidity, and I'd begun to sweat like a polecat. I took a last look at the downtown city lights, four miles away, and headed back inside to welcome air-conditioning.

Chief of Detectives Henry Morris had dispatched half a dozen men from Burglary (offense against property) and Robbery (offense against people) to canvass the motel, an almost unprecedented allocation of personnel. These six men represented the *entire* shifts of their respective units.

Pulling officers from other details to work Homicide attested to the importance of the case, at least to the brass—Harry Connick for sure, and who knew what others. I suspected the fuse burned short. One good newspaper exposé and the case could explode in their faces.

The complete Homicide shift—six men—also worked the case, under my direction, though "direction" did *not* mean I served as their boss. How could I? One of these men, the veteran Pascal Saladino, was nearly legendary throughout the Department, a big, tough, jovial cop to whom the motto of the Canadian Mounties applied: Pascal didn't *always* get his man, but he *usually* did. Pascal's recommendation had gotten me accepted into the proud, elite New Orleans Homicide unit, one of the nation's best.

But the HoJo murders was *my* case. My number had come up. I imagined the brass, waiting impatiently in Tom Duffy's office, would have preferred Saladino, or my friend Fred Dantagnan from day watch, or the brilliantly thorough Clem Dasalla of graveyard. Regardless, "direction" meant the Homicide men would follow my suggestions, offering their own if they believed them of value.

Officers were still knocking on doors and waking guests when I came back inside after midnight. Before the morning ended they interviewed every guest, save a few who evidently reserved rooms and didn't use them. Some of the interviewed guests expressed fear that the killers might still be in or near the motel.

"How's the canvass going?" I asked Pascal Saladino, who lolled in an easy chair in the lobby, watching the comings and goings. He smoked his trademark, a fat, smelly cigar, and appeared amused. He'd handled too many murders to let these knock him off stride, no matter how anxious his superiors.

Younger detectives looked to Saladino for advice and example, considered him, correctly, a wise and unshakable veteran. He knew things worked out if you stayed after them, no matter how disastrous they appeared at the moment.

It once took Saladino *twelve years* to solve a murder case, but solve it he did, long after most detectives would have given up. Two armed robbers shot up a New Orleans tavern, wounding eight people, three of them fatally. Two of the dead victims were the parents of a New Orleans cop.

With virtually no clues to go on, Saladino nonetheless kept digging. And digging more. He never let himself forget the bloodbath in that bar. *Ten years later,* armed only with a prison inmate's recollection of overhearing a conversation about *different* homicides, he matched the bullets taken from the bodies in the bar to bullets found at other unsolved murders.

Two years after this, with help from the FBI, Saladino's evidence led to convictions for *eight* murders, including the three in the tavern. Other victims included a nun, a priest, and a bank teller. Saladino's remarkable investigation solved a multiple murder case even his most optimistic superior believed hopeless.

"Not too good, Skinny," Pascal said to me, answering my question about the canvass. "We've got the names of the people who saw Williams stagger out to the swimming pool. About twenty minutes before that a few individuals in rooms near two-fifteen heard what sounded like firecrackers. Gunshots, no doubt. But nobody saw the perpetrators. Came. Saw. Conquered. Left. Can the guy at the hospital make the hitters?"

"I think so."

"Skinny, who should have been on top of this?"

"Connick, I think. The taxpayers sprang for their room."

Saladino thought this enormously ironic. He tried to relight his cigar, but his laughter blew out the match. I thought he might roll out of his chair, so convulsed had he become. I waited for words of enlightenment, but all he finally offered was, "Better you than me."

"Thanks a lot. You're a great help."

"I'll tell you this," he said. "Hang onto that witness's ass. It looks like he's all you have. Take him home with you if you have to."

"Diane would love that."

"No one with them at all," Saladino said, shaking his head. "They were just left hanging."

"No, they were just left dead."

Emmett Thompson and I drove to Charity Hospital to check on our witness; we ignored increasingly frantic messages to contact Tom Duffy. We could always tell Duffy we'd turned the radio down low to concentrate on the investigation. I felt fairly certain that once the brass cornered us, necessary legwork would stop dead in its tracks, possibly for hours, as debate raged on how best to handle the murders.

Emmett Thompson agreed. "To hell with them," he said, and said no more.

Medium height, medium build, average features, Emmett Thompson possessed two distinguishing qualities: his utter cynicism about everything, and his brilliance as an investigator. Thompson ranked right with Saladino as the *crème de la crème* of Homicide.

A few months before we'd stopped for a French Quarter traffic light when a tourist raced into the street and started pounding on the driver's—Thompson's—side windows. Though we wore civilian clothes and we drove a plainclothes car, we must have looked too much like cops to be anything else. Emmett rolled it down a few inches. The tourist combined equal portions of panic and outrage in his facial and verbal expressions.

"You're police, aren't you?" he asked, his voice rising.

Emmett nodded slightly, allowing this might be true. His eyes were hooded.

"There's a guy in the next block," the tourist said, "a *bum*, and he's trying to panhandle everybody who walks by. Outrageous, in a so-called fine city like this! But it gets worse. I wouldn't give the tramp a quarter, so he unzipped himself and urinated all over the sidewalk."

Emmett looked at the man blandly.

"Well, do something!"

Emmett scratched his head.

"He pissed on the sidewalk! He almost hit my shoes!"

"Mister," Emmett said, while rolling the window back up, "obviously you've mistaken me for somebody who gives a damn."

But Emmett did give a damn. He showed it by transferring numerous vicious killers from the streets of New Orleans to the state penitentiary at Angola.

At Charity Hospital we talked to both Eddie Clogher and our witness, Samuel Williams, valuable as gold and infinitely more rare. Eddie had arranged for Williams to stay in the hospital for several days, with a twenty-four-hour armed guard at his bedside. Williams could be released only into my custody.

Clogher had obtained descriptions of the three killers. Here's what we had:

1. Black male. Approximately 23 years old. Height 5'10". Weight 140 pounds. Slender. Dark complexion. Seen wearing blue and white scarf around head. Subject has mannerisms of homosexual.

2. Black male. Approximately 25 years old. Height 5'10". Weight 150 pounds. Medium build. Dark

complexion. Close-cropped hair. Subject clad in
dark clothing and armed with nickel-plated revolver.

3. Black male. Approximately 23 years old. Height
   5'10". Weight 160 pounds. Medium build. Dark
   complexion. Medium Afro bush. Subject clad in
   dark clothing and armed with nickel-plated revolver.

It wasn't much, and most of it surely mistaken, but
Clogher had followed procedure and sent the descriptions out
over each of the eleven police broadcast channels in New
Orleans. Officers were told the three men were wanted for a
double murder and should be considered extremely dangerous. This meant, unfortunately, that if a policeman pulled
over a car containing three black males for running a stop
sign, the officer would employ a professional yet aggressive
manner until he could determine the occupants weren't
suspects in the two homicides. It's sad but true that the
number one cause of police deaths involves an unsuspecting
cop approaching a vehicle containing individuals who have
just committed a major crime.

Before leaving Charity Hospital a little after 2:00 A.M., I
called my wife, Diane, and told her I didn't know when I'd
be home. The call woke her up, which she said she preferred
to awakening and not knowing what kept me. Working
beyond midnight on the four-to-twelve shift occurred frequently enough that I figured she'd know: A murder investigation can't be left, like a partially finished auto repair, until
the shift begins again sixteen hours later. Still, I counted
myself lucky to have a wife who worried, though I wished
she wouldn't.

Also, phoning Diane always did more for my spirits than
hers. Observing a homicide firsthand, after five years of
being *saturated* with murder ranging from mutilations an

individual has to see to believe to little children dead from
batterings, keeps the detective in need of stabilizing remind-
ers that good things do exist in his life. I most often received
these reinforcements from Diane, while in return she got
awakened in the middle of the night.

Police work would put stress on any marriage. Even
simple plans for a family picnic can't be made with certainty
because something could, and often did, arise to make them
impossible.

Diane couldn't be sure I'd show up for the nice dinner
she'd planned, or be able to take our children on outings we
promised: I might have to be in court on my own time, or any
of a hundred other duties that didn't fit neatly into a shift.

The worst part for her was the worry. She feared I'd be
hurt or killed. Often I was afraid also, but dealing with it
came easier for me. In many situations I'd be able to control
what happened. Diane could only live in a state of tension
and anxiety, shouldering more than her share of the load
raising the children, and worrying about her husband's
safety.

"When will you be home?" she asked.

"I can't say, Di." Usually I could give her a pretty good
idea.

"I'll go into the bedroom and kiss Todd and Amy for
you."

I rode to headquarters with Emmett Thompson, who
seldom spoke. Just as well. My thoughts jumbled with
bodies laid in military-neat fashion on a carpeted floor, with
killers who came and went unseen, with normally confident
men suddenly become fearful; and overshadowing everything
a room with *only women's clothes*.

I tossed that last bit of information around in my head.
Unusual often means significant, but what I searched for
eluded me.

CHAPTER
—2—

"What took you so long?" Tom Duffy asked, bustling out of his third-floor police headquarters office to greet me.

"I was at the crime scene. Then at the hospital to interview the witness."

"People are anxious to hear what you've learned." Duffy raised his brows, rolled his eyes, a "this is crazy" look on his expressive face. "They want to know if you've solved the case yet."

Duffy took my elbow and guided me into his office. All manner of human beings paced and argued in the not-overly-large enclosure, often raising their voices, and the place looked as if it had just been on fire, the smoke hung so thick.

Duffy introduced me to the group, which did indeed appear disappointed that I didn't have the hit men in leg irons, babbling confessions. The only confession the assemblage got was mine, as I explained what we'd learned so far. Before I had narrated myself out of Room 215, but long enough to divine that no breakthroughs were forthcoming, Assistant District Attorney Tim Cerniglia began telling, not for the first time I guessed, a poker-faced DEA agent just at whose doorstep the blame for the killings should be placed.

"Judge Jerome Winsberg," Cerniglia said. "Don't you agree that what he did is absolutely unbelievable?"

The DEA agent, hair in a ponytail, wearing blue jeans and a Memphis Chicks baseball cap, nodded gravely but noncommittally.

"I just know it ain't our damn fault," said a second DEA man. He wore a purple tank top, Bermuda shorts, and thong sandals. As out of place as the men might seem in Duffy's office, they blended right in to the colorful French Quarter. Both DEA agents were in their late twenties.

"Figure it out," Cerniglia said. "Winsberg's the one."

"All I know," said Tank Top, "it ain't us."

"No, it sure ain't us," said Ponytail.

"Gentlemen!" said Chief of Detectives Henry Morris. I think that's what he said. Morris, who later became chief of police, rising all the way from patrolman on the beat, was a grumpy man who spoke in mumbles. No one worked harder or knew more about police business, though, from bottom to top, and Morris achieved the near-miracle of being liked and respected by everyone in the Department. "Who gives a damn who's to blame," this bear growled. "Goddamn. Dope fiends running around killing people in our motels, and all I hear is Winsberger."

"Winsberg," someone corrected.

"I know his name. Goddamn. Two dead victims and all I hear is talk about who's to blame."

"Ain't us," said Tank Top.

Morris looked disgusted. "Dillmann, you in charge of this case?" he asked.

"Yes, sir."

"Well," Morris said to Duffy, "give Dillmann whatever he needs. If he's gotta dip into day watch or graveyard, so be it."

"Right," said Duffy.

"Dillmann," Morris said. At this time he knew my name, but a few years down the road he invariably called me "Dantagnan," while greeting Fred as "Dillmann." "You canvassed the motel?"

"Yes, sir. Almost finished."

"You protecting that witness?"

"Yes, sir."

"You broadcast descriptions?"

"Yes, sir."

"You doing background on the victims?"

"Not yet, Chief. It's three A.M. All I know is they came from Alexandria."

"Goddamn. It's three A.M. and I'm here awake. Get some people out of bed in Alexandria and find out what you can."

Homicide detective Sam Gebbia handled the calls to Alexandria. I stayed in Duffy's office. They'd summoned me to deliver a preliminary report, but it turned out they had more to offer me than I them. Through the bickering and finger-pointing over where blame should be placed, which I understood and had a certain sympathy for—a single mistake, albeit a serious one, could destroy careers—I learned the name of the man they believed hired the killers.

"David Joseph Sylvester," Cerniglia said. "It's got to be him."

Alarms sounded in my head. David Sylvester: The New Orleans detective who didn't know that name should find a new line of work. Sylvester was the biggest heroin dealer in the city, literally a one-man crime wave because the poison he peddled pushed hundreds of people to perform *any* act to appease their overpowering craving. Sylvester created muggers, maniacs, murderers. People made desperate by his heroin committed many of the city's most heinous crimes.

I tell Diane everything—confiding in her keeps the nightmares from destroying me—but I never told her about the time I was sent to check out a suspected murder victim in an abandoned apartment. I found a teenager who'd been dead for seven days, his face eaten away by maggots crawling through his body, the stench so trenchant a slaughterhouse in summer would have seemed as fresh as a Colorado breeze.

The body was identified as a seventeen-year-old honor student from an uptown upper-middle-class family. He had decided to experiment with heroin.

Two other teenagers had also been listed as missing for seven days. It couldn't be, I thought, but I went back to the apartment anyway—and found them there. I'd missed the bodies the initial time huddled in the corner of a dark closet, because, I suppose, the stench of the first boy's heroin-ravaged corpse had subconsciously made me unwilling to search further. Perhaps I didn't *want* to find anyone else. I'd known instances of infants fresh from the womb trembling spastically in need of a fix; of a young mother so desperate to score she leaves her children, ventures to a street corner, and returns to find them dead in a fire; of young people so addicted to heroin they commit murder to feed their habits, meaning they'll spend the rest of their lives behind bars—an awful waste; of fathers forcing their daughters (and sons) into prostitution to pay the drug dealer; and of innocents, young and old, killed in crossfires, à la "Miami Vice," when dope deals turn sour.

"David Sylvester," I said to Cerniglia. "So you figure he's a player in this?"

"Got to be. You can bet he put out the contracts."

"How's that?"

"Sylvester has been arrested for possession of heroin," said Ponytail. "For other raps, too. But not a hundredth of what he's guilty of. He's smart, calculating, and dangerous. He uses other people to carry his narcotics, which is the main reason he's been hard to bust. But we've now got him charged in both state and federal court with possession of heroin with intent to distribute.''

"Why hit Paulette and Eddie?"

"Let me paint the whole picture for you," Cerniglia said. "You'll see the D.A.'s office wasn't to blame for these deaths. It was Judge Winsberg—but I'll get to his part later."

I figured he would. Cerniglia, a young prosecutor, admired by police for his gung ho pursuit of convictions, always came into court thoroughly prepared, and even other lawyers enjoyed listening to his bang-up summations to a jury. In Duffy's office, however, he carried two crosses: As a prosecutor he wanted killers caught, but as Harry Connick's loyal employee he sought to keep his boss's name free of any taint of negligence.

"Eddie Smith and Paulette Royal," Cerniglia said, "were runners for Sylvester. The DEA's tried for years to nail Sylvester. Eddie and Paulette finally turned, and the Feds were able to make a strong conspiracy case. But here's the rub. If the Feds prosecuted Sylvester, he wouldn't receive the stiff sentence we could go for. If *we* prosecuted him, he could get life. So the DEA turned its entire case over to us for prosecution. Witnesses, evidence, the whole ball of wax. We were scheduled for trial in Section C of Criminal District Court—Judge Winsberg—on July twenty-second."

The witnesses were killed *thirty-five hours* before the start of the trial.

"What happened?" I asked.

"Yesterday—Christ, only yesterday?—Winsberg forced the state to produce one of its witnesses, Eddie Smith, in court. Bob Glass, Sylvester's lawyer, had filed a discovery motion requesting his appearance, and Winsberg granted the motion. We had kept his whereabouts secret till then.''

"Did Winsberg make him give an address?"

"No. Hell, though, all Sylvester needed was to have him followed back to Howard Johnson's. That's what he must have done. A few hours after leaving court, they're dead. What kind of deal is this?"

I didn't know. I had trouble enough keeping the facts straight, much less playing the assign-the-blame game, which I intended to stay out of. But it did seem, on the surface, that if the prosecution feared for the lives of the witnesses—as obviously they should have—the prosecution should have provided some protection.

Looking in Sylvester's direction, however, seemed eminently reasonable to me. *Cui bono?* The drug kingpin, if not involved, was the beneficiary of a phenomenal piece of good luck—only a coincidence? With Paulette and Eddie testifying, Cerniglia assured, Sylvester was dead meat. Without them, he'd likely walk.

Unless led in other directions, and I had to keep my eyes open for them, I intended our investigation to focus on the Sylvester connection. One of the victims, summoned to court two days in advance of the drug dealer's trial, gets executed gangland style just a few hours later. Exactly the way I believed Sylvester would handle such a grave threat to his freedom.

But believing is not proving. I probably couldn't break the tough, savvy, streetwise Sylvester, even if I could talk to him, which I couldn't. Glass, the lawyer, would summon thunder and lightning if I approached his client.

Sylvester, thirty-two, owned a record of arrests (though little jail time) dating back fourteen years, a rap sheet testifying to rapid graduation up the crime ladder:

Vagrancy
Burglary
Arrest as fugitive
Burglary
Carrying concealed weapon
Carrying concealed weapon
Gambling
Carrying concealed weapon
Possession of heroin
Battery
Battery
Possession of marijuana
Automobile theft
Possession with intent to distribute heroin
Possession with intent to distribute heroin

Murder didn't seem farfetched as a next logical entry on Sylvester's arrest registry. I knew I'd love to put it there. If so, he would beat a serious drug indictment only to find himself charged with homicide, which carried a potential life sentence. He'd surely spend many more years in prison for murder, probably most, if not all, of his life, since Louisiana law views contract killings with the same severity as the killing of a police officer.

Sylvester didn't qualify as a one-dimensional stereotype of the evil drug dealer, which perhaps partly explained why he'd been sent to jail only once. In fact, some people in the projects viewed him as a sort of Robin Hood and could be counted on to come to his defense.

Sylvester had been known to help poor families pay pressing bills, whether as a good public relations ploy, or part of an otherwise well-hidden social conscience, I didn't know, but certainly there were people who would hesitate to testify against him. The Mafia itself has been known to

provide various beneficial services, like Sylvester perhaps
delivering a sack of groceries to a needy family, which didn't
mean their other activities should be ignored. In this case,
the issue was dealing heroin, and murder, activities which, if
guilty of, qualified Sylvester as a monster.

But I couldn't attack this monster at its head. Arms and
legs had to be chopped off first. When I left Lieutenant
Duffy's office I had warnings not to talk to the press ringing
in my ears, plus urgings to "move fast," because, though not
put so crudely, arrests might deflect attention away from *why*
the murders had been possible (any way you cut it, the D.A.
should have protected Paulette and Eddie). I also had a plan
of how to start.

I parked the new red Cadillac by the Jaxson Brewery on the
bank of the Mississippi River in the French Quarter and
walked four blocks to the Mid Ship bar on Iberville Street.
I'd driven the flashy car several times around the block and
slowly cruised by Mid Ship, wanting to be seen. Now, at
4:30 A.M., less than eleven hours after the killings at Howard
Johnson's, I strolled into this bar frequented by transvestites
as if I owned it. Mid Ship has no door—you just walk
in—and the first person I spotted was the bartender, a big
bruiser with forearms the size of hams, dressed in drag:
straight skirt slit to midthigh, high heels, black fishnet
stockings, frilly lace blouse, red wig, and makeup so heavy
that he must have piled it on with a trowel. I was surprised his
plastered face allowed his skin to move and form words.

"What are you drinking, Honey?"

"J and B and water in a tall glass."

I wore a shiny gray silk suit, pink shirt open halfway down
my chest to reveal three heavy gold chains, four diamond
rings, gold watch on one wrist, gold bracelet on the other,
dark glasses, pink silk handkerchief in breast pocket, and a

wide-brimmed gray hat. Vince the Fence provided me with the duds and the flashy Cadillac on virtually no notice, assuring me that they'd "fool anybody." But he warned, "The problem's going to be *you;* you're too mother's milk, too uptight. Loosen up so you don't look so much like a cop."

Every big city has a number of Vinces whom the police allow to operate, within carefully defined illegal bounds, in exchange for information (and in this case clothes, car, and gold). Hardly the most salutary arrangement imaginable, and impossible to justify to the individual whose TV has been stolen, but justification isn't necessary, publicly at least. Most people don't know about the fence/police relationships of this world. Still, they probably do hold down crime. Busting Vince puts only one person—Vince—behind bars. Using his information (often his motivation is ridding the city of bothersome competition) plants dozens of criminals in the slammer. In any event, when the HoJo murders made it desirable to go underground in the French Quarter, Vince's name popped immediately to mind.

"Haven't seen you before, Honey," said the bartender, his voice as deep as Chief Morris's.

"I'm looking for somebody," I said.

The somebody's name was Sticks—that's all I had—a female impersonator, transvestite, and prostitute first cultivated as an informant by Emmett Thompson, and later by myself. Streetwise, with an ear finely attuned to French Quarter gossip, Sticks pointed Homicide in the right direction on two previous murder cases. I hoped, if I could find him, he'd make it three.

Sam Gebbia learned from his phone calls to Alexandria that murder victim Eddie Smith, a New Orleans native, worked nightclubs as a female impersonator and was well known in the city's relatively large transvestite community.

Dressed as a woman, Smith was considered lovely, good-looking enough to enter the transvestite beauty contest, which attracts thousands of spectators, held annually at St. Ann and Bourbon streets each Fat Tuesday, Mardi Gras Day.

Gebbia's information coupled with what Tim Cerniglia advised—that David Sylvester employed transvestites as heroin runners—made Mid Ship's fringe French Quarter location as good a place as any to start. It also might explain why Room 215 contained only women's clothes.

I refused to let myself calculate the long odds I faced—that would only discourage me—but I knew a hit commissioned by a gangster of Sylvester's savvy wouldn't solve easily. The hitters already demonstrated their professionalism by getting in and out of the busy Howard Johnson's unseen.

Still, I did have motivation: nailing David Sylvester, an undesirable in almost anyone's reckoning. And another, worded best by Captain Tony Polito: "If we don't catch these assholes, no witness will ever come forward again in this city."

After a couple swallows of J & B, I had my bearings in Mid Ship; I looked around and decided I might be too conservatively dressed. The bar, no larger than the living room of a middle-class suburban home, featured perhaps fifteen patrons, a jukebox playing Barry Manilow and Elton John (easy dance music), and wreaths and colored lights usually associated with Christmas.

I scanned the room and took the following predawn Mid Ship clientele census: a cab driver; a pair of young girls, probably runaways looking to be picked up; a drug dealer; a nutso talking to himself; a drunken tourist who'd wandered dangerously off the beaten path; eight men dressed as women; and me, a cop dressed as a pimp.

Two couples—transvestites—danced slowly and seductively to a Barry Manilow tune. Several of them were real knockouts; without their Adam's apples, which are very difficult to change surgically (a costly, quite complicated operation usually only performed for cancer patients), they could have fooled me. Other possible giveaways may include the size of their hands, shoulders, and backs. Transvestism, contrary to popular belief, is a practice distinct from homosexuality; it is related to finding erotic pleasure by dressing in the clothes of the opposite sex (women also dress as men), and is more frequent among heterosexuals.

Three of the men-dressed-as-women sat at a small corner table engaged in earnest conversation. The last of the transvestites, a cute blonde *with* breasts, sat at a separate table massaging the tourist's thigh. Booze-befogged, a beautiful blonde goddess smiling at him and quoting a 1930s price, the conventioneer, or so I judged, thought he'd died and gone to heaven. Sex, if he obtained any, *could not* be of the straight variety, and just as likely he'd be amazed when the gorgeous "woman" turned nasty and robbed him, at knife or gunpoint, or hurt him if he resisted. The people in dresses should not be regarded as weak.

"President Ford's crazy if he thinks I'm eatin' with him tomorrow!" It was the nutso. Barefoot, pants barely more than rags, wearing a raincoat with nothing underneath, he resembled a down-on-his-luck prophet.

"Give my friend a drink," said the cab driver in a pure Brooklyn accent. His eyes twinkled. He probably stopped by a couple of mornings a week after work to catch this show.

"Oscar's a dear, isn't he?" said the bartender, referring to Nutso. In his high heels the bartender walked like Fred Munster on stilts.

"We've got a car for a president," said Nutso.

"What you say, Flash?" the drug dealer said to me. He was the only black, except for one of the transvestites, in the joint. "You sure lookin' good tonight." He slid onto a stool next to mine.

"Yeah," I said. A big-timer like me wouldn't pass the time of morning with a petty pusher.

"Been here before?"

"First time." The dealer was a start. The French Quarter, approximately one square mile in area, is a very small place if you know it. Permanents, like the dealer, often know where other permanents, in this case Sticks, hang out. But the Quarter, like a colossal haystack, can render a needle like Sticks unfindable.

"You waitin' on your old lady?" The street name for a girl who works for a pimp. The dealer's curiosity didn't surprise me. Rather, it heartened. He'd check me out and the word—rumor, gossip—would race through the Quarter with the speed of light. Such a transmitter of information is also an excellent receiver.

"Not waiting," I said. "Looking. You know Sticks?"

"Sticks? Sticks ain't got no old man."

Time to get tough. "Look, motherfucker," I said, "don't tell me Sticks don't have no old man. What the fuck does an asshole like you know, anyway?"

"Whoa, Flash, take it easy. No cause to get hot. You ain't from here, huh?"

"Atlanta."

"How you know Sticks?"

"From Atlanta, six months ago. She told me the action's good here. Plenty of tourists with lots of money to spend. But she says people don't know how to treat their old ladies right."

"Yeah, they don't look out for 'em like they should."

"I run it right in Atlanta."

"Man, I know some *fine* women. *Real* women. Why you foolin' with he/shes?"

"That's where the money's at, Baby."

"Shit."

"Believe it."

"If you're gonna set up, you're gonna need somebody who knows the people. These pimps around here are crazy. They'll cut you from asshole to elbow. Yeah, you'll need help."

From him, no doubt.

"What's your name?" I asked.

"Tell 'em you're lookin' for Frankie."

"Frankie, I need to find Sticks."

"Man, she's workin' the street. She'll be in and out of the joints."

"You know where she stays?"

"Sticks could be stayin' anywhere."

"You think you might see her?"

"Might, Man. I'm on the street all the time, rippin' and runnin'."

"If you see her, tell her Dillmann's in town."

"Where's your crib?"

"Sticks knows."

"If you want real women . . ." Frankie said, but I interrupted.

"Maybe you're right," I said loudly, getting off the stool and heading for the runaways. What I planned to do, I shouldn't; the job belonged to Vice. Had he known, Duffy would have been upset.

"Here's some sweet meat," I announced, grabbing each girl by an elbow and jerking them to their feet.

"What the hell?" one of them snapped at me. Fifteen years old, I figured; the other about a year younger.

"Sweethearts, you need an old man to take care of you," I

said, sensing Frankie's admiration as I roughly pushed and pulled the teenagers through the opening where a door should have been.

The last words I heard from Mid Ship came from Nutso: "Ford's crazy if he thinks I'm gonna bail him out!"

Half-dragging the frightened, protesting girls back to the Jaxson Brewery and Cadillac, I spotted a marked unit and flagged it down. "Jesus Christ, Dillmann," the uniform said. "What in the world are you supposed to be?"

"Can't explain right now," I said. "Do me a favor, will you? Take the Bobbsey twins to Juvenile. They were sitting in Mid Ship when they should be home with hot milk and cookies. They're probably runaways."

I cruised the backwaters of the French Quarter, by bars like Mom's Society Page and Dungeon, the former a hangout for female impersonators, the latter a rough place where individuals can get hurt. I didn't know anyone other than Sticks with whom I could even start the murder investigation.

I also drove near Pirate's Alley, where Nobel laureate William Faulkner wrote his first novel, *Soldier's Pay;* by the historic Cabildo, where visitors can see the "founding stone" of the colony (1699), the death mask of Napoleon Bonaparte, and the spot where France ceded the territory of the Louisiana Purchase to the United States; and by night-spots like Pat O'Brien's, Lucky Pierre's, Old Absinthe House, and Lafitte's in Exile. But by 5:30 A.M. even the Quarter had wound down, and street cleaners would soon be making their rounds. I'd have to find Sticks later.

I returned the clothes, gold, and Cadillac to Vince, and myself to a saner space in time at a favorite hangout, Cafe du Monde, for some soothing café au lait and hot *beignets*. I relaxed a few minutes, shifted gears from pretend pimp to detective, and read an early edition of the *Times-Picayune*, which had front-page coverage of the HoJo murders.

The story related how Judge Winsberg, acting on a discovery motion filed by the defense attorney, Robert Glass, ordered Eddie Smith and Paulette Royal into court just a few hours before their deaths. "It's a shame," the *Times-Picayune* quoted Harry Connick. "We should not have been compelled to produce these people in court. It's sad, very sad."

"If we had not been ordered to produce them," Connick added, "we feel these people would still be alive."

No harm had yet been done to the D.A.'s office, but the feisty Winsberg hadn't said his piece yet. I suspected he'd burn some ears when he did speak out.

CHAPTER
—3—

Bone-tired, but needing to do background on Paulette and Eddie, I arrived at the Homicide office, a big gray room on the third floor of police headquarters, at a carefully timed 7:45 A.M. With the graveyard shift leaving, day watch taking over in fifteen minutes, and a big hunk of luck, maybe I could capture my own desk.

Detectives share desks in the cramped Homicide unit, a depressing and spiritless enclosure except for walls decorated with homemade attempts at humor, itself pretty depressing when you think about it: a picture of a nun wearing her habit and Saladino's face, leering and sinister; a sign, "When All Else Fails, Try the Truth"; a photograph of an Old West hanging, captioned "God Bless Judge Roy Bean"; and a poster, "Shoot BEFORE You See the Whites of Their Eyes."

I intended to slip niftily onto my desk chair at the instant graveyard's Paul Drouant abandoned it, amazing my friend Fred Dantagnan of day watch with my speed and grace. I chatted with Fred about the Saints' upcoming season—he is a diehard fan with unswerving faith in a football team that's *never* had a winning season—and watched the eyes of this powerful block of granite grow misty with cruel hope when I

mentioned several new offensive linemen I confidently predicted would provide previously unimagined protection for
beleaguered star quarterback Archie Manning (a player of
unquestioned ability who viewed the world mainly from his
back).

Waiting for Drouant's move while mesmerizing Dantagnan with dreams of Saints' glory, I gauged the distance he
needed to cover against my own. It was important to win.
The desk's telephone served three detectives, one from each
shift, and I needed to use that blower. A world of phone work
beckoned on yesterday's killings, and I imagined a small
cheering section rooting for my victory: Certainly Harry
Connick wanted me to reach the phone first, as did Chief
Morris, Captain Polito, and Lieutenant Duffy.

I knew reasonable pleas wouldn't budge Fred. He'd
empathize with the victims, but his philosophy—one murder's as important as the next—didn't allow for cases with
priority gradations, and he had plenty of homicides of his
own to handle. Besides, he probably took pleasure knowing
the brass squirmed.

Drouant moved. Like a bullet I aimed my backside for the
valuable chair, but the bearish Dantagnan, only faking his
hibernation, proved just as quick. Our hips collided midchair
and we thudded to wood sharing the precious perch. But
Dantagnan performed a couple of hard-hipped hula bumps:
He sat on the chair and I on the floor.

"Dammit, Fred," I pleaded as I pulled myself up, "I'm
working Howard Johnson's." A "heater" case, even he
would agree; a high-profile investigation promising pro-
tracted pressure from press and public, not to mention the
criminal justice hierarchy.

"I'm working a John Doe," he said.

I knew he wouldn't listen to sense. He sat immovable as
Gibraltar, except for his right hand, which reached to pick up
my phone.

"Give me a break, Fred. We're friends."

"Leave me alone, Dillmann. Get away."

"I'll view your next autopsy for you."

"I like autopsies."

And I remembered, he did. The only man in Homicide who liked autopsies. I once saw him eating a ham sandwich during an autopsy.

"I'll work for you Labor Day."

"That's six weeks away."

He began dialing the phone. I put my hand carefully on his to stop him.

"I'll give you one of my details." Our $14,000-a-year homicide detective's salary didn't provide many extras for a family, and the details I spoke about were part-time jobs— security guard at the Superdome, night watchman at a warehouse, etc.—most of us worked when we could. Such jobs were hard to find—and hold. Not many employers would hire someone who might or might not show up, depending on police overtime duty. You couldn't cut it in Homicide if, while hot on the trail of a killer, you glanced at your watch, saw quitting time (moonlighting time) had arrived, and decided to go to your second job.

"I already got more details than I can get to," Dantagnan said.

"I'll buy lunch today." I'd reached panic time.

"Where?"

God.

"Popeye's?"

"Forget it."

"Wise Cafeteria?"

"No deal."

"Brennan's?"

"I guess I could get out of here for a while and do some legwork."

I guessed he could, too. Jesus. Brennan's. One of the

fancy tourist places, internationally known for its champagne brunch. Brennan's, once the Casa Faurie mansion, was built around 1801 by the maternal grandfather of French Impressionist painter Edgar Degas. President Andrew Jackson ate at Casa Faurie, which later belonged to Judge Alonzo Morphy. Morphy's brilliant son, Paul, was acknowledged as the world's greatest chess player by the time he was twenty-one, retiring undefeated in 1859 when he was twenty-two.

Had I lost my mind? Frea would probably order the ultra-expensive eggs benedict. But I knew I'd better not complain, not now, or he might reconsider, park himself here, and tie up the phone for hours.

"See you at noon?" Fred suggested, sweeping some papers off *our* desk.

"Yeah," I said.

"Noon," he said gruffly. "On the dot, Dillmann. At Wise's."

It took a second to catch his meaning. When I turned to thank him, he had already rounded the corner and headed for the elevator. For a moment I dwelled on our friendship—our families were very close, and on the job we'd squeezed through several tight spots together—but then I reverted more to form and groused about a penny-pinching system that didn't provide enough desks, phones, or cars. The scene with Fred wasn't unusual: two detectives needing the same equipment. This time the guardians of the system—the D.A., Chief Morris—had been its victims, if only for a brief period.

I had one phone call to answer before doing background on Paulette and Eddie. The message, addressed to the "policeman in charge of Paulette Royal's death," came from a Janet Belton and listed a number probably assigned to the sprawling, government-subsidized, low-income Calliope Housing Project.

"This is Detective Dillmann," I said when I established Janet Belton was on the line.

"Are you the policeman in charge?" she asked, a telltale crack of concern in her voice. A friend or relative of the victim, I guessed. "Have you caught who killed Paulette?"

"I'm in charge of the murder investigation," I said. "No, we haven't caught the killers yet."

"Well, I don't know who killed her, but I can tell you who had it done."

"Who?"

"I'm not afraid. I'll tell you. It was that dope dealer, Sylvester."

"Miss Belton . . ."

"Mrs."

"Mrs. Belton, could I come and see you? At your earliest convenience, please."

"You come right ahead. I'm not afraid. 'Bout time someone speaks up about what's goin' on."

I'd hassled with Fred for *one phone call*. But a caller fingering David Sylvester, whom I believed lurked behind the homicides, promised too much hope to put off. It behooved me to see Mrs. Belton right away. The call might produce nothing—detectives are often besieged by phony leads—but I judged Janet Belton to be a genuine article.

On my way out I noticed Sam Gebbia for the first time since the meeting in Duffy's office. Sam probably hadn't gotten any sleep either. He sat at his desk, asking questions, taking notes, saying yeah yeah yeah to the replies. I imagined Gebbia frozen in amber, the phone physically linked to his ear. Morris wanted information about the activities of Paulette and Eddie in Alexandria? Sam would get more than even the meticulous Morris could ever want.

As a uniform, in 1971, before being promoted to Homicide, Sam and his partner jumped a pair of burglars

scrambling out a store window at Canal and North Robertson. The perpetrators fled, Sam and his partner pursued, the
cops quickly narrowing the gap on the robbers. Suddenly,
one of the felons stopped on the figurative dime, whirled,
and opened fire on Sam, still hurtling toward him full-speed
from a distance of just a few yards. The gun's explosions,
like the sonic booms of a jet breaking the sound barrier,
didn't stop Gebbia, nor did visions of death; he'd been
trained to react, not think—a split-second hesitation to think
can stop you permanently—and pumping adrenaline drove
him instinctively forward. He heard a bullet whiz by his ear,
an inch or so from killing him. Still Sam came, a man
possessed, firing his weapon and wounding the burglar. The
bullet's force spun the felon, dropped him to his knees, and
Sam made the arrest. The actual gunfire constituted an
infinitesimal fraction of the whole, but forever in the
remembering.

Gebbia still wonders how at almost point-blank range the
burglar missed him. He believes he should be dead. But I
think he also feels the worst is behind him, and it probably
won't get any more dangerous than that; having survived the
really bad part of life at Canal and North Robertson, the
remainder is a relatively relaxed coast downhill. I know
Gebbia is brave and largely without fear, two qualities that,
taken together, do not, as some might think, signal a lack of
common sense.

"You got something, John?" Gebbia asked, putting down
the phone as I walked by his desk. His five o'clock shadow
matched mine.

"I'm headed out to the Project to interview someone who
knew one of the victims."

"Which one?"

"Paulette. What have you learned about her?"

"She was hooking, in New Orleans, then hiding out with Eddie in Alexandria after the Sylvester indictments came down. Looks like she was trying to straighten up her act."

Janet Belton told me the same thing when I got to her apartment. Mrs. Belton, twenty-two, a year older than Paulette, was an attractive single black mother working as a nurse's aide and trying to save enough money to move out of Calliope. Her toddler played as we talked.

"How long had you known Paulette?"

"We'd been friends for years. We grew up in the same neighborhood. *Good* friends, Detective Dillmann. I was a year older than Paulette, but I considered her my little sister. It broke my heart the way life went bad for her. Anyway, we stayed friends. You don't give up on a friend. I hope you punish that man Sylvester."

"Did Paulette use drugs?" I wondered if drugs led her to Sylvester, to running *for* him, then running *from* him, ultimately to her death.

"Never. Paulette hung around all those people, but she never used the stuff. Sylvester used *her*. He used all of them."

"Them?"

"The freaks. The ones who dress as girls. That Eddie who died with her. A lot of others. Cops don't like to mess with those freaks. Sylvester's smart. He knows that. He used the freaks to spread his drugs all over the Project, all over New Orleans."

Janet Belton was right. I'd known earlier that employing transvestites had been a stroke of evil genius: Most police officers, traditional thinkers in the common-man mold, would view a male or female in drag as bizarre, laughable, and harmless, would take second, third, and fourth looks but never stop to question. Who imagines an ogre lurks behind the gay, smiling clown costume? I wondered what I'd find when I dug deeper into the largely unknown world of transvestites.

"Why did Paulette associate with these people?"

"She liked the nightlife and late hours of the French Quarter. She hung out there, fell in love with what she saw. It was glamorous. Not like here. *Here*. My God, you can't imagine. But in the Quarter she was equal with the beautiful people. Like most kids her age, and she was only fifteen when she moved there, Paulette was a thrill seeker."

"Was she a transvestite?"

"Nah." Janet Belton laughed. "You mean dress as a man? Good Lord, no. But she hung around all those guys who dressed as gals. I guess the cops figured she was a man, but she was the real article."

"Did Paulette run drugs for Sylvester?"

"Yeah, her and Eddie."

"You say she didn't use them. Why did she run them?"

"You kidding? She could make as much in one night's carry as she could in a month on a regular job."

"She have other ways of making money?"

"I don't know." Janet Belton looked down at the worn carpet. A place of despair, this crackerbox Project, and I admired her for setting her heart on escape to make a better life for herself and her child. She had selected a course different from Paulette, who ran drugs *and* hooked, but preferred not to dwell on her friend being a prostitute.

"When's the last time you talked to Paulette?"

"Talked to her? Or saw her?"

"Both."

"I hadn't seen her in over a year. I last talked to her three days ago."

Three days ago?

"She call you on the phone?"

"Yeah, said she'd gotten back to New Orleans. She just wanted to check in and talk."

I didn't realize the extraordinary significance I should have attached to this call.

"Did she sound frightened? Nervous? Anything unusual that you can remember?"

"Man, she sounded *happy*. The court business with Sylvester was coming up, and when she got that out of the way she'd be free. She sounded real good, Detective Dillmann."

"She never said she was afraid?"

"That was earlier. Months before."

"What happened?"

"Well, Paulette called me every now and then. Never would say from where. Like I told you, I was her big sister. I guessed she was out of town. Anyway, Paulette was going to appear in court against Sylvester, and the cops had offered her protection. She told me she wanted the protection, but Eddie didn't. She'd fallen for Eddie. He claimed he couldn't relax with police around all the time, so she gave in to him."

"Did she tell the police she wanted the protection they offered?"

"That's what she said. She was afraid."

Incredible. Not only would common sense have dictated a close guard on the witnesses, but Paulette thought it was needed.

"Then because of Eddie," Janet added, "she said forget the protection."

"When was the last time you saw Paulette?"

"More than a year ago. Before she left town. I found out later, when she called, it was because of the trial."

"Why do you think it was Sylvester who had her killed?"

"Paulette told me."

"She *told* you?"

"Before, when she called from out of town. She said Sylvester would do anything to keep her from testifying. Is that man gonna be punished, Detective Dillmann?"

Maybe not. First we had to catch the hitters, men unconnected to the victims with only money as a motive.

"Mrs. Belton, we're going to do the best we can." I stood up to go, silently wishing her luck. The small living room in which we sat, paint peeling from thin walls, had two chairs, a coffee table, and a TV. The type of place, I supposed, from which Paulette had fled.

I called Diane from a gas station pay booth, telling her I couldn't give a time—I didn't say day—when I'd be home.

"Is it the murders at Howard Johnson's I read about in the paper?" she asked.

"Yes," I said.

"Who would do a thing like that?"

"His name's David Joseph Sylvester."

"Will you find him? Is he dangerous?"

"Finding him is no problem, Diane. And yes, he's dangerous, but not the way you think. He hired other people to do the murders for him. Di, I'm going to be all right. I really am. Give the kids my love. I'll catch you up on everything when I get home."

I drove by a pumping station—New Orleans is below sea level, almost half the land area is already under water, and when it rains hard, which is often, water must be pumped into canals that lead to Lake Ponchartrain, or else the entire city will flood—and over the Broad Street overpass to the Orleans Parish Coroner's Office. Pipe-smoking Monroe Samuels, a distinguished-looking pathologist who always wore a bow tie, had performed the autopsies on Paulette and Eddie. This long-time respected doctor, now in his late fifties, shook my hand and offered that I probably wanted to hear about the Howard Johnson's homicides.

"Right," I said.

"Those two," Dr. Samuels said, "never had a chance. I don't know how you boys keep your sanity seeing such terrible violence every day."

How *we* keep our sanity? Except for Dantagnan, I didn't know anyone who viewed Samuels's job with anything other than horror.

"Did you recover any bullets?" I asked.

"One from each head."

"The bullets in good shape?"

"Good enough for ballistics comparison. I'll have them over to the lab by this evening. I understand you boys also located some."

The two I'd found in the pools of blood, one under the carpet, plus fragments. The one beneath the carpet could sober up a man real fast. It was *flat*. It blasted straight through the head of one of the victims, bolted through the carpet as if piercing tissue paper, and slammed into the concrete slab with such force that the bullet's head flattened like a pancake.

"I know the wounds weren't contact," Dr. Samuels continued. "I understand the firing was through a pillow. But still, the shots were fired at extremely close range. I'd say the killer shoved the gun into the pillow against the victims' heads and boom boom boom."

"Any other sign of trauma on the bodies?"

"No, nothing. They weren't roughed up before they were shot."

Nor had they put up a struggle. At gunpoint, most people don't.

I drove from the coroner's office to Howard Johnson's to pick up the photostated registration records. A pair of uniforms, unrelated to the investigation, drinking coffee in the restaurant, were the only signs even remotely suggesting something out of the ordinary happened the night before.

I wanted the registration records to be checked against the list of people actually interviewed during the canvass by Burglary and Robbery. We could have placed an officer all night at every door and *someone,* deciding to check out early and unannounced or not returning to the motel after revelry in the Quarter, could still have been missed. And that individual might have seen the killers arrive or leave. It wasn't much, but I didn't have much to go on, and time ticked off the clock, as Lieutenant Duffy reminded when I got back to Homicide headquarters.

"What have you learned, John?" he wanted to know. I'd given the registration records to a secretary to cross-check— normally I'd do this myself, but the circumstances of the HoJo investigation were special, requiring utmost speed— and hoped to escape unnoticed by the brass. Discussing my relative lack of progress with Duffy or Morris would depress them, take up time, and serve no purpose.

"We've thrown out a lot of lines," I said.

"What lines?"

Duffy looked worried. *His* superiors must be tightening the screws on him, too. Ordinarily, Duffy's detectives, me included, couldn't ask for a more patient, empathetic boss, probably because his long hard struggle up the ladder to commander was still fresh in his memory. However, the heat from upstairs had started to melt my boss's understanding nature. I had to cough up some answers that he could accept and pass on.

"I've already been underground in the Quarter. [Drinking and rubbing elbows with Nutso and a pair of runaways.] We're doing deep background on the victims. [Gebbia on the phone to Alexandria.] I've found a source who's certain

Sylvester is behind the killings. [Janet Belton, whose specu-
lations, no matter how informed, were inadmissible in a
court of law.] I'm close to locating a C.I. [confidential
informant] who, if drugs or transvestism are involved, knows
about it. [Sticks, whom Frankie the drug dealer from Mid
Ship said could be living 'anywhere.'] And I'm off to an
important meeting right now. [Lunch with Fred.]"

"I guess I can say you're making progress," Duffy said
and sighed.

I didn't think my short speech impressed him much, but
Duffy, a cop's cop, as opposed to an administrator's cop,
knew times come when a detective needs to be given his head
and left alone.

I arrived at Wise's Cafeteria at 12:30, a half hour late, and
Dantagnan waited just inside the door, pawing the carpet like
a bull about to charge.

"I'll bet management loves you," I told him.

"How's that?"

"Would you go into a place where *you* guarded the door?"

Fred looks fierce—stocky and powerful. He can be fierce,
too, but with family, friends, most of the public, he's the
gentlest of men. Yet how could a customer, hand on
doorknob, wife and little kids in tow, know that? The casting
director of *Godfather III*, if such is ever made, should give
Fred a screen test.

"I need help," I said, when we put our trays on the table
and sat down to eat.

"What can I do?" he asked.

"I don't know. Listen, I guess. This Howard Johnson's a
heater, the brass want it solved yesterday, and I'm not even
sure where to start."

"What do you mean, don't know where to start?" His
face registered impatience and so did his voice. "You know
as well as I do that you need a source of information from

deep in that cesspool of humanity. What do you know now? You know Sylvester. Find out everything about him. It may lead you somewhere. But your cause certainly isn't hopeless. For God's sake, you've got a witness.''

"But no suspects.''

"Anything unusual about the killers?''

"One was probably gay. So, possibly, was one of the victims. It looks like we'll be dealing with transvestites.''

"And you don't know where to start? Get your ass into the Quarter and find out what's the word on the street.''

Fred forked a portion of roast beef into his mouth. He made the investigation sound easy. What did I expect him to do? Make the case look hopeless? No one can do his best if the goal seems unattainable, disappointment and defeat foreordained.

"John,'' he said, "we've been through this before. When things look darkest, that's just when something breaks.''

CHAPTER

—4—

"I heard a gunshot," said Samuel Williams, a lucky man, "and felt a buzz in my head. I knew I was shot. I thought I'd been killed."

I'd come directly from my lunch with Fred Dantagnan to Charity Hospital to obtain a detailed statement from the only person known to have been in Room 215 during the murders. "Let's back up and start from the beginning," I said. "Why were you in Howard Johnson's?"

"I'm from Alexandria. I shouldn't have been there at all. I came to New Orleans looking for work."

Samuel Williams, our star witness, propped up in his bed, looked worse than he really was with his head swathed in bandages. Williams, an impatient patient, nervous and scared, wanted to go home.

"How did you get hitched up with Eddie and Paulette?"

"I met them in a bar in Alexandria. They'd been living in Alexandria for about a year, but were headed back to New Orleans. We got to talking, had a few drinks together, and they asked if I wanted to ride with them. They said I could stay with them while I looked for a job, and I said 'What the hell' and took a room at Howard Johnson's with them.

What's this all about, anyway? We didn't have much money. Why did those people shoot us?''

"When did you check in at Howard Johnson's?"

"Monday the nineteenth. Why did those people smoke us?"

I hoped he'd stop asking. It's never good for a police interrogator to allow roles to be reversed. He might say something a defense attorney can use to smokescreen an otherwise airtight case. Moreover, in this instance, though I knew I'd personally see to the witness's safety, Williams might not believe me if I told him about David Sylvester, hit men, and drug-related murders.

"Did you leave Howard Johnson's at any time during your stay?"

"Sometime Monday night—the nineteenth—me and Eddie and Paulette went out to a bar in the French Quarter. Actually, Eddie dropped us off and went somewhere by himself. He picked us up about three hours later."

"Did either Eddie or Paulette leave the room at any other time between the nineteenth and when the shootings occurred on the twentieth?"

"Yes, twice on Tuesday. Once real early. I was sleeping. But I was awake when they got back. And then they left again Tuesday afternoon."

Tuesday. Leaving in the afternoon had been for Winsberg's court, with Paulette staying at the D.A.'s office while Eddie made the mandatory appearance. I wondered where Paulette and Eddie had gone the first time they left Room 215 that Tuesday.

On Tuesday the twentieth, the defense attorney, Robert Glass, had through discovery procedures forced the state to produce Eddie Smith, which enraged the D.A.'s office. They didn't want Glass questioning the witness beforehand because they'd then lose the element of surprise during the trial. Glass, on the other hand, needed the opportunity to question in advance those slated to testify against his client. He needed to tie down what Eddie Royal intended to say (three months earlier, Glass had questioned Paulette in court—she was the more important witness of the two). Glass's strategy: strengthen the defense by tying down the offense.

It wasn't my position to judge, but I felt Glass had the right to know what he faced. I saw nothing wrong with his demand that the prosecution produce its witnesses. Once their testimony was disclosed, however, they should have been provided the finest protection. Paulette and Eddie could have been arrested as material witnesses and held in protective custody at the city jail apart from the rest of the inmate population. The prosecution often hesitates to take this drastic step for fear of alienating witnesses who don't want to be behind bars, and conceivably could retaliate by refusing to testify. But given the circumstances of this case, the risk should have been taken. Actually, it could be argued that Paulette and Eddie should have been provided around-the-clock guards *in Alexandria*.

A sensitive, delicate situation. The D.A.'s office blamed Winsberg, who countered by pointing out that under the law he had no choice. Connick claimed he did have a choice: He could have denied Glass's motion. It was obvious to me that the debate would never be resolved.

Regardless of legal niceties, the drug charges against Sylvester carried a possible life sentence, not the six months a minor burglary might bring, and once Winsberg issued his ruling, *the witnesses should have been protected*. The facilities and manpower existed to provide that protection.

The prosecution may have underestimated Sylvester. If so,

it must not have talked to any of the scores of New Orleans street cops knowledgeable about his nature.

"On Monday night," I said to Samuel Williams, "when you and Paulette went to the Quarter, where did Eddie Royal go?"

"I don't know."

"Where did you and Paulette go?"

"Several places. I don't remember the names, but Eddie picked us up where he dropped us off."

Looking at Samuel Williams I wondered if Paulette or Eddie had told anyone in the French Quarter where they were staying, and if that information had found its way back to Sylvester. Maybe he didn't need to have Eddie followed from Judge Winsberg's court.

"What happened the night of the murders?" I asked.

"I was in the bed closest to the front door, sleeping, and Eddie and Paulette were in the other bed next to the sliding doors that lead to the pool. I heard somebody knock, and saw Eddie get up and go to the door. He asked who it was, but I couldn't make out the answer. Eddie came walking back into the room, and here comes this fag with a blue and white bandana tied around his head walking behind him. Then came two goons carrying pistols. They told us to get on the floor, and they put pillows over our heads. I couldn't understand what anybody said with the pillow shoved against me. Then I heard gunshots—three, I think. Then three more gunshots. Finally I heard a last gunshot and an awful buzz in my head, and I knew I'd been hit. I stayed on the floor under the pillow a good while, trying to lie still as a dead man. After what seemed like a long time of total silence, I lifted the pillow off my head. That's when I saw Eddie and Paulette lying in puddles of blood. I made my way out the sliding glass doors to the pool and told some people I was shot and hurt real bad. They called the police. I laid my head down on a patio table by the pool until the ambulance showed up and brought me here to the hospital.''

I followed some elementary logic. Before opening the door, Eddie Smith asked who was there. After receiving an answer, he allowed the killers to enter. This meant he must have recognized the voice of one of them and didn't think the individual posed a threat. Eddie Smith knew David Sylvester intimately and had to fear for his life. There had been no forced entry. Ergo, Eddie voluntarily opened the door for those who killed him.

"When you heard the knock and saw Eddie at the door, did you hear conversation?"

"Just Eddie asking who it was."

"And Eddie let them in?" I wanted Williams to repeat it.

"Must have. The door was locked and Eddie opened it."

"Did Eddie give the impression that he knew the people?"

"I thought it was one of his friends, because Eddie was homosexual, too."

"How long after the 'friend' came in did the others enter?"

"Right on his heels. They busted in."

Simple enough: The killers used the man in the bandana to gain entrance into the room. Kicking the door in would have alerted other motel guests.

"Describe the men Eddie let into the room."

Williams answered as he had earlier to Clogher. His descriptions didn't fill me with optimism that we'd soon have the trio under lock and key. He told me all three were black, dark complexioned, close to the same age (twenty-three to twenty-five), similar in height (five feet eight to five feet ten). One had a slender build and a bandana on his head; the other two average builds, one with close cropped hair and the other a medium-length Afro. Not much to go on. Williams didn't recollect either man having any visible moles, marks, scars, or physical deformities to distinguish them from thousands of others on the streets of New Orleans.

I wondered if we faced sifting through the multitudes in an attempt to cull out two nondescript hit men and one nondescript homosexual. Why couldn't we have recognizable offenders? I remembered Saladino, talking about another case, sneering, "The job would be easy if each killer had orange hair cut in a mohawk, missing front teeth, a purple birthmark splashed across his cheek, and a gimp leg." It didn't happen. And here, although "ordinary-looking" is not a requirement on a hit man's job application, it makes for job security and seniority.

"Was the gay man armed?"

"No."

"Could you identify these men if you saw them again?"

"I sure could."

A detective with my job couldn't help loving Samuel Williams. I thought for a moment about adjusting his bed to make him more comfortable.

"You said when the three subjects entered the room, the two 'goons' demanded everyone lie on the floor. Did they actually place you on the floor, or did they direct you where to lie?"

"They told me to get out of bed. I wasn't moving fast enough for them, so one dude grabbed me and pushed me to the floor, and pressed a pillow down on my head. They meant business. They weren't playing around. Their guns looked like cannons. I figured my time had come and I said a quick prayer."

"Before the pillow was placed over your head, did you observe where Eddie and Paulette were forced to lie?"

"No, not until after I was shot and everybody was gone."

"What were the lighting conditions in the room when these people entered?"

An important question. Samuel Williams said he could identify the killers. I pictured a defense attorney assuring a jury that Williams couldn't.

"It was still light outside. The light was off in the room, and the drapes drawn, but I could see good because the TV was on in front of the two beds."

"Describe the man who jerked you out of bed."

Williams described the shorter of the two hitters. I needed to establish who did what. A defense attorney, again, would drip sarcasm and heap abuse in court if we didn't know which killer did what.

"Are you sure of the number of shots fired?"

"Seven. I think."

"And you were shot first?" I hadn't forgotten what he said. I was testing it.

"Last. I told you."

And, like Clogher, I believed a gun probably jammed. That's why Williams got shot only once. Most revolvers hold six rounds—if one hitter used all six, and the second gun jammed after firing once, there'd be no way remaining to hit Samuel Williams, unless the first gunman wanted to reload.

"Do you know who shot you? Do you know who shot Paulette and Eddie?"

"I don't know who shot anybody."

"Did the pillows on both your beds have pillowcases on them?"

"Yes."

"Are you sure?" He'd already said he was.

"Yes, all of us had pillowcases."

That was interesting, because when I'd conducted the crime scene investigation, two pillowcases—the ones that should have been on the pillows covering the heads of Eddie and Paulette—were missing.

Why would pillowcases be missing?

"Except for Paulette and Eddie, had you ever seen any of these people before?"

This might seem an unnecessary question, but I'd risen to my feet to leave, so why not? Some witnesses won't state the most obvious fact until asked. As I neared the door, Williams answered, "No."

The uniform guarding the room stood right behind me. I wanted to leave before our witness let loose his inevitable flurry of questions. I was too late.

"Detective Dillmann, how did I get involved in all this?"

"It was just bad luck," I said truthfully.

"When can I go home?"

"Not right now. We're going to take care of you for a while." I didn't want to get into it. The hitters had killed two people to save one. They would kill one to save four: Sylvester and the three who charged into the motel room.

"I don't want to be taken care of," Williams said.

"You'll like it."

"But—"

"Trust me," I said, stopping his next comment, and went out the door. What else could I say? That his life would be forfeit if we let him go?

My watch read 2:30 P.M., twenty-eight hours since I'd gotten out of bed to report for the nightshift culminating in the killings at Howard Johnson's. I called Emmett Thompson at Homicide. "We have to find Sticks," I told him.

"You won't find him now. It's daytime."

"What do you think?"

"We've been up forever. Let's crash and start again when the sun goes down."

"Meet me at the Submarine at eight?"

"You got it."

I drove to my small, three-bedroom home in Metairie, a New Orleans suburb. Diane knew from the time (I was fifteen hours late), I'd been on a case. Usually she'd know from TV bulletins, but in this instance the only news story had appeared in the *Times-Picayune*. So far the brass had kept the media pretty much at bay.

"Would you like scrambled eggs and a cold beer?"

Diane had become accustomed to life as a cop's wife, and she always registered curious about important ongoing investigations. She knew beer and eggs—even your diet gets messed up—tempted and she'd glean news about the case.

"No food, Di. I need sleep. Wake me at seven, will you?"

"Make it ten at least."

"Seven. And Di, please, I'm not home to anybody."

No doubt the brass would call. Let them imagine me as rested as Rip Van Winkle out solving the crime. They'd be less nervous than if I waxed pessimistic; the way I felt, I'd probably tell them that the killers were most likely already in Chicago or Detroit, or wherever hit men go after they do their work. I knew I shouldn't think negatively—if you expect nothing you'll probably get it—and blamed my poor attitude on lack of rest.

I was asleep before my head sank to the bottom of the pillow. Often I can't sleep, not in the middle of an important case, but after being up so long, I simply zonked out.

"Honey, will you want breakfast or dinner?" were the words that woke me.

"Breakfast. Eggs and coffee."

I realized Diane had put our two-year-old in bed with me. Amy's warm hugs and slobbery kisses didn't make getting up and back to work any easier. At the table I groggily ate breakfast while Diane, Amy, and our son, Todd, had dinner. We had meals together as often as my erratic schedule would allow.

Diane told me the phone rang almost constantly while I slept. She ran down the two dozen or so messages, and I didn't hear a single one I wanted to answer.

Instead I called Fred Dantagnan at Homicide. "Anything new?" I asked.

"That's what everybody wants to know from you. Where are you?"

"At home."

"Good for you. Stay away from here."

"That bad?"

"All bosses, not a single worker. If you want to shoot the breeze, do it on the street where it might accomplish something. You won't find what you're looking for up here. They'll just talk you to death."

At 8:00 P.M.—twenty-six hours after the murders—I stood in front of the Civil War submarine on Chartres Street in Andrew Jackson Square. Looking like an elongated football, the submarine had held two to four men and was driven by a manually operated propeller. Deliberately sunk in 1862 in Lake Ponchartrain, it was discovered in 1878 and raised for public viewing.

Crowds of tourists and ever-present conventioneers bustled by in the warm early evening. I wore tan slacks and a casual short-sleeve shirt, okay attire for either Mid Ship or Brennan's. Emmett Thompson, dressed similarly, pulled up in his white unmarked police car and I got into the front seat. Emmett had also grabbed a few hours' sleep. His police radio, which we wouldn't be answering, was turned on low.

"Where to?" I asked. Emmett knew Sticks better than I did. He'd developed Sticks as a snitch.

"Let's cruise Decatur Street. Sticks will be prowling. Once he gets a date into bed, we'll never find him."

What Emmett meant by Decatur Street, which he knew like his own front yard (he'd worked it as a uniform), comprised a narrow four-block strip near several big convention hotels. Decatur Street: tourists passing through on their way to Bourbon Street, dodging panhandlers, and being propositioned by prostitutes—straight, gay, transvestite, you name it. Decatur Street: inexpensive restaurants, and bars frequented by sailors off the Mississippi River. A rough place, dangerous, with muggings and drug deals commonplace. It's New Orleans's Times Square, but not as well lit.

We could have witnessed practically anything, but this night we saw a local step off the curb and slam himself with a loud thud into the right rear fender of a limousine turning a corner. The local screamed, a chilling, primeval cry, and, faking pain, crumbled into a heap on the pavement.

The limousine's chauffeur, a carbon copy of Mario Puzo's tough guy muscleman Luca Brazi, charged out of the driver's seat, an enraged Fury, and around to the rear of the car where the "victim" writhed in agony. A visitor from the provinces, not wise to big city scams, might have mistaken the driver's haste for that of a Good Samaritan eager to offer aid.

The Luca look-alike picked the local up by his collar, held him in the air, and began shaking him. "You ain't collecting any goddamn insurance money from me!" he roared. "You understand that, you stupid son of a bitch?"

The frightened pedestrian seemed to understand.

In the next block two little dogs on leashes fought each other furiously as their owners, two respectable old ladies out for a walk, tried unsuccessfully to tug them apart.

And still another block further we spotted the guy in the

black raincoat, the flasher, wearing black shoes, scraggly hair and beard, and nothing else. He stood alert waiting for a group of ladies he could surprise.

We covered the four blocks, turned right onto Canal, then right onto Chartres to go back and cruise again. Unfortunately a production crew filming a movie blocked our progress. We had to back onto Canal and go several blocks before we could return for another pass on Decatur. Whatever their script, the movie guys had missed a better one just a block away.

When we hit Decatur Street a second time, Emmett said, "I know that guy," and pulled to a stop.

Guy? He looked twenty-five years old, white, with shoulder-length sandy brown hair, and makeup to rival what a mad cosmetologist might apply—garish lip liner, mascara, eye shadow. He wore a pink frilly blouse, tight chic jeans, and platform sandals. Emmett left the car and I followed.

"Rhonda," Emmett greeted. "How's business?"

"Just fine, Mister Emmett, but it's hot as hell. There's no use hitting the street until the concrete cools. But you're looking good, Mister Emmett. How does it feel to be out of that uniform?"

Street informants, and Rhonda so qualified, often call police officers by their first name, prefaced by "Mister." Though the relationship usually is one of nonhassle (I wouldn't bust a prostitute for being a prostitute), the informant knows the individual is a cop, a fact he'd prefer to forget. The informant wants to show respect, thus the "Mister," and at the same time block out that he's talking to an arm of the law.

"You look great, Rhonda," Emmett complimented, not a patronizing note in his voice. "You must be taking most of the action on Decatur."

"It's these new tits, Mister Emmett. Do you like them?"

He unbuttoned his blouse, cupped one in each hand, and held them forth for display.

"They're pretty, Rhonda. What did they cost?"

"A bunch. I had my ass done last year. I never thought I'd save enough to get the tits, though. I just love them, don't you?"

"Right now I need to talk business. I need to find Sticks."

"What did she do now?"

"No trouble, Rhonda. Just talk. Where is she?"

"I haven't seen her in weeks, Mister Emmett. I heard she got into trouble here on Decatur Street. I hear she's working Basin Street."

Basin Street is about as far from Decatur as you can get and still be in the French Quarter.

"Don't bullshit me, Rhonda," said Emmett, for the first time a hint of menace in his voice. I knew he didn't fake it. He wanted the HoJo murders solved as much as anyone. "There's no action on Basin Street."

"I'm only telling you what I heard. You sure Sticks isn't in trouble? I don't need trouble."

It often happened this way. You obtained information, and when the source began fearing for himself you could pretty well count on its accuracy.

"My God," Emmett said, shaking his head when we were back in the car. "I save all year for Disney World. Rhonda saves for tits."

The radio crackled for us to call the office. Instead, we stopped at a corner pay booth and phoned Dantagnan, who'd differentiate between a radio message signaling a break in the case and a roundup for a time-consuming, blame-affixing meeting.

"Fred? What you got?"

"It's dead up here. We hoped you'd have something."

"Not yet." *I* hoped for fewer radio calls. If I kept refusing to respond, I'd be on the carpet. I was, after all, only a detective, with a duty to follow the instructions of superiors. I knew I needed to be on the street, but if brass brought down enough heat, I'd have to submit.

We headed for Basin Street, one of the oldest and most historic thoroughfares in New Orleans. Tennessee Williams wrote *Cat on a Hot Tin Roof* on Basin Street, and elsewhere you can see the Streetcar Named Desire. A park on Basin Street bears jazz musician Louis Armstrong's name, and you can't help, on a hot, quiet, lazy afternoon hearing strains of "Basin Street Blues," with Marlon Brando yelling "Stella!" in the background.

I didn't even want to think about where we'd be, or what we'd do, if we couldn't find Sticks. This streetwise/transvestite/hooker/police snitch embodied a walking directory on the underside of French Quarter life, at least one portion of it.

What did we have? *Black* transvestites. *Black* hitters. A *black* prostitute murdered. A *black* heroin kingpin dealing out of the Quarter. Rhonda, a white, would know no more about such matters than a Scarsdale matron would about life on a Harlem street. Sticks was our best shot. If we didn't hit the mark with him, I feared we'd fire blanks the rest of the way.

Emmett and I cruised Basin Street for an hour, quite recognizable—unmarked police car or no—to street people. But they wouldn't take particular note. Basin Street registering its high crime rate would really look suspicious with a *lack* of police presence.

I felt like talking, but most of the time—like right now—Emmett could make the Sphinx look like a blabbermouth. I kept quiet and watched as he drove, knowing his inward calm matched his outward exterior. The only emotion showed in a twinkle in his eyes that took in everything and laughed at the madness they recorded.

He came all at once into view, flouncing around the corner of Bienville onto Basin Street. Laughing. He clung to the arm of a distinguished-looking, graying, fifty-year-old man in coat and tie.

Sticks wore a black sequined dress cut eight inches above the knee, spiked heels, and carried a satin evening bag slung over his shoulder. A human string bean five feet eleven, an even hundred pounds, so skinny he made me gape, toothpicks for arms and legs, a walking razor blade; but I had to admit, he looked jaunty, peppy, full of life. Sticks might seem a heavenly vision to the businessman who wobbled on liquory legs.

We hopped out of the car and approached the laughing couple. Sticks spotted Emmett, put a this-is-a-good-deal, I-don't-need-this-now, please-leave-me-alone expression on his face and hoped we'd let him walk right on by.

We stopped directly in front of them, blocking their progress. "Step over here, Sticks," Emmett said, gesturing toward a doorway. "I need to talk to you."

"Mister Emmett, give me a break."

Sticks looked sideways at his escort.

The man seemed less distinguished close up. He reeled, frozen-faced from hooch. Numb. A needle thrust into his face wouldn't have hurt him.

"I don't have a lot of time," Emmett said roughly. "Let's walk."

Sticks knew the score. He could tell Emmett wouldn't go away, and I heard a low groan of disappointment at giving up this minimum fifty-dollar trick.

The man *didn't* know the score. "Leave the lady alone," he said, with breath a match could ignite. He lurched, shoved his arm out to push Emmett away.

I clamped my right hand down on the arm, spinning him halfway around, squeezed hard, and with my left hand shoved my police badge up against his face, not an inch from the tip of his nose.

"Look, Cap," I said. "You don't know what you're into. You're drunk. Go back to your hotel and sleep it off."

"Let loose of me. I'm the president of—"

"I don't care, Cap. Get up the street."

This ludicrous man who'd picked up another man he thought was a woman wanted to argue more, but I increased the pressure on his arm. Even through the booze it hurt. I felt I did him a favor. Would he, in days to come, prefer to explain to a wife or a board of directors how he happened to be with a transvestite prostitute? When the belligerence left his eyes, I released his arm and he stumbled along unsteadily.

Ten feet away, just when I hoped we had him out of our hair, he turned and asked, "Do you have a warrant?"

What to do? The man was too intoxicated to understand an explanation, and reasoning with him—that is, explaining that he had no business stumbling around the French Quarter like a fawn in a cage of tigers—would have been useless. We could have him carted off to jail for interfering with a police investigation, but we didn't want to fool with it. Nobody would gain by his arrest.

"Go back to the hotel," I told him again. "You're going to get hurt here."

This was the plain truth. He was lucky to have not already been hurt, lucky Sticks picked him up. Sticks would have charged him $50 for oral sex, but if a different transvestite had latched onto him, it could have cost him his life.

"You need a warrant," the drunk persisted.

Good Lord.

I strode up to him, pushed him, while at the same time holding on for dear life so he wouldn't fall, and said, "Get the hell out of here."

This time he left for good, turning only once, twenty-five feet away, to shout, "I'm reporting this to the police!"

At last we could turn our full attention to Sticks. "For heaven's sake, Mister Emmett," he said. "At least handcuff me and put me in the car. Make it look right to any eyes watching."

Handcuffing him, we got in the car and drove in silence to a dark, secluded wharf overlooking the Mississippi River. On the black water ships passed back and forth in the night.

CHAPTER

—5—

A beautiful night. Absolutely enchanting. And a lovely, perfect spot, if you're a teenager, to bring your girl—or if you're married, your wife. Songs get written about places like this.

Sticks sat in the backseat, handcuffs removed; Emmett and I were in front. From our position on the wharf we looked out on a gorgeous, take-your-breath-away evening, the sky sparkling with stars, the great river not five feet in front of us, but we couldn't enjoy it. Sticks smoked up a storm and the warm slight breeze off the river couldn't cope with it. The moment we parked, Emmett had to roll up the windows and keep the engine running so the air conditioner would save us from asphyxiation.

"Sticks," said Emmett, wasting no time, "we've known each other for years. You've helped me. I've taken care of you. I'll tell you right now, what I have to ask is strong. What's the word on the street about the murders at Howard Johnson's?"

"Paulette and Eddie."

"Right."

"It's scary, Mister Emmett. Nothing's kicking at all. Some heavy people involved, I guess. You know these queens, they gossip about everything. But this time it's real spooky. Nothing.''

"Sticks, you don't need to bullshit me. I know you. I know when you're bullshitting.''

"Dammit, Mister Emmett, you picked me up off the street right in front of God and everybody. I told you this is heavy. You trying to get me killed?''

Sticks couldn't hide his fright. The moonlight streaming into the car played no tricks on his face. His hands trembled when he lifted his cigarette to his lips. A tough situation for him, but just as tough for us. We knew he was lying: The French Quarter buzzed with talk about the murders at Howard Johnson's, however uninformed that talk might be. Homicide investigations didn't get much more major than this one, and both of us groped for the right way to handle Sticks, the prize informant. Someone to treat with respect, but someone who *had* to help. We needed it desperately.

"Sticks," said Emmett, his voice low, "don't make me keep reminding you. You owe me. You know you owe me. Besides, have I ever let anybody hurt you?''

"Mister Emmett, I'm telling you, we're dealing with dangerous people.''

"We'll take care of you.''

"Like Paulette and Eddie?''

"That wasn't us.''

I thought of Ponytail and Tank Top passing the buck. It *really* hadn't been us, but what difference did it make? What Sticks said carried weight, and police officers in New Orleans and perhaps all over the nation might face living with the horrible blunder already made.

"Sticks," I said to keep the dialogue going, "did you know Paulette and Eddie?''

He nodded quickly, once.

"I saw it," I said. "They were lying on the floor with

pillows over their bloody heads. All head shots, Sticks. They died like dogs. Nobody deserves to die like that.''

I knew Sticks possessed a certain decency, and that's where I tried to aim my appeal. In ways he wasn't a bad person. I couldn't understand how he lived, and I imagined it wrong, but he also carried something good in him.

"The murders were awful," Sticks said, his voice breaking. "But what good does it do for me to get killed?"

"You've got Emmett's word," I said. "You've got mine."

"I won't testify."

"Nobody's asking you to testify," Emmett said. "We just need to know the names of the players. We'll keep you out of it."

"You promise?"

"We promise."

Sticks lit one cigarette with another. I looked at the moon and stars and said a prayer.

"The word is," Sticks said, "a queen named Cris is involved. She got into a car with two guys—I think they're the ones who took the contract—about an hour before the killings came down."

"Who were the guys?" I asked.

"I don't know."

"What kind of car did Cris get into?"

"I don't know."

"Who put out the contract?" Emmett asked.

"I don't know for sure, but Cris was talking with David Sylvester right before she got into the car."

I glanced at Emmett. As cool as he appeared, I knew he fought to keep from slapping me a high five.

"Do you know Sylvester?" I asked.

"Everybody knows Sylvester." A shudder ran through his whole thin body. "He's the main man."

"Did you see Cris talking to Sylvester?"

"No, a friend did."

"Did you see Cris get in the car?"

"No, it was the friend."

"Who is that?"

"She won't want to get involved."

"The name, Sticks. Give us the name."

"I don't want her in trouble."

"We'll treat her just like she's you."

"I can count on you? Do you swear I can count on you?"

"We swear."

Sticks sank into silence. It didn't take extra compassion to realize he faced a tough choice. I watched a paddle steamer, *The President,* churn up the old river, the boat blazing with bright lights, the jazz band's music wafting across the water to us. I promised myself that some night I'd take Diane to this place.

"Her name is Trixie," Sticks said.

"Where can we find Trixie?"

"She won't talk. I'll have to talk to her first."

"When can you do that?"

"Some time tomorrow. She lives in my neighborhood."

"It's just before midnight now," I said. "Do you really mean tomorrow?"

"Yes, but Trixie's on the street now. She'd be almost impossible to find."

We had no reason to keep Sticks, and no choice but to trust him. He'd always come through in the past, and could be counted on to know if a witness would likely clam up. If we put the heat on Sticks to get us to Trixie faster, we might lose everything.

"Call me on the straight line number," I said, "when you've talked to Trixie." The "straight line" allowed Sticks to reach me without going through the police switchboard. It's a number I rarely give out.

We left the solitude of the river for the chaos of the city, dropping Sticks at the foot of Canal Street, just a stone's throw from the Quarter. Bad enough his friends had seen him picked up in a cop car, but chauffeured back?

With the exception of Samuel Williams's survival, the information Sticks provided represented our first break of any kind; possibly a gigantic one. Sylvester's name had popped up! It made us want more. When a case stalls on dead center, depression often takes over and affects performance, something always to guard against. But a break, especially a potentially big one, injects energy into the investigator, sets his adrenaline pumping.

Emmett and I chuckled about "lettin' 'em wait" as we enjoyed a cup of coffee at Cafe Du Monde. But we both knew there was a big difference between aggravating the brass for good reason and doing it out of perversity, so after one cup we returned to the Homicide office.

The big, almost vacant, Homicide room glowed with lights at 1:00 A.M. The people on the graveyard shift, if caught up on their paperwork, had dispersed for the first of endless cups of coffee or they cruised the city—maybe two or three guys teamed up to keep one another company while they waited for murder. Day shift, the busiest of the three, clamors with a steady stream of calls from witnesses, other cops, newspapers. Reporters spend more time with homicide detectives than any other type of policeman.

This early morning, except for a lone typist, only maintenance cleanup people worked in the room.

Duffy was still up.

"Come into my office," he said. "I've forgotten what you guys look like."

"You didn't forget, Tom," Emmett joked. We called him "Tom" when alone with him, "Lieutenant" in mixed company. We sat down in his office.

''Fine time to show up,'' Duffy said. ''Everybody's gone. You guys come like thieves in the night.''

His words sounded tough, but he showed no anger.

''We couldn't get any work done answering questions,'' I told him.

''I know,'' Duffy said. He had worked the street, knew how it went. ''You got any breaks yet?''

We told him about Sticks, never mentioning his name, and how he brought up Sylvester. We wouldn't reveal a confidential source, not even to our boss. You learn to treasure informant's, protect them, and not just because it's something that makes you important to the Department. Kept in the dark, Duffy could honestly tell a judge he didn't know the name of our snitch. The fewer people who knew an informant's name, the better. Duffy knew this and respected it. Because of excellent cops like him, New Orleans's Homicide unit had one of the best solve rates, 76 percent at this time (nationwide average: 70 percent), in the country, despite Mardi Gras murders committed spur-of-the-moment by transients, cases extremely hard to solve.

I knew cops, like reporters, who opted for jail, and would do it again, to protect such people as Sticks. Once you divulge a source, you may never find another one.

''All your eggs in this snitch's basket?'' Duffy mused.

''It's all we've got,'' I said. What could we have? We considered ourselves lucky to have Sticks.

''What if the snitch doesn't produce?'' Duffy knew the answer to this. He sighed.

''We'll find him,'' I said, ''if we have to interview every transvestite in the city.''

Though it remained unsaid, Duffy longed for hope, blessed hope, to offer his own very nervous superiors.

Duffy represented the best of bosses. He *understood* our jobs and gave us some slack; simultaneously, he understood and placated the upper brass, gave them hope that ultimately they wouldn't end up facing a bank of klieg lights in some congressional hearing room squirming to a righteous senator's questions.

The NOPD possessed one advantage over other cities with its practice of placing one person, in this case myself, in charge of a homicide investigation. During the Charles Manson investigation in California, so many different individuals and agencies had pieces of the action, each one striving for the glory of cracking the case, solving it probably took longer than necessary. I've heard of numerous examples in New York City of one detective withholding information from another. But in New Orleans, I had one person to report to, Duffy, and then he sent the information up the ladder. I could call on a battalion of detectives, and I might later—to find Trixie, or to perform other investigative tasks—but right now I didn't need them. We had to cool our heels and give Sticks a chance. Otherwise, we'd lose him. Higher-ups might want speed *now,* and I'd oblige as much as possible, but a quick solution, which might prove no solution at all, weighed more heavily on them than me. Turning loose an army of detectives in the Quarter would warn the killers, and at worst get Trixie killed. What Emmett and I gave Duffy constituted very little, but *something;* it would temporarily hold off the frightened wolves.

When we left Duffy's office I told Emmett to go home and get some sleep; two people weren't needed for what one could handle.

I went to the "alias file" in our computer. When an individual gets arrested, his or her aliases and nicknames are listed on the arrest report and then input into the computer. Later, we can instruct the computer to pull out every alias and start a new file, and that is what I now checked. I entered the name "Trixie" along with the proper code; when the file showed on the screen, I had to go through each individual Trixie ever arrested in New Orleans and then call up separate records. A tedious process of elimination, but I needed this data for an alternate plan in case Sticks failed.

Sixty-eight people named Trixie showed up on the computer. I narrowed them down to fourteen. Then I made a handwritten list with their pertinent stats: name, age, address, previous addresses, social security number, arrests, and people they'd been arrested with. Luckily, I had only fourteen; a "John Smith" entry can spit out hundreds of possibles.

I searched for a female impersonator who frequented the area where Sylvester lived, the Sixth District (the New Orleans equivalent of a New York City precinct), who'd been arrested for prostitution, vagrancy, narcotics, or simple robbery—especially busts for narcotics.

Trixie saw Cris get into a car with two men. I strongly suspected Cris as the individual used to escort the shooters through the door of Howard Johnson's Room 215.

The tedious two hours of computer work complete, I called the Vice and Narcotics offices and set up a meeting with an on-duty officer from each. I told them I was working the HoJo murders, which meant "urgent."

A little before 4:00 A.M. I met the man from Vice in a bar, Lucky Pierre's, on Bourbon Street. This night Frankie Ford, maybe the best in the world at a piano bar, still took requests. New Orleans, like Las Vegas, never closes, but it does have clocks.

I didn't envy the man from Vice. He had one of the worst jobs in the police department, dealing with prostitution, gambling, pornography, low-degenerate crimes. Hanging around public restrooms doesn't edify, nor does peeping through holes cut in restroom partitions. I couldn't hack that kind of duty. It gets almost suicidally depressing seeing eight- and nine-year-olds used for prostitution, and probably explains why I've never met anyone from that detail devoid of a sour attitude.

The undercover Vice man wore an expensive suit, but his tie was pulled to one side, his shirttail was out, and his hair mussed—his role that of a drunken conventioneer, a big spender with a credit card. The Department gave this detective money to throw away on booze, but he had to buy his own clothes, a costly proposition.

"I'm trying to locate a queen named Trixie," I said.

"What's he look like?"

"I don't know."

"Is he local?"

"I think so."

"What area does he work?"

"Lives in the Sixth, I think, but works the Quarter."

"Don't you have any more than that?" He'd help, but he wouldn't be impressed. The HoJo murders might be a big deal to some people, but not him.

"That's it," I said. "I'm trying to jam David Sylvester."

"Yeah?" His interest increased. "Sylvester put out those contracts?"

"Looks like it."

"Well, good luck to you, Dillmann, and believe me when I say I'm rooting for you. Trixie, huh? Could be one of several. With just a name, it's going to be tough."

Like a computer, he rattled off half a dozen possibilities. I jotted down what he said. Then he did the same with the name Cris.

At 4:30 A.M. I met the Narcotics undercover man at a Tastee Donut. He, too, dressed for his part: tattered jeans, sleeveless sweatshirt, four-day beard; a portrait of grubbiness. This time I mentioned Sylvester right away, which got his attention. Being from Narcotics, he owned a wealth of

Sylvester stories. He also had six possibilities, two were the same Vice had given. "Sylvester," the narc said, "often links up with tranvestites. One of the ways he moves his dope. That's why he's so hard to pop. We don't have many undercover narcs who dress in drag."

"I guess not," I said. I wasn't familiar with the day-to-day operations of Narcotics, but I imagined it a macho crew, not unlike Homicide, and getting someone like Saladino to dress in drag would be a joke. Not to mention the detective would need the acting skills of Laurence Olivier to play a role so completely foreign to him.

"Sylvester is cunning," the narc told me, which I'd heard before. "Transvestites, by necessity, form their own little community. Like the Amish, you might say. They figure people can't understand them, and they're probably right, so they don't try to get through. They confide in one another, and keep their mouths shut. Wouldn't you if experience has taught you that you're going to be laughed at or, more likely, beaten up? Add to this clubbishness a healthy dose of fear of Sylvester, and you've got people who keep quiet."

At 6:30 A.M. I was back at Cafe Du Monde, thinking and sipping coffee with an early edition of the July 22 *Times-Picayune* spread in front of me. Judge Winsberg had indeed struck back, calling District Attorney Harry Connick "obnoxious" and "half-cocked."

I never believed for a moment Judge Winsberg would sit quietly and let blame for the Howard Johnson's murders be dumped in front of his bench. Why hadn't Harry Connick raised an objection when the defense demanded that Eddie Smith be produced in court, Winsberg wanted to know.

Connick, in turn, told the newspaper that Eddie Smith had refused protection; true enough, though perhaps not relevant. The *Times-Picayune* had not yet sent up the loud cry about witnesses going unprotected, which I knew was the reaction certain officials most feared. Not much consolation, I guessed, with the story still a front-page item.

Lethargically I read a few other stories: the Olympic Games beginning in Montreal, and the upcoming Republican National Convention, pitting President Gerald Ford against Ronald Reagan.

I watched the sun clear the horizon over the Mighty Mississippi, and then went home to sleep.

CHAPTER

—6—

"John," Diane said, shaking me awake. "It's your dad. Come to the phone and talk to him."

My father, a distributing company executive, had been sandwiched between detectives. His grandfather, my great-grandfather, clocked in one of the longest police careers in New Orleans history, 1902 to 1946. Thus, my father, John, Jr., became a frustrated detective, just having grown up listening to and hearing about my great-grandfather George, and then living vicariously through me. Dad always pumped me for information, rooting as avidly as a kid of the 1940s did for Roy Rogers and Tom Mix when they chased bad guys. He took pride in what I did, never more than in 1971 when at age twenty-four I became the youngest homicide detective the city ever had.

"What are you working on?" he asked.

"Nothing unusual."

"You haven't been home."

"I know." I didn't want to get into the HoJo case with my father. He'd have more questions than the D.A.'s office.

"I've been calling Diane. I know something's up. What is it?" Dad was a born snoop.

"I told you, nothing unusual." I didn't yet know the time of day, but by the way my head pounded I knew I hadn't slept long.

"It's those murders at Howard Johnson's, I'll bet. There's a lot more to those homicides than what I read in the newspaper, isn't there?"

"I can't tell yet," I hedged. If I verified his hypothesis, he'd milk me hard for information. I'd never get back on the street.

"Are you going to catch those killers?"

"Dad . . ."

"Who hired them?"

"Dad, I have to go."

"Your great-grandfather always confided in me."

I doubted that. Maybe he confided after he solved the case. I eased off the phone and into recollections of George: He had died when I was a year old, 1948, two years after he left the force. Police work was his life, and he died when they made him retire. I wish I had known him.

George Dillmann was something. I have old newspaper clippings from his career. One, from the *New Orleans Item* dated April 25, 1915, ran on the front page and featured George in straw hat, suit, and tie. The case in question earned him the moniker Single-Handed Dillmann, a nickname that stuck.

Harry Lester, a bandit, shot and killed a baggageman for the L & N Railroad during a train robbery. Carrying purloined cash, jewelry, and other valuables, Lester leaped off the train near Honey Island and fled into the swamps at night.

A big posse armed with shotguns and bloodhounds decided to wait the ten hours for daylight. The Honey Island swamp posed a nightmare whatever the time, but especially at night. Swarms of mosquitoes and insects could drive a man mad, and the poisonous snakes, alligators, and quick-sand could kill him. A fearful place.

George, who hunted there often, knew the swamp like the back of his hand. He went in alone. Several hours later he came out, shot in the face (he carried the scar his whole life), dripping in mud, utterly exhausted, but he had a handcuffed Harry Lester in tow.

When George retired in 1946, the *New Orleans Item* ran a feature story on him and his wife, Sophie, whom I did get to know quite well. "Oh, it wasn't easy like now," Sophie told the reporter. "A policeman was a real man in those days. George caught yellow fever carrying out the dead and dying from the houses in the epidemic about 1908."

"I did my duty," George said during the interview, "and I always tried to be fair. I got that combination behind me, and that's why I got friends today."

It was more pleasant to think of George this early afternoon on July 22 than to refocus right away on the Howard Johnson's case. My father and Sophie told me so many stories about him. One time, off-duty, he walked into a grocery store being held up by two men with sawed-off shotguns; they spun on him and fired, and he returned the fire, wounding one of them and killing the other. When he returned home, Sophie told me, his overcoat was riddled with bullet holes.

George stood a very strong five feet eight and weighed 220 pounds; and he didn't carry an ounce of fat: sort of an early day Dantagnan. My great-grandfather's hands looked like catchers' mitts. He was a tough, old-time street detective who would have stayed on the force until he died except the Department made him retire.

The Mississippi River brought many immigrants to New Orleans, including George's ancestors, who arrived from Germany and France in the eighteenth century. By 1840, with a population of 102,193, and professional opera and theater companies, the nation's fourth largest city became known as the Paris of America.

George saw New Orleans change a lot in his own seventy-two years. The streetcars he rode have just about vanished, and so, too, have the beat cops who knew everyone by name. The old-time police motto, still used—"Protect and Serve"—became somewhat meaningless. Police often can't guarantee protection anymore.

I ate red beans and rice about 2:30 P.M. and gave Diane an edited version of the case, deleting the David Sylvester portion. The shooters were frightening enough; talk about the heroin dealer would only provide extra cause for worry. She had enough of that without me filling in details. While we talked, Amy toddled around the table performing her repertoire of tricks sure to amuse Mommie and Daddy. Todd was in school.

I sympathized with Diane and the problems of being married to a cop. The routine isn't routine: Plans for family outings, dinner with friends, trips to movies can't be made with any certainty. While usual working hours are predict-able—the regular eight-hour shift, the holiday duty, spend-ing one of every three nights working—there are times, as with heater cases like the HoJo killings, when massive doses of overtime are required. Also, Diane could hardly enjoy seeing me strap on a gun every day, and seldom when I returned home did I have cheerful stories to tell.

Diane often asked how she could help, and I tried to convince her she did in invaluable ways by keeping part of my life steady and sane. She couldn't be mistaken for streetwise, and I didn't want her to be, which was another reason why I couldn't, and shouldn't, tell her about people like David Sylvester.

"Will you be home on time?" Diane asked as I prepared to leave at three.

"I don't know," I said, kissing her, the same answer I always gave. The answer made me feel terrible, and I wished with all my heart I could be more specific.

I sat desultorily at my desk in the Homicide office "clerking"—doing paperwork, but prepared to look busy if a superior wandered by. Usually I wouldn't have bothered, but the brass wanted to think I was right on top of the Howard Johnson's case; sniffing out clues, running down witnesses, collaring the perpetrators. In reality, the inertia broke only when the phone rang and three heads— Emmett's, Gebbia's, and mine—snapped to attention.

A little before 5:00 P.M., running out of time and patience before we had to start looking up those people on the computer list, the call came through on the straight line.

"Detective Dillmann?" asked a deep, feminine voice.

"Speaking."

"This is Trixie. Sticks says I can trust you."

"What's your location? I'll come and get you."

"I'm at a pay phone at Claiborne and Melpomene."

"I'll be there in ten minutes."

"The source came through," I said to Duffy, as we literally jogged past his office on our way to the garage. "We'll want to use your office in a half hour or so," I called over my shoulder.

We brought Trixie back to Homicide and ensconced him in Duffy's office. The commander went downstairs, probably for coffee.

Trixie, five feet ten, slender, wore tight jeans and a short blouse exposing his navel. Frightened, his hands couldn't control the cup of coffee I handed him.

"Did you know Paulette and Eddie?" I began.

"Oh yes, they were my good friends."

Right away I permitted myself a breath of relief. Scared Trixie might be, but what he knew bothered him, and he had obviously made up his mind to tell it.

"What information do you have about Cris?"

"I know the bitch had something to do with the murders."

"How do you know?"

"On Tuesday I was sitting on my porch—"

"That's the twentieth?"

"Right."

"Where is your porch?"

"Twenty-eight twelve Philip Street."

"Go on."

"I saw Cris on the corner talking to David Sylvester. I figured it to be a dope deal—Cris is always strung out. After Sylvester left in his big car, Cris came over and sat with me. I didn't think anything about it, but then this big black Lincoln with red pinstripes along the side pulled up in front of my house. The dude driving the Lincoln blew his horn, and Cris went and got in the backseat. Three hours later, about seven thirty that night, the two dudes in the Lincoln dropped Cris off, right where they'd picked her up. She was a nervous wreck, shaking. I thought she wanted to cry. I didn't find out until later about Paulette and Eddie, but I'm sure Cris brought those two over to the motel."

"Why are you sure of that?"

"Because Cris was a close friend of Paulette and Eddie, and would have known where they were. Cris told me she talked with them earlier on Tuesday."

Before the appearance in Judge Winsberg's court. Again it seemed possible Sylvester hadn't learned their whereabouts through the pretrial hearing.

"What's Cris's connection with Sylvester?"

"She's on dope, what else? Sylvester's her supplier."

"Can you describe the individuals in the black Lincoln?"

"No, I didn't want to stare at them."

"Where can I find Cris?"

"I don't know where she lives, but she hangs around my house on Philip Street. A lot of the girls do."

"What was Cris wearing when she got in the Lincoln?"

"Blue jeans. A blouse. A blue and white bandana tied around her head."

Bingo! Let the bells ring! I felt like hurrying out of Duffy's office to share the good tidings.

"You say Cris talked with Paulette and Eddie on Tuesday the twentieth? How did Cris hook up with them?"

"They used to live with Cris and Mae West. The four were good friends. Cris told me Paulette and Eddie came over to her house on Tuesday morning."

That explained where they went on the twentieth when Samuel Williams woke up and learned they'd left the motel. Such running around would never have been permitted if they'd been under guard. Obviously, Paulette and Eddie felt safe with Cris. They would have opened a door for Cris.

"Cris lived with Mae West?"

"Yes."

Mae West. The legendary (in New Orleans) Mae West. Not, of course, the actress of the 1930s, but a female impersonator as famous in his circle as the other in hers: large breasts, flamboyant blond wig, great body. Our Mae West headlined female impersonator shows on Bourbon Street, the sex symbol to transvestites that his namesake had once been for straights. Mae West was big time, sort of.

"Do you know what Paulette and Eddie talked with Cris about?"

"No, they just recalled old times, I guess. Like I said, they'd been close."

And Paulette and Eddie could have given an address to these "close" friends, I guessed. Cris, an addict, might have traded information to Sylvester for drugs. Increasingly, I believed Sylvester hadn't needed Eddie Smith followed from Judge Winsberg's court. He could have learned his location from Cris. Then it was wait for the first opportunity, hitters, and on to Howard Johnson's.

"You say you're sure picking up Cris in the Lincoln tied into the Howard Johnson's murders. Why couldn't it have been something else? A ride with friends? A trick, maybe?"

"It all fits. I knew it when I heard on the news that Paulette and Eddie had been murdered. Those were bad dudes in that Lincoln. I knew Cris wasn't going on any trick. It all fit."

I thought so, too. What else could it be? But what Trixie told me didn't *prove* anything. Getting the proof might be difficult, and I could see only one obvious way. Neither the hitters nor Sylvester would talk. And catching the hitters with guns whose bullets ballistically matched those at the crime scene was a pipe dream. The *only* way to get proof was to turn Cris before the hitters threw him away. I knew I had to get to Cris first. I had to consider it a race.

"Listen to me closely, Trixie. I'm going to put you back working the street. Find Cris and call me immediately. I'll give the word to the desk sergeant. You leave a number with him. He can get hold of me either by radio or telephone, and I'll be back to you in seconds." The higher-ups trying to reach me earlier might have found this interesting.

"Paulette and Eddie are dead, Trixie," I continued, trying to convey how serious matters were, "because they opened their mouths. Please don't make the same mistake. Don't say a word to anyone except me. If Sylvester even suspects you saw Cris with those people in the Lincoln, *both* you and Cris are dead meat."

When Trixie left Duffy's office, I gave him ten minutes, then went to the coffee shop downstairs, found Duffy, asked him to come back to the office, and brought him up to date.

"What do you intend to do now?" he asked. He knew what I should do, but wanted to hear it from me.

"I'll stake out the Philip Street house round the clock. Dantagnan will work with me. Gebbia, Clogher, and Thompson can work the Quarter. We're bound to catch him."

"How will you recognize this Cris if he's in drag? The description you have is of an individual dressed straight, so to speak."

"We'll have to hope. Remember, I've got Trixie looking. I think he'll come through."

"Do you need more personnel, John? You can have all you want."

"Not right now. Five of us can handle it."

Duffy appeared more relaxed than usual when I left, hopeful and eager. He could report action to his superiors, but he especially liked the chance, however long, of his Homicide unit nailing Sylvester when so many had failed for so long.

I called Fred at home, picked him up there, and drove to Philip Street. Normally Fred wouldn't like surveillance *or* working a case on a shift not his own. Family time counted a lot with Fred. But a heater case possessed an irresistible appeal.

For my part, I wanted him nearby. He was my best friend, I knew all his moves, and I needed someone I could trust absolutely in a dangerous situation.

The 2812 Philip Street address turned out to be a large, wood, two-story house converted into multiple apartments. From a big porch, a hallway went deep inside, with apartments on each side. Fred and I parked a block and a half

away in a van with one-way glass and viewed the comings
and goings through binoculars.

Who could not be intrigued by this show? A constant flow
of some of the most beautiful women in New Orleans, and
they weren't women, paraded in and out the door. All
shapes and sizes and colors, but no johns allowed, the Philip
Street address reserved itself for transvestites; a hideaway, a
place to rest and talk, change clothes, freshen makeup—a
haven.

Fred and I took turns watching. Usually surveillance is
deadly dull, all cops hate it, but this I would have paid
admission to see. The straight-arrow Dantagnan claimed not
to be impressed, while I wondered aloud about the tangled
lives of those he/shes.

"I don't want to know," Fred countered. "They leave me
alone, I'll leave them alone."

Fred did say working another shift besides his own would
be worth it if he caught a glimpse of Mae West. But when I
suggested he dress in drag and try to infiltrate "this nest of
beauty," he responded with, "Get lost, you asshole."

"They don't make stockings big enough for your ugly
legs," I said.

"Lay off, Dillmann."

"You'd look cute in a dress, though."

"Lay off, I said."

A good idea, since I couldn't tell if he was kidding or had
really steamed into the angry zone. Hand-to-hand skirmish
in a crowded van with this short, white version of the
Steelers' Mean Joe Greene made no sense, particularly since
we camouflaged ourselves to see out, not raise a ruckus and
cause everybody on the street to want to see in.

Perhaps ten minutes later, Fred, manning the binoculars,
leaned forward, stiffened, and began to quiver. "I think

that's him,'' he whispered excitedly. ''I'm almost sure of it. Yes! It's Mae West!''

''Let me see!'' I said, snatching the binoculars from his hands. But 2812's doorstep was empty when I focused. I'd been had.

''Hah!'' Dantagnan said. ''You're the one who ought to be in drag.''

So it went until 6:00 P.M. and beyond. A score of transvestites entered and exited the house. But there'd been no sign of Cris, no word from Trixie. The van became an oven; we could smell each other.

At 6:45 P.M. the alert came over the radio that Trixie had just called. I phoned him immediately and learned Cris minutes before had gone into 2812, Apartment #1, the first door off the hallway to the right. ''Good news,'' I said to Dantagnan, and the powerful detective jammed a thumbs-up.

Trixie, it turned out, set up his own surveillance, just two blocks from where we cooked in the van. Duffy's fear had been justified: We'd seen Cris go inside and didn't recognize him.

It hadn't hurt, fortunately. Now we made hurried plans to raid the residence.

CHAPTER

—7—

At 7:30 P.M. on Thursday, July 22, forty-nine and a half hours after the HoJo murders, Fred, Emmett, Gebbia, and I gathered at the door of Apartment #1 at 2812 Philip Street.

I thought four detectives just the right number. Few enough not to trip over one another, yet adequate to control violence or an escape attempt. I disagree with those police administrators who contend an overwhelming show of force paralyzes a suspect, demonstrates to him the impossibility of escape, and persuades him to give up. The strength-in-numbers theory also holds that a massive show of police prevents a fugitive from taking hostages, or opening fire and hurting innocent people.

Of course, every situation is different, but I didn't think raiding this French Quarter apartment required squads of detectives. A dozen cars converging on a residence, and two dozen policemen fanning out in all directions, can create havoc. The whole neighborhood takes notice, bringing out bystanders—potential victims. Worst of all, the confusion can trigger gunfire from the cornered offender.

Besides, if the situation merits, you can always call in reinforcements.

Fred and I once handled a triple-murder, drug-related case

in the black Projects. We knew the name of the killer and the apartment in which he lived. Our chief of detectives at the time wanted to send in five black cops, five white cops, plus the Tactical unit.

Fred and I pleaded to be given four hours to see what we could do on our own. I went to the front door, Fred to the back, and we made the arrest; the killer's mother let us in: She feared her eighteen-year-old murderer son, whom we found sleeping on a couch. A police army invading these Projects could have provoked a terrible scene.

Another time homicide detective Mike Rice and I traced a killer, who'd all but decapitated a man with a butcher knife, to a restaurant/bar on Bourbon Street. Pretending to be drunk, Rice and I staggered over next to the suspect, and quick-as-you-can shoved guns up against his head. We had an overpowering case against the individual, warrants for his arrest, and he never stood a chance. The *Times-Picayune* praised Rice and me for an arrest most patrons in the restaurant/bar didn't know had taken place, but actually the job had been much easier and simpler than if we'd laid siege to the establishment. Rather than deserving praise, we'd merely demonstrated a method preferable to a mass show of force, which could have turned out disastrously.

Emmett lifted his fist to knock on the door of Apartment 1. We knew another detective guarded the only rear exit from the apartment, a precaution against the very likely chance Cris would rabbit. He faced a murder charge.

Cris had been in the motel room when Paulette and Eddie were killed, of that I was sure. He probably hadn't pulled a trigger, but we needed to treat him as armed and dangerous. Cris was a drug addict, and drugs added to double murder spelled trouble.

We knew the others in the room would be transvestites;

some of them very likely violent transvestites who made their living by mugging. None of us outside that door joked about taking down "pansies."

Emmett pounded on the door. "Police! Open up! Police!"

No one responded. We heard scurrying around inside, probably a quick move to flush drugs down the toilet. We hadn't come about drugs.

"Police! Open up!"

Nothing. Just more scurrying.

"Police! Open up, or we're coming in!"

We approached a neat legal question. I hadn't obtained a warrant. Because of the urgency of the case, I didn't believe we could afford two hours getting one. Maybe I rationalized, but I told myself we could actually be saving Cris's life.

The law says if an officer sees a suspected felon enter a house, he can follow in hot pursuit. We'd seen Cris. We just didn't know it had been him.

We decided to go in. In two hours Cris could be dead or on a plane to Brazil.

"Police! This is the last warning!"

Nothing.

I stationed myself directly in front of the door, moved back a few feet, lifted my right leg, and, using it as a battering ram, kicked forward with all I had, right at the lock. The sound resembled a double report from a .22 rifle as the door flew all the way open and banged against the wall.

Emmett and Fred rushed in first, revolvers drawn. Emmett fanned to the right, Fred to the left, and I came in behind, straight ahead, a .357 Magnum in my hand.

Five transvestites, three blacks and two whites, occupied the front room, and four of them began screaming like frightened schoolgirls when we came through the door. Attired in varying degrees of dress, including a ball gown, two wore only panties. We lined them up against a wall, spread-eagled. Three of them were crying.

But not Mae West. It was really him! He wore only lace panties, and not the slightest hint of panic.

"What is this?" someone sobbed.

"What do you want?"

"What did we do?"

I answered as best I could. "Cris," I said. "We want Cris. Where is he?"

They asked more questions, and the lineup against the wall grew ragged. Dantagnan, who would be comfortable controlling half of the FBI Most Wanted list, desperation on his face, knew he'd found himself out of his element among all the squealing. A beached fish. Grateful to be "in charge," I figured this left me free for duties more important than maintaining order.

"Where's Cris?" I asked again, to an audience that didn't listen. "Are one of you Cris?"

Mae West turned his head, his eyes glinting with amusement, mocking, no fear whatever. Looking straight at me, he inclined his head slightly toward the bedrooms at the back of the apartment.

I went alone, holding the gun down beside my knee, and came through the first bedroom door sideways. Step. Look. Stop. Look again. Another step. Look. Stop. Step.

Cris sat on a queen-size bed, smoking a cigarette, wearing a long-sleeved, bright blue cocktail dress, rhinestone earrings, and silver high heels. He looked decked out for the Rex Carnival Ball, New Orleans's biggest Mardi Gras bash. Instead, his destination was an interrogation room at Homicide.

I gauged Cris to be five feet ten, twenty years old, and thought Samuel Williams had given us a pretty good description.

"Cris?"

"Hi." He answered in a deep voice. No squealing. His eyes didn't go with the dress. They shone watchful and hard. "Get yourself up against the wall."

He followed instructions, moving with a calculated swish, and I brought his hands, one at a time, to handcuffs behind his back. Calm, not the least flustered, though surely he knew the reason we'd come for him, Cris nonetheless lacked the poise and monumental disdain of Mae West. No matter. Mae West played in a solo league. I judged Cris a tough cookie, not easy to break, and his hard exterior reaffirmed my belief that he'd witnessed the killings at Howard Johnson's.

Trixie had told me Cris cried and appeared badly shaken when the men in the Lincoln brought him back to Philip Street, and I imagined it might take something like a double-murder to shake this iceberg.

After I handcuffed him, I read him his rights. "Do you understand what I said?"

"I certainly do."

I led him to the living room where a look of permanent puzzlement had etched itself onto Fred's face. How was he to maintain order? Jack the Ripper he could handle. In an apartment full of women he could turn on a certain firm, teddybear charm. But what should he do here? Getting rough didn't seem to be the answer, but he sure wouldn't play the role of gentleman either.

The names of the others were Mae West, Linda, Dawn, Jessica, and Polly. We took all of them to Homicide.

What a parade when we came in, and I must say New Orleans's finest showed no class. Uniforms downstairs saw our group first, and felt obliged to whistle and request introductions to our "dates." It got worse at Homicide on the third floor. The elite of the murder squad lowered themselves to the level of driveling degenerates with front-row seats at a strip show. Of course, we'd allowed the transvestites to dress before making the trip, and they'd done it to the nines. Mae West, alluring in underwear, glowed regal in a floor-length gown.

"Dillmann, you gotta fix me up," leered one homicide detective.

"Why don't I ever get cases like this?" mused another sadly.

"What's shakin', baby?" a third chimed in. "Damn, you sure look good!"

By now, only Cris among the transvestites looked grim. He knew what was coming, and I could see him steeling himself for it.

The other transvestites gave as good as they got. Mae West might have been standing behind a microphone, in front of adoring fans, as with grace and elegance he parried crude asides from my Homicide unit buddies.

I questioned all six, one at a time. I bore the ultimate responsibility for the case, and knew before we finished I'd have to go one-on-one with Cris, a murderer, in probably the most important interrogation of my career. To give Cris my best shot, I wanted to interview the other five first. Making Cris wait gave him time to think, to become nervous— possibly an edge in my favor. An individual in Cris's shoes, staring at a murder rap, might remain calm and in control for a short time. But for a long time?

We placed Cris in a separate, isolated holding cell. Linda, Dawn, Jessica, and Polly cooled their heels in chairs far apart in the big Homicide room while I questioned Mae West. Making Mae wait would do no good. That cool exterior would remain in place forever.

I sat, feeling off balance, across from Mae, real name Samuel Johnson, in Duffy's office, ten feet by twelve feet in size with lots of pictures and awards on the walls. Duffy had left, probably to apprise anxious superiors of a possible breakthrough.

I blinked twice and reminded myself this beautiful woman was a man. He smoked a cigarette held in an expensive gold holder. Mae ranked primus inter pares in the transvestite community. A guru. Others went to him, sought advice, heeded it. If he'd talk to me the others likely would, too. I drew breath to ask my first question, but Mae spoke first. "Look, I know why I'm here. It's those motel murders. I don't like what happened. It's vicious and ugly. I'll answer any questions you have."

"Did you know Paulette and Eddie?"

"Very well. They lived with me before they moved to Alexandria."

So they hadn't kept Alexandria a secret.

"Did others know they stayed in Alexandria?"

"Everybody knew. They just didn't know *where* in Alexandria."

"Did you know why they went up there?"

"Of course, it was a choice between that or jail. They were going to testify against David Sylvester, and more power to them. Too bad they ever got involved with him. They always looked for the quick buck."

Fear caused most people to hesitate before saying the name David Sylvester. Not Mae. He had spunk, arrogance, and a matronly concern for the other transvestites.

"Did Paulette and Eddie keep in touch with you from Alexandria?"

"No, the next I saw of them was Tuesday."

"This last Tuesday?"

"Right. I was really happy to see them. We had a nice visit, and I wished them luck on doing in Sylvester. It worked out the other way around, bless their hearts."

"Did they tell you where they were staying here in New Orleans?"

"Yes, Howard Johnson's."

"Mae, I want you to think carefully. Did you tell anyone else Paulette and Eddie were staying at the motel?"

"Positively not. I would never have done that. Only me, Linda, and Cris knew where they were."

"Cris?" I stared at Mae for several moments. "How did Cris know?"

"She and Linda were with me when Paulette and Eddie came over."

I asked point-blank: "Do you think Cris is involved in these murders?"

Mae hesitated, fighting a battle with himself. While this went on, I kept telling myself, *Man, Man, Man, this is a Man.* A person has to see Mae West to believe him.

"I won't point my finger at anybody," Mae said. "All I know is Cris hasn't been herself since the killings. She's a nervous wreck."

Mae could provide enormously valuable testimony that Cris had knowledge of Paulette and Eddie's location if the case ever came to trial. When I told the gorgeous transvestite I had no more questions for now, he took a seat in the Homicide room. I promised him a ride back to Philip Street with the others when we finished the interrogations.

I interviewed Polly, Jessica, and Dawn, now more relaxed after the bantering outside. Maybe too relaxed. I had to tell them we investigated murder, which won their attention, but they didn't know Paulette and Eddie or anything about the killings at HoJo. They just happened to be in the apartment when we raided it and got picked up in the sweep.

Then came Linda, the other participant along with Cris and Mae West in the Tuesday tête-à-tête when Paulette and Eddie revealed their Howard Johnson's address.

Linda, real name LeRoy Anderson, looked more like a

LeRoy than a Linda. He had a horsey look and voice, red hair, and although he tried, didn't come across as feminine at all. Transvestites, like everyone else, can't be stereotyped. In casual conversation, most men have a story to relate about a luscious-looking transvestite. But percentage-wise, the gorgeous ones, the beauties, don't outnumber the fair-to-middling in appearance, any more than they do in the mass of the general female population.

"Did you know Paulette and Eddie?"

"I only met them once. Last Tuesday."

"Did you know they'd been living in Alexandria?"

"How could I know that? I never heard of them until Tuesday."

"Where did you meet them on Tuesday?"

"Philip Street. I was there with Mae and Cris when they came over."

"Did Paulette and Eddie say where they were staying in New Orleans?"

"Yes, at Howard Johnson's on Old Gentilly Road."

"How long have you known Cris?"

"Not long; she's a friend of Mae's. I don't like her."

"Why not?"

"She shoots dope. She'll do anything for a fix, and that's bad news. It can lead to trouble for everybody. I don't need that kind of trouble."

"Do you think Cris had anything to do with the murders of Paulette and Eddie?"

"I don't know. I wouldn't put it past her."

I arranged for Linda and the others to be chauffeured to Philip Street. I didn't think such an accommodation would be necessary for Cris.

Much has been written about the nervousness of a suspect facing police questioning, and no doubt it can be a nerve-testing experience. But in important cases, the detective often becomes just as shaky. He knows or at least believes that everyone—his peers and superiors—watches and measures his results. Most wish themselves in his position, and believe they would succeed. He wins acceptance, very important to him, from other detectives if he comes through. If he doesn't . . .

I took some time before summoning Cris from the holding cell and perused the rap sheet Gebbia had obtained while I questioned the others:

5-29-74 Aggravated battery
7-26-74 Simple burglary
6-28-75 Armed robbery
8-16-75 Possession of stolen .38 revolver

The record of Cris, real name Jessie Ford, showed an individual well on the road, at age twenty, to becoming a career criminal. Remarkable. Most kids at that age are enjoying friends and college, perhaps thinking ahead to a lifetime of loving and raising a family, maybe even making contributions to mankind. But Jessie Ford—Cris—had instead become a violent drug addict transvestite facing a future of squalor, misery, and meanness in a state penitentiary called Angola.

I put my head down on the desk for a couple of minutes, then asked a detective to bring in our suspect. I watched Cris sashay into the office with exaggerated feminine mannerisms. He wore the fancy, long-sleeved cocktail dress we'd nabbed him in, and I knew why it held importance for him.

CHAPTER
—8—

Cris and I faced each other alone in Duffy's office: the door closed, the lighting normal, no one could see in, we couldn't see out. The handcuffs had come off, and I told Cris he could smoke. I wanted him comfortable; denying him cigarettes or making him stand wouldn't work. A person won't confess to murder to get a cigarette or ease some minor annoyance.

Right away I had to assess the intelligence of our young suspect. A bright individual might capitulate to hints of prison horrors, but not Cris. Although smart, this youth's hide had toughened to resist such scare tactics.

Besides common decency, an ulterior motive spawned my attempts to make Cris comfortable. If I did get a statement, a defense attorney would pound on it for days, and if all else failed he'd work his way around to accusing me of exercising undue pressure, and probably worse. If Cris did confess, I intended to take him immediately to a doctor in the coroner's office for an examination and photographs—a good precaution, because experience taught that a defense attorney might try to convince the court I'd roughed up and/or brutalized his client to get him to talk.

Often the hard cop/soft cop routine nets positive results.

Dantagnan could play a great hard cop. I wasn't very intimidating, so the role of soft cop usually fell to me. Sometimes I couldn't tell if Fred's anger was an act or for real.

But each case dictates its own course of action. This time I judged it best to go one-on-one with Cris.

From what Samuel Williams said, I didn't think Cris pulled a trigger. Although the law said Cris was as guilty as the gunmen and Sylvester, I believed justice and the community were better served by getting all of them, not being forced to stop with the prosecution of an accomplice. Cris represented a small, easily replaceable cog in the mighty narcotics machine that ground out big bucks for Sylvester, and destruction for so many others.

At the same time, I couldn't make promises to Cris—only the D.A. could do that. Without Cris's cooperation, Samuel Williams still might make a positive I.D. of the hitters (if we ever identified and caught them), but we'd likely never nail Sylvester. I questioned Cris alone because I wanted him to realize how much trouble he had gotten himself into, and that cooperation with me represented his best chance. Also, he needed to eschew the often common "I'm not a rat" attitude. Hard cop/soft cop in this situation would merely divert his attention.

When Cris sat down and got comfortable, I told him he was a suspect in the murders of Paulette and Eddie, and then read him his rights under *Miranda*. Just as important, I made sure he once again understood them. I kept reminding myself how often murder investigations were blown at precisely this crucial stage.

"Cris," I began, "did you know Paulette and Eddie?"

"Yes, they were my friends."

"Cris, tell me: Why did you kill them?"

It might work. I didn't think so, but why not try? At the

least, the question allowed me to look for and gauge a reaction. But Cris gave none. He stared at me with hard, old man eyes that showed nothing.

"I didn't kill anybody," he said in a barely feminine voice. "I had nothing to do with those murders. You've got no cause to have me up here."

I stared at the transvestite, trying to maintain a mild expression of disbelief. Beneath the blue dress lurked arrogance, defiance, toughness.

"If those girls," Cris said, referring to Mae West and Linda, "are telling things about me, they're lying."

So it would resemble teeth-pulling, which I'd feared all along. Cris should have asked for a lawyer. He hadn't. I counted that as a big break.

"Tell me about yourself, Cris. Do you work? Or do you just hustle? How do you get money to eat?"

"I live on Felicity Street. I don't work. I just kind of get along."

Felicity Street. The Projects. I wondered if somebody with deliberately sick humor named those streets: Piety, Abundance, Humanity, Treasure, Industry, Benefit, Pleasure. Despair Street would make more sense. Dirty Needle Street. I thought of David Sylvester, and only partially succeeded in choking down my anger.

"Cris, don't lie to me," I said. "Do you want me to read your rap sheet? Burglary . . . armed robbery . . . should I go on? You're no angel, you're a hustler. Tell me the truth."

"You got it in front of you. I work the streets. I hustle just like all the other girls."

I stood up, walked around Duffy's desk, hovered over Cris, and pulled up the sleeve of his cocktail dress. His arm revealed a maze of needle punctures and track marks, with scars from old track marks right alongside.

"How bad is your habit?"

"I don't have a habit." He told the truth as he saw it. Like alcoholics, an addict seldom admits he has a problem.

"How much do you shoot a day?"

"I don't shoot every day. I chippie on weekends."

This meant, if you believed him, he took a bag or two of heroin a week, exclusively on Saturday and Sunday. The tracks crisscrossing his arms told an entirely different story.

I held his arm up so he could see it. "What do you mean, 'chippie'? You don't chippie. You're a stone junkie."

With this line of interrogation I tried to gain the upper hand. Take charge. Disarm him by reading through his lies. It came down to unpleasant work with which I didn't feel comfortable. I walked back behind the desk and sat down.

"Pull your chair up closer," I said. This again to establish who held the reins here. Cris had been casually leaning back, smoking.

"You're not stupid," I said. "Listen to what I'm about to tell you, possibly the most important words you'll hear in your life. *I'm looking down your throat.* I didn't pick you up at random; you're here for a reason. Remember what I'm saying. There's only one person who can help Jessie Ford, and that's Jessie Ford. You're in more trouble than you've ever thought about, ever dreamed about. You're up to your eyeballs in this mess, and you've got only one way out: me."

I watched him think. No feminine mannerisms now; just a youngster with his chin on his chest.

"What did you say your name was?"

Most suspects don't want to know the name of their interrogator; they don't want to become personal. I took Cris's question as a good sign and answered, "Dillmann. Detective John Dillmann."

"Mr. Dillmann, you have to believe me. I didn't kill those people."

I stood up again and raised my voice. "I know you didn't

kill them. You didn't pull the trigger. But you're stupid, Cris. You're going to the penitentiary just like the two idiots who did because you were there. The law is clear. You're just as guilty as if you put the pistol to Paulette's head and to Eddie's head and pulled the trigger. You're stupid, and you're going to spend the rest of your life in jail. Sit and think about that. Think harder about it than anything else you've ever thought of.''

I walked out of the office, slamming the door, and felt I'd won a measure of his confidence. Also, I'd conveyed what deep trouble he faced, revealing just enough to scare him while holding back all the trump cards. Nervous and frightened, rightly so, he now had a few moments to cool down and think. His best interest surely involved talking to me and coming clean. I felt confident I could prove his guilt, that Samuel Williams would identify him. But I really wanted the shooters and Sylvester.

Outside the office, Duffy passed time with several detectives, obviously waiting to hear from me. I dropped my head to the side and kneaded neck muscles knotted tight from tension, cursing the one advantage I didn't have: rest. I worked on less sleep than Cris. It didn't bother me during the questioning, but outside the pressure cooker office I realized how tired and close to the edge I ventured as exhaustion began to take over.

"John, how we looking?" Duffy asked.

"I have hope we'll get there. I'm letting him cool."

"Do you have anybody going to the hospital to make an identification?" Duffy was asking if I'd sent a picture over for Samuel Williams to see.

"No need to. Cris was the one with the bandana. Williams shouldn't have any trouble at all identifying him."

"What about Sylvester?"

"Nowhere near that point yet."

I drank a cup of coffee, called Diane to say I might be three or four hours late (I'm a terrible time guesstimator!), reentered Duffy's office, and closed the door. Cris paced a path in front of the desk.

"Sit down," I said. And he did, lighting a cigarette. I opened Duffy's drawer, took out a legal pad. "Let's get down to business," I said, poising pen over paper. "Tell me everything, Cris. Start at the beginning."

"All I can tell you is what I heard."

"Go ahead." I'd seen it happen before. Cris would tell me what happened, portraying himself as a nonparticipant. Fine. Anything to get the ball rolling.

"Eddie and Paulette were killed," said Cris, "to keep them from testifying against this guy Sylvester. Sylvester's a major dope dealer—mainly heroin. He faced a long stretch in jail, but no jail time if he got rid of the witnesses. Sylvester was willing to pay a lot of money to off Paulette and Eddie. You understand? Now I don't know who took the contracts, but I saw them in a big black car."

I put the pen down, not having written a word. "Cris," I said, "I told you fifteen minutes ago I was looking down your throat. Sure you know about the black car, because you were in it. Now give me the names of the two people in that car."

Sweat jumped from every pore on Cris's face. The hard eyes showed fear, uncertainty. His face screwed in thought. He knew he had a Rubicon to cross.

"I didn't go in that car. I don't know the people in that car."

"You're acting stupid. I can prove you were in it. I can prove you were in the motel room."

"Who told you that?"

"I'm asking the questions, Cris. You're not." I still hadn't played my trump card: Samuel Williams.

Cris thought some more. He wondered if I bluffed. Still I

didn't mention Williams, but I did decide to scare him some more.

"I'm going to get up, Cris, and put these handcuffs on you. Then we'll walk across the street where I'll book you on two counts of murder plus one count of attempted murder. I can prove that at approximately six P.M. on July twentieth you entered Room two-fifteen of Howard Johnson's. But listen up to this: Maybe a week from now, or a month, or six months, one or both of those killers may sit in the exact same chair you're in. I'll question them, and they'll talk. They'll talk good. Do you know whose hand they're going to put that gun in? Yours. Are you actually willing to take the whole rap, be the fall guy? Do a long stretch in Angola for somebody else? If you are, you're not smart enough to be called stupid."

Again, I hadn't lied. I'd told what *would* happen—if we caught the hitters. I wasn't against bluffing, but the most powerful hand doesn't need to. The truth rings clearer than any bluff.

"Didn't you tell me earlier the court will say I'm just as guilty, even if I didn't pull the trigger?"

I finally had him in the right spot: looking for an out.

"Yes, under the law. You're just as guilty under the law. But the law's reasonable. There's room to recognize differences."

"Will I have to do time?"

Incredible. Of course he'd do time. A lot of it. But this often-asked question confirmed my belief that Cris would talk.

I pulled my chair around the desk right over to him—we actually brushed knees—for the most difficult part. I needed to explain that I had no authority to make a deal, but I would talk to the district attorney for him.

"Cris, I could sit here, lie to you, and promise you'll walk

away from this completely. But two people are dead.
Executed. I don't have authority to make any kind of deal,
but I will promise you this: I'll talk to the D.A. in your
behalf and find out his best offer. By telling me what
happened, you can't do anything but help yourself.''

True. We could pile a world of hurt on Cris while Sylvester
flew free as a bird, laughing at us. Besides, in my own mind,
there *were,* despite the law's lettering, extreme variations of
guilt. At the highest level sat David Sylvester. Next: the
cold-blooded, professional, contract killers. Last: though
certainly responsible for a heinous crime, Cris, a weak-
willed drug addict.

The transvestite hung his head. Even the crisp blue dress
seemed to droop. ''You really think it's in my best interest to
tell you everything?''

Amazing.

''Yes, I do.'' I'd already told him. I got up and said,
''Would you like some coffee? A Coke?''

''A Coke, please.''

Good. I wanted to go out and give Duffy the news. That
done, I grabbed a soft drink from a machine in the basement,
took the elevator back to the third floor, and with Emmett
Thompson went back inside Duffy's office to fetch Cris.
Emmett, who'd played such a major role in the case, wanted
to hear and ask questions, and so did Sam Gebbia, and Ben
Morris of the Drug Enforcement Administration. Morris had
learned everything against Sylvester might not be lost after
all.

Again we read Cris his rights, this time in an interrogation
room considerably larger than Duffy's office, and then he
made the following statement:

I was at the corner of Clara and Philip Street about a week
ago, and I saw David Sylvester. David told me Eddie and

Paulette were in Alexandria, and he wanted me to drive up there and locate them for him. He told me Eddie and Paulette were coming down the following Thursday to go to court to testify against him.

David said he had a contract out on Paulette and Eddie and he wanted to find them. He said he'd rent a car for me to go to Alexandria. I told him I would think about it, and he said to make up my mind before Thursday.

About 2:15 P.M. on Tuesday, the day Eddie was shot, I was sitting on the steps of a house across from 2812 Philip Street when I saw David Sylvester standing on the corner of Clara and Philip. He motioned me over and asked if I had seen Smitty yet, that Smitty wanted me to go for a ride with him. I told him no and walked over to 2812 and sat down on the steps there.

About 5:00 P.M. Smitty came to the house with his brother-in-law. Smitty wanted me to take a ride with them because they knew where Eddie was. I told him no. Smitty said I had to go with him, knock on the door, and check for police. We left in a black 1972 or 1973 Lincoln Continental with red pinstripes and red interior. In the car were Smitty, Smitty's brother-in-law, and me.

We drove to the Howard Johnson's motel on Old Gentilly. Smitty's brother-in-law led the way to the motel room. When we got there, Smitty knocked on the door with his gun. I saw the door crack open, and Eddie asked who it was. That's when Smitty made a motion with his head to me. I said, "Eddie, it's Cris," and he opened the door a little more, and Smitty busted through.

We went on into the room and Smitty's brother-in-law closed the door. Smitty told Eddie and Paulette to get on the floor. The other guy in the room was in bed. Smitty looked at him, giggled, and told him to get on the floor, too. Then Smitty put a pillow over Paulette and Eddie's head, and the brother-in-law placed one over the other guy's head. Smitty and his brother-in-law shot them. I didn't do any shooting. I didn't even have a gun. When they finished, Smitty and his brother-in-law took the pillowcases and we left.

We drove back to the city and stopped by Smitty's old lady's house in the Calliope Project. Smitty took the pillowcases with the guns inside into the house and came right back out without them.

Next we drove to Two Jacks Bar at 2101 South Liberty Street. The brother-in-law and I sat in the car while Smitty got out. He walked up to David Sylvester on the sidewalk. A lot of people were around, so David and Smitty didn't talk with each other. Instead, Smitty made a palms-down, side-to-side motion with his hands, like the "safe" sign in baseball, to David, who returned the hand gesture and nodded his head.

Smitty and his brother-in-law dropped me off on Philip Street. Smitty told me not to say anything or Homicide would get me.

The next morning I saw David Sylvester at Clara and Philip Street. He said I should wait until Knucklehead, who is Smitty, came by to give me something. Sylvester wanted me to think it was dope. Quick as I could, I left. I figured Knucklehead was coming to kill me.

That we suspected key elements of Cris's statement served mainly himself—especially his refusal to acknowledge that he'd provided Sylvester with the HoJo address—didn't prevent us from firing a barrage of questions at a witness who would certainly be key in any future prosecution.

Q: Did David Sylvester tell you how he knew that Eddie and Paulette were staying in the Alexandria area?

A: No. He just knew they were there.

Q: At the time Sylvester asked you to go to Alexandria, you say he said he'd placed a contract on Eddie and Paulette?

A: Yes.

Q: Did Sylvester tell you how much money he offered?

A: No.

Q: At any time prior to your going to Howard Johnson's with Smitty and his brother-in-law, did you have occasion to be in the company of Sylvester and Smitty when they discussed the contract?

A: Yes, on Monday night, at Two Jacks Bar. Smitty told David that after the job was finished, he wanted his $20,000. David said there wouldn't be any trouble he already had the money.

Q: Do you know Smitty's real name?

A: No. His nickname is Knucklehead, that's all I know.

Q: Do you know the name of Smitty's brother-in-law?

A: No.

Q: Can you describe Smitty's brother-in-law?

A: Negro male, 21 or 22 years old, about 6-feet-1-inch tall, 165 pounds, dark complexion, a short Afro hairstyle. He wore dark clothes the night we went to Howard Johnson's.

Q: What did Smitty wear that night?

A: Gray pants, gray shirt with a black design, and a green T-shirt.

Q: What did you wear?

A: Blue jeans. A multicolored shirt. A blue handkerchief on my head.

Q: Describe the pistols used during the shooting.

A: Smitty had a .38-caliber, nickle-plated revolver with

a long barrel and pearl handle. His brother-in-law had an automatic. I think a .45 caliber. He said it got stuck.

Q: Who shot Eddie Smith?

A: Smitty.

Q: Who shot Paulette Royal?

A: Smitty did.

Q: Who shot Samuel Williams?

A: Smitty's brother-in-law.

Q: How many shots did Smitty fire?

A: Six.

Q: How many shots did the brother-in-law fire?

A: One time—the gun jammed.

Q: Do you know Smitty's address?

A: No, I don't.

Q: Do you know where the brother-in-law lives?

A: He said he stays with his mother in the St. Thomas Project.

Q: Do you know who owns the Lincoln Continental?

A: The brother-in-law said it belonged to his mother.

Q: Was there any conversation between any of you while en route to the motel?

A: The brother-in-law talked about throwing the guns in the river afterward. Smitty said, no; he was going to keep them. After it happened, on the way back, the only thing said was, "We did what we had to do."

Q: Did they force you to go with them or did you go of your own free will for the money you could make from the contract?

A: I didn't get no money. Smitty said he had something on me he would tell the police. He threatened me. He forced me to go.

Q: What did Smitty hold over your head to make you go with them?

A: A long time ago I was involved in an armed robbery. Smitty said if I didn't go along, he'd tell the police about it, and I'd go to jail.

Q: Were the shots muffled, or did they make a loud noise?

A: Muffled, because they stuck the guns down in the pillows.

Q: Had you ever seen Smitty before that Tuesday?

A: Yes. I knew him.

Q: Had you ever seen the brother-in-law?

A: Several times in the St. Thomas Project.

Q: Could you identify these men if you saw them again?

A: Definitely.

Q: Did you hear David Sylvester say he wanted Eddie and Paulette dead?

A: He said it that night at Two Jacks. He told Smitty he wanted them killed.

The clock said 11:20 P.M. this Thursday, July 22, when the interrogation finished. I brushed by Lieutenant Duffy himself as I headed for the computers, specifically the alias file, to learn more about Knucklehead.

"Well?" Duffy asked, trailing behind.

"We may break the case wide open."

"Sylvester?"

"He's tied in."

It turned out I spoke too hastily. My own inexperience, combined with the elation engendered by Cris's statement, made me think we approached the end when actually we'd just begun.

CHAPTER
—9—

Only one Knucklehead came out of the alias file: Nelson Davis, aka Smitty, five feet six, 125 pounds, age twenty-four, last known address 1114 South Johnson Street in the Calliope Project. Nelson Davis's arrest record made murder for hire a not unlikely next entry:

6-69   Aggravated rape
8-72   Possession of stolen property
5-73   Possession of marijuana
9-74   First-degree murder

The first-degree murder charge had been dropped because witnesses became too frightened to testify. They had good cause to worry. Phrases such as "armed and dangerous," "multiple offender," and "career criminal" didn't adequately begin to describe the man who pulled the trigger on Paulette Royal and Eddie Smith.

The deeper we dug into Nelson Davis's background, the more terrifying the picture. He hadn't wanted to throw the murder weapons used at Howard Johnson's into the Mississippi River because he intended to blast Sylvester if the drug dealer dealt him any static about the $20,000 promised for the killings.

Small in stature, Nelson Davis loomed as a gargantuan ogre to everyone who knew him in the Calliope Project. His eyes, always blazing with anger and apparently half-crazed, intimidated men twice his size. "He'd just shoot you for no reason, no reason at all," said an acquaintance—we found no friends—interviewed in the Project.

Nelson Davis sported a heart and dagger tattoo on one arm, that of a champagne glass on the other. When he learned we issued a wanted poster, he announced he wouldn't be captured alive, and everyone in the Department took him at his word.

Veteran prosecutor Nick Noriea, later becoming more familiar than he wanted to with Nelson Davis, ranked him as one of the two most dangerous men he'd run across during his career. The other: Charles Mathiesson, a white stickup artist who blew off an old woman's leg with a shotgun because she didn't turn over her purse to him fast enough, and at close range blasted another woman's head onto the wall and ceiling during a beauty salon holdup. When asked in court why he routinely carried a double-barrel, sawed-off shotgun, Mathiesson replied, "The streets of New Orleans are dangerous. A man's got to protect himself."

Fred Dantagnan helped capture Mathiesson an hour or so after he splattered the beauty salon with pieces of the proprietor's head. The killer had gone to a nice restaurant to treat himself to a steak dinner.

I combined Nelson Davis's photo with pictures of five other black males who fit the same description and brought them to Cris. He sat minus handcuffs in the Homicide room among plenty of detectives whose presence assured he wouldn't make a run for freedom.

The photo identification was critical. Everything had to be just so to withstand the inevitable attack a defense attorney would launch against it in court. The men in the five other photos really had to resemble Nelson Davis. Pictures of blocky football players wouldn't do, nor would snapshots of seven-foot basketball types. The defense attorney, doing his job, wants the jury to believe I showed Cris a picture of Nelson Davis in the same lineup with five white society sorts attired in tuxedos.

Photo identifications *always* get challenged, the lawyer's voice filled with disbelief: "You really think *this man* looks like my client?"

"Sit over here, Cris," I said, gesturing toward my desk. "I'm going to place six photographs face up in front of you. I want you to look closely at all six. Say nothing until you've carefully studied each one. Then tell me if you know any of these men."

Cris looked at them closely. He shot me a quick, furtive glance, then focused back on the pictures. I didn't think for a moment that his problem involved identification. He thought about crazed-eyed Nelson Davis and whether he really wanted to go through with this.

Five minutes ticked by before Cris slowly picked up the photograph of Nelson Davis from the desk and said, "This is Smitty."

"Are you sure?"

"That's Smitty."

I didn't think a defense attorney could successfully suppress the photo lineup. I hadn't influenced Cris's identification either verbally or by actions. Caution as always had been the key. A case can easily be destroyed at this stage if the detective, perhaps exhausted, perhaps simply in a hurry to have done with depressing details, makes a mistake. As Saladino had pointed out when I first joined Homicide, cutting a corner never pays off. Saving ten or fifteen minutes, even a thousand times, doesn't balance out a murderer walking free.

At this point, Cris's statement worried me more than the legality of the photo lineup. The transvestite refused to admit he'd given Sylvester the Howard Johnson's address. I believed he feared, correctly, that such an admission—being the one to finger the victims—would stand as a big negative against him.

But Sylvester learned from someone where Paulette and Eddie stayed, and who else but Cris? Cris talked to them the day of their deaths. Moreover, Sylvester had to know they weren't guarded. He wouldn't send hit men to a room full of cops.

Emmett Thompson and I went through Nelson Davis's arrest record, hoping for clues to help identify his brother-in-law. We found nothing.

Additional questioning of Cris at this time didn't represent a prudent course. Again, because of possible court rulings, we had to keep one eye firmly fixed on the future. The defense could try to prove we had broken Cris down through marathon sessions or, more likely, he had caved in under withdrawal from lack of heroin and had been willing to testify to anything in order to stop his agony.

Most critical now, I needed to reach a district attorney to nail down Cris's statement before he had a chance to renege. Each of the things I fretted about had in the past become nightmarish realities for detectives I knew. In this instance, Cris could say I'd held a gun to his head to get his confession.

I called First Assistant District Attorney William Wessel, second-in-command to Harry Connick himself, waking him at his home. I explained to this increasingly delighted prosecutor exactly what we had, and he said, "Hold him in protective custody until morning when we can get him a lawyer. Bring him to Chief Morris's office at nine. The Feds are involved in this; they'll have to be present."

Wessel also proceeded cautiously. Connick could make deals with Cris's lawyer until the Gulf of Mexico dried up, and the Feds could still turn around and make his life miserable. Therefore, the presence of a U.S. attorney was mandatory.

"Are you going to pick up the tab for a motel room?" I asked Wessel.

"You don't want to take Cris home with you?"

Where had I heard that before?

"I take it that means yes."

"Yes."

I didn't want to keep Cris in jail for fear of alienating him. Also, if anyone in the jail recognized him, word would get back to Sylvester. The jail pipeline occasionally appears to rank as the modern world's most efficient means of communication. Prisoners can transmit messages through guards or visiting friends or the simple expedient of using the telephone. If news reached Sylvester, he could alert the hitters, who might flee the city, the state, the country. Sylvester could have evidence destroyed (the guns), arrange alibis (if he suffered from overconfidence, he might not have thought them necessary), or hit the hitters. So far, we did not have a strong case against Sylvester, although we did against the two shooters. Cris could identify them, and so could Samuel Williams.

We took special precautions to get Cris out of police headquarters. Parish Prison faces headquarters, and at all hours inmates, seeking breaths of fresh air and dreaming of freedom, look out the jail windows. One of them could spot us if we walked Cris into the street.

Emmett, Gebbia, and I escorted Cris down the elevator to the garage, told him to lie down on the backseat, and drove away. We went to the Calliope Project, and Cris pointed out 3505 South Prieur, where Nelson Davis said he had dropped the guns off at his "old lady's house," which we assumed meant girlfriend, Apartment C.

We needed to prepare a search warrant, and that required a description of the premises. We looked at a low-income, federally funded, brick, three-story apartment building. No shrubs, trees, or gardens. Trash everywhere, and also crime. Only a bright moon shone this 2:00 A.M., and young kids sat on every step, a sad and terribly depressing sight.

Residents heralded our entrance into the Project with dozens of whistles, a human warning system that signaled police were coming. The whistles echoing between the buildings cut eerie, frightening slices into the otherwise silent night, and my cold, clammy hands told me I feared a shot ringing out at any moment. The darkness, broken only by the moon and our headlights, seemed almost total, yet I could feel eyes watching.

People in the Projects suffocate in summer, shiver in winter, and are not sustained by hope of escape. Victims and criminals live side by side in a quagmire of fear, poverty, and desolation. The police are overwhelmed, but they keep trying, like little boys with their fingers in the dike. Patrols do not work. While an officer investigates one crime, ten more take place. Probably an army of police would be helpless, and they wouldn't be tolerated.

Calliope represents the highest crime rate in the city. It breeds young people who *want* to be caught committing a crime, who consider it a badge of honor, a passage into manhood, to serve time at Angola. A wretched prison, even as prisons go, life at Angola, for some, takes preference to Calliope.

After checking out 3305 South Prieur, I dropped Sam and Emmett off at headquarters, telling them Cris and I would be staying at the Best Western across from the Criminal Courts Building, near Miracle Mile, a police watering hole. Most of

us at one time or another sought solace at the Mile;
unfortunately, too often some tried to drown their depression
from the job.

Cris still wore the blue cocktail dress, now slightly
sweat-wilted from a wrestling match with himself over
whether to give a statement. And I certainly didn't exude the
charisma of Prince Charming.

The desk clerk eyed us with total distaste. I decided to
stare him down. *He* decided to demand cash and a deposit up
front. I told him to charge the room to the district attorney's
account. Other prisoners were housed at this convenient
motel when incarceration at city lockup proved a disadvantage; still, he couldn't resist being a comedian: "One bed,"
he quipped, "or two?"

"Two," I said.

Figuring this as the absolute low point of my police career
(instead of snuggling in my cozy bedroom with Diane, I
shared a room at Best Western with Cris), I derived
satisfaction from Cris's not seeming delighted about room-
ing with me either. He took makeup out of his purse and
started doing his face in front of a mirror, while I bleakly
mulled over six hours locked up with him.

Fate smiled on me this morning. No, not smiled. Fate
came down, patted my back, shook my hand, and pinned a
medal on my chest. And not just because it saved me from
six hours with Cris. This morning would prove lucky in a
pleasant variety of startling ways.

Ten minutes after checking into Best Western, a call came
from Emmett.

"Get back over here with Cris right away."

"What you got?"

"A make on the brother-in-law. We need Cris for an
I.D."

How did this good fortune come about? An anonymous

caller with a deep voice, obviously high on drugs, told Emmett the individuals we wanted were "Clarence" and "Smitty." Then the caller laughed and hung up.

When I arrived back at Homicide, I saw Emmett playing with the computer. He threw a seven, though he had to be more than good for the luck to come. Guessing that "Clarence" might be a brother, not a brother-in-law (actually he was a brother-in-law), Emmett typed in the name Clarence Davis and came up with a strong possible for our second hitter. Clarence Davis: six feet one, 180 pounds, thirty years old. Address: 1331 Spain. Clarence Davis's rap sheet read:

7-73	Attempted shoplifting
5-74	Theft
8-74	Armed robbery
12-74	Armed robbery and aggravated battery

The aggravated battery entry represented shooting a victim during a $13 holdup.

Once again we arranged a photo lineup, and Cris, evidently not as terrified of Clarence Davis as he'd been of Nelson, immediately identified the suspect.

"Fred," I said to Dantagnan, as I approached the husky detective where he sat scowling at his desk. "I need a favor."

"Forget it, Dillmann. I'm not helping you anymore."

"We've got a make on the brother-in-law. We've got to take a look at his house."

Fred brightened. "You gonna pop him now?"

"If he's there."

"Sure thing, buddy. Count me in." Dantagnan smiled, getting up to find the keys to the armory that contained, among other things, shotguns, sniper rifles, tear gas, flak jackets, bullhorns, and floodlights.

"Fred," I said, "we've got it covered. Me. Emmett.

Sam. What we need is someone to baby-sit Cris at Best Western. The room's in the district attorney's name. There's Cris. Here's the key." I held it out to him.

He looked at Cris, lip curling into a sneer, and then at me. I hoisted myself to the balls of my feet, in case I required a quick getaway.

"You want me to spend all night in a motel room with *that?*" He drew back a step and began clenching his fists.

"Not all night. Just till eight in the morning. Then get him over to Morris's office."

Most cops, despite the macho image they project, would prefer accompanying Cris rather than a potentially life-endangering attempt to arrest a killer. I told that to Fred, but it didn't impress. The consummate man of action, he enjoyed the danger part of a detective's job. Asking him to tend a transvestite while others tried to collar a killer in a heater case equated to asking a dedicated all-pro to sit out the fourth quarter of a close Super Bowl game.

I understood how Fred felt: cheated. The best part of detective work comes when, after working hard and well to obtain evidence, you venture out to make the arrest. A cop can't convict—that's for a judge and jury. The closest he comes to making an impact is the bust.

My friend walked away from me. "Get somebody else," he said.

I followed him. "Fred, you know Cris is crucial. We can't afford to lose him. He's our whole case against Sylvester. I don't know anyone on the force I trust more than you."

Actually, because of friendship, Fred represented the *only* person I thought *might* do it.

"Get real, Dillmann. Anybody can protect him," he said stubbornly.

"Maybe, but I don't want just anybody. I want you, Fred. Think of Paulette and Eddie. Think of future victims of Sylvester. You owe it to them—and to the public."

"The public be damned."

I'd read in history books about someone famous saying the same thing—and getting away with it.

"You don't mean that," I said. But it looked like he did.

Then, all at once, he relented. "Jesus, a whole day with that!"

I put the motel key in his hand. "You're a good guy, Fred."

"Don't tell Bea." His wife. Bea would kid him something fierce if she found out.

We headed for 1114 South Johnson Street, the last known address of Nelson David, aka Smitty and Knucklehead. We went without arrest warrants or search warrants, to save time, something that wouldn't be done today but a common practice in 1976 when we often arrested on probable cause.

Sam drove; I sat next to him; Emmett leaned forward in the backseat. Sam and Emmett carried pump shotguns; I packed a .357 service revolver. We'd decided that Emmett and I would knock on the front door; Sam would cover the back entrance. If Nelson Davis answered, or if we suspected he hid inside, we intended to take him. We'd notified district communication that we were on a wanted check, so the district would be prepared to send backup if a shootout occurred.

We made plans as we drove. Tension in the car was palpable; all of us fought fear, but no one admitted it. We collected courage from each other. We had to penetrate the Calliope Project, a virtual arsenal, at 3:30 A.M. to flush out an extremely violent suspect. What worried us most, though, was our own exhaustion.

On many emergency trips to hospitals, I'd seen bedraggled interns struggling to complete a thirty-six-hour shift without sleep. They couldn't possibly make required critical life-and-death decisions as intelligently as if they'd been well-rested and clear-headed. The same applied to detectives. Weariness led to mistakes, mistakes led to death—ours or others. At least we knew, and the danger of the moment surged more awareness through us than we rightly could expect.

No way around it, we knew knocking on doors in the Project at this hour of the morning invited trouble, but not as much, perhaps, as during broad daylight. At 3:30 A.M. we had the element of surprise.

Nevertheless, woe to the detective who stands in front of a door and knocks. He should always stand to the side. If a suspect decides to shoot it out, he'll likely do it through the door. The best scenario: When the suspect himself answers the knock, you grab him. The worst: When the individual answering the door tells you the perpetrator is hiding "somewhere" inside, and is armed.

Suddenly Emmett's voice dashed all our dark dread of dangers lurking in Calliope.

"Look at that!" he shouted. "It's the Lincoln!"

Two miles from police headquarters, just a few blocks from Nelson Davis's address, on Melpomene Street, the big black car passed us headed in a "lake" direction, toward Pontchartrain, as we traveled in a "river" direction, toward the Mississippi. I didn't know if Emmett actually recognized Clarence Davis, or if he reacted from a hunch: a big automobile in this neighborhood at 3:30 A.M. stood out like the Hope Diamond in a costume jewelry rack.

Sam swung a quick U-turn and pulled to within a half block of the Lincoln, a safe distance. Tailgating might panic the driver into shooting. Worse, he could keep his cool, jam on his brakes, let us take the brunt of a rear-end collision, and *then* come out firing.

I radioed in the Lincoln's license number, my eyes riveted

on the big black car ahead of us. It stopped for a red light.
The driver waited. Sam could do little other than pull wearily
up behind. With a green flash the signal transformed the
street into a drag strip. Zoom! It was off to the races as the
Lincoln peeled rubber up Melpomene. Sam stomped pedal
to the metal in hot pursuit. In no time flat we hit 60 mph and
soon 70.

Our car was chaos. The radio crackled the Lincoln's
registration: Clarence Davis. In the backseat, chambering
rounds into his shotgun, Emmett shouted, "Sam, stay
behind! Behind!"

Sam didn't need Emmett's entreaties. Both training and
experience taught him how to handle himself in a chase. No
way, as TV often depicts, would he pull alongside the
Lincoln and try to ram it off the road. That would be plain
suicide. Juxtaposing the two cars in a nose-to-nose dead heat
would give the advantage to Clarence Davis, who could shoot
us while we tried to jockey him off the road. Sam intended to
stay behind and hope the suspect ran into something unconnected to humans.

I readied my .357. Sam yelled, "Emmett, make sure both
shotguns are loaded!"

Up deserted Melpomene, two lanes on each side of a
median, we raced, the Project buildings, bars, small homes,
businesses, and restaurants a blur as we passed. Our siren
wailed. Clarence Davis ran red lights and stop signs, which
gave him the edge since we had to make every effort to avoid
placing a third party in jeopardy. I put out a hurried 10-8,
officer needs assistance, a call that takes priority over
everything. Even policemen on their way to other calls come
to help.

Sam, the better driver, kept Clarence Davis no more than a
block in front of him. At last it dawned on the Lincoln's
driver that he couldn't shake us. At Melpomene and South

Liberty he pulled to the curb. Sam stopped at an angle behind the left rear of Davis's car, in his blind spot, giving us every advantage. Our suspect had an obstructed shot—he'd have to turn and fire virtually blind—and the three of us had clear views. If Clarence Davis decided to resume the chase, we'd positioned ourselves ready.

The three of us, Clarence Davis still behind the Lincoln's wheel, came out of our car at once. Sam leaned across the front fender and leveled his shotgun at the suspect. Heart pounding, I squatted behind the open passenger door, aiming the .357. Emmett raced to our right and trained a second shotgun on Davis.

"Stay away from the car!" Emmett yelled to Sam and me. "Stay back!"

"You, inside the car, put your hands on the dash!" Sam roared at Clarence Davis.

Davis looked over his left shoulder. He calculated, figured, measured his chances. He saw Sam and the shotgun. He looked over his right shoulder. He saw Emmett and another shotgun. Still, he didn't put his hands on the dashboard.

"Hands on dash, goddamn you!"

No compliance.

Holding the .357 with both hands, I crept toward the Lincoln. "Get those hands on the dash!" each of us yelled, seemingly by plan. "Watch his hands!" Emmett kept yelling to me. This I did, but I also had to be alert for someone else possibly hiding in the vehicle. Two steps from the Lincoln's front door, Emmett and Sam still screaming, as officers must do in combat, I stopped, and tried to detect any movement inside the car. I hoped he wouldn't bring his hands up suddenly. I'd have to kill him if that happened.

"Put those hands on the dash!"

And at last, ever so slowly, he did.

Looking for weapons, watching his hands, I opened the car door, grabbed him by the collar, and yanked him outside. Sam and Emmett were there in an eye's blink, and we threw the murder suspect onto the hood of the Lincoln.

"I didn't do anything," Clarence Davis said. "I didn't do anything."

Emmett placed his shotgun on the back of Clarence Davis's neck, while Sam frisked and I handcuffed. Then we placed him in the back of our unmarked squad car, and Emmett read him his rights.

While Emmett and Sam took the suspect to Homicide headquarters, I drove the Lincoln to the crime lab cage for a thorough inspection. Maybe our luck would continue and we'd get Cris's prints or, better yet, those of Nelson Davis.

Lieutenant Duffy arrived at the Homicide office just about the time I did, and we went to the desk where a surly Clarence Davis sat flanked by Sam and Emmett. Duffy called the three of us aside. "One of the hitters?" he asked.

"Yes," Emmett said.

"Well, they'll be happy at the district attorney's office. They think it's about time you started making arrests."

About time? I thought we'd been setting records for this type of case. I could see a vein throb in Emmett's temple.

"Who's 'they'?" he asked Duffy.

"Don't get twisted, Emmett," said Duffy the peacemaker. "They want to prosecute this case bad. They don't understand our end."

THE HOWARD JOHNSON'S MOTOR LODGE ON OLD GENTILLY HIGHWAY. THE KILLINGS TOOK PLACE HERE.

(Don Guillot)

THE PARKING AREA THROUGH WHICH THE KILLERS ENTERED THE MOTEL.
(Don Guillot)

TWO JACKS BAR. THIS IS WHERE FINAL DISCUSSIONS WERE CARRIED OUT FOR THE MURDER CONTRACT.
(Don Guillot)

EMMETT THOMPSON. HIS CONTACTS IN THE FRENCH QUARTER LED
TO THE FIRST BIG BREAK IN THE CASE.
(Don Guillot)

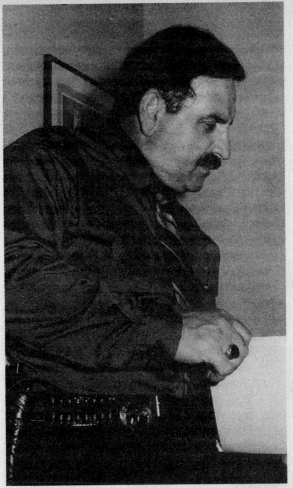

PASCAL SALADINO. STILL WORKING HOMICIDE AFTER TWENTY-EIGHT YEARS ON THE NEW ORLEANS POLICE FORCE.
(Don Guillot)

FRED DANTAGNAN. DILLMANN'S BEST FRIEND, TODAY WITH
DILLMANN'S PRIVATE INVESTIGATION AGENCY.
(Don Guillot)

HENRY MORRIS. HE BECAME SUPERINTENDENT OF POLICE BEFORE
HIS RETIREMENT.

DISTRICT ATTORNEY HARRY CONNICK. AT HIS BEST WHEN THE
PRESSURE WAS GREATEST.

CHAPTER
–10–

I hadn't lied to Cris.

Seated in Duffy's office, Clarence Davis kept our momentum going by rendering a verbal statement. He said he wouldn't waive his rights on self-incrimination, but since he went ahead anyway, it could be used in court, with the officers, including myself, testifying to what they heard, though the prosecution might choose not to use the statement because what Clarence said wasn't entirely true.

Here's what Clarence Davis told us:

Last Tuesday I was approached by Nelson Davis. He asked me to give him a ride to make a drug score. Nelson doesn't have a car, so he needed me to give him a ride. We got into my Lincoln, and I asked him where we were going to buy the dope. He told me to drive to Philip Street; I think the 2800 block. When we arrived the sissy got in the car. I'd never seen him before.

Nelson Davis told me to drive on the interstate, and I thought we headed for the Desire Project. Plenty of drugs there. When we got to Louisa Street he told me to turn left, instead of right toward the Project. Then he told me to pull into this Howard Johnson's motel.

That's when I figured we were in for a big dope deal, not just a bag from the street.

We got out of the car, and I thought the sissy just came along to score some dope with us. We went to a room, 215 I think, and the sissy knocked on the door. This guy let us in the room, and when we walked inside I saw two people on the bed.

All of a sudden Smitty, that's Nelson Davis, upped with a pistol; and when I looked, the sissy had a gun. I thought they were going to rob these people for their dope.

Then Smitty shoots two of the people through pillows he put over their heads, and the sissy shoots the guy from the other bed, also through a pillow.

I was the wheel man. I didn't shoot anybody. I was so scared I just wanted to get out of that room. I didn't even know they'd brought guns.

I drove Smitty and the sissy back to the Calliope Project, and dropped them off at Two Jacks Bar on South Liberty Street. I haven't seen either one of them since.

Indeed I hadn't lied to Cris.

And I couldn't resist taking a certain pride in having predicted that one of the shooters would place a gun in the transvestite's hand.

Regardless, Clarence Davis outsmarted himself. He figured we'd picked him up for a reason, and he thought it had to be because someone connected the black Lincoln to the Howard Johnson's killings. Thus he concocted a story placing minimum blame on himself, but still admitting the car had been present at the scene.

No sense in lying about the murders either, he felt. He believed himself safe with the I-was-just-the-driver-on-a-dope-deal story, not understanding that the tale he told made him as guilty as the people he said did the shooting.

The value of the verbal statement: Clarence Davis put the same three men at the murder site as Cris did. The best sort of corroboration. And Samuel Williams could be counted on for the cake's icing.

Not only did his mainly self-serving statement dig a deep hole for Clarence Davis, it painted him as unreliable and devious. I didn't believe Cris had pulled the trigger on anyone. In addition, Clarence Davis said Cris had knocked on the door of Room 215 to gain the murderous crew their admittance. I didn't believe that version, though in this instance I should have. I underestimated the self-serving extent of Cris's own confession.

It took about an hour to pry out Clarence Davis's account of the HoJo killings, and he told the story right after informing us "I'm not waiving any rights." We'd have been remiss in our duty if we'd *insisted* he not proceed, though we warned him he shouldn't.

Clarence Davis talked because he believed we could prove most of what happened anyway, regardless of what he said. He wanted his account on the record. Street smart, but not smart enough, he perceived an advantage in being the "first" to open up. He knew Nelson Davis, Knucklehead, hadn't been apprehended yet, and he assumed we didn't have Cris. It appeared to him he had a clear field to toss out whatever served his cause.

This rather handsome killer, who once shot and seriously wounded a victim for $13, had clean features and a slender, muscular build. He might have been a young minister, or an upcoming politician. He wouldn't have stood out in a crowd, however, not at six feet one and 180 pounds, though an observer would have been impressed if he looked closely at him.

If we really had Clarence Davis for murder, as I believed, some unknown people might now live out their lives. His blend-in features made him perfect for the role of hit man, and I suspected he'd kill again and again if not stopped. He certainly showed no hint of remorse about what happened at Howard Johnson's. He might have been only thirty years of age—just a year older than myself—but he was thirty going on a hardened, cynical fifty.

Looking at Clarence Davis, his life ruined whether he knew it or not, I thought of the Projects and drugs. A young man in Calliope has three main choices for a big, escape-from-the-Projects money-making career: drug pusher, hit man, athlete. The first two lead inexorably to disaster, even for a David Sylvester, who clawed his way to the top, however briefly.

I asked Clarence Davis several questions:

Q: What happened to the guns?
A: I don't know. Knucklehead and the sissy still had them when I dropped them off at Two Jacks.
   [Lie.]
Q: Why were these people killed?
A: I guess for their dope. But we didn't get any dope.
   [Lie.]
Q: Do you know David Sylvester?
A: No.
   [Lie.]
Q: Didn't David Sylvester pay you and Nelson Davis to kill two people because they were going to testify against Sylvester?
A: I didn't kill anybody. I never heard of this guy Sylvester.
   [Lie.]
Q: Where does Nelson Davis live?

A: I don't know. I just see him around the Project. I
haven't seen him since the killings. I don't want to
see him. He's crazy. Crazy and dangerous.
[True!]

At 6:00 A.M., not able to remember the last time I slept, I
took Clarence Davis to central lockup and booked him for
two counts of first-degree murder and one count of attempted
murder. Before leaving I made arrangements assuring he'd
be safe from the rest of the prison population.

I returned to my desk in the now-silent Homicide room,
too tired for elation, put head in hands, and tried to lock the
pieces of our puzzle into place to form a picture of the
investigation. Events had moved too rapidly—the killings
occurred less than two and a half days before, and already
we'd captured two of the three who busted into Room
215—for reflection and stock-taking. Mainly I'd operated
on adrenaline and instinct, spurred on by the concern of
superiors, but the time for a thoughtful overview of the case
was past due.

I forced myself to think, blotting out everything else, a
task more difficult because my mind dwelled at 1114 South
Johnson Street in the Calliope Project where, while I'd
questioned Clarence Davis, Sam, Emmett, Joe Miceli, and
Lynn Schneider, all of Homicide, looked for Nelson Davis.
The mission of these detectives ranked as the most dangerous
thus far, and though I was the least likely cop to go searching
for trouble, I felt I should have been with them. The case had
been assigned to me. By all logic, Nelson Davis had been the
shooter who killed Paulette and Eddie, and in terms of a
penchant for calling on extreme physical violence, he stood
head and shoulders above even Sylvester. The drug pusher
would likely think before acting. Nelson Davis acted first.

What stage had the investigation reached? All the perpetrators had been identified, and both shooters picked out of a photo lineup by Cris (Samuel Williams would soon do the same). I believed if the D.A. and the Feds hammered out a deal for Cris, we'd convict both Davises. Locating the guns and matching them ballistically would add further muscle to the case, but even without them the prosecution would be a heavy favorite in the courtroom.

What about Sylvester? Would he get away with murder? I knew the case could never be classed a success if Sylvester went free, and as matters stood we'd be underdogs against him and the high-powered Robert Glass. Sylvester never put his hands on anything. *He* didn't hand over dope on some dark street corner. *He* didn't go to a motel and shoot anybody.

Settling a plea bargain for Cris would garner four trial points linking Sylvester to the HoJo murders: (1) Sylvester asked Cris to go to Alexandria to locate Paulette and Eddie; (2) Sylvester told Cris he'd be picked up at Philip and Clara by Nelson Davis, and the pickup did indeed take place, whereupon they drove straight to Howard Johnson's and committed two homicides; (3) Sylvester returned a "safe" sign to Nelson Davis after the killings; and (4) Cris heard Sylvester tell Nelson Davis at Two Jacks that he wanted the witnesses against him dead, mentioning $20,000 as "no problem."

Not enough.

I harbored no illusions that the two Davises would ever implicate David Sylvester. Nelson and Clarence were too tough and too scared. They would opt for the penitentiary over what they felt Sylvester would do to them if they talked. Also, as hardened professional criminals, they'd hate bearing the brand of snitch burned into their hides. Nelson Davis's tattoos of a heart and dagger (violence) and champagne glass (good-time guy) would be replaced by an invisible "rat"—a symbol in which Sylvester would wrap Nelson's entire body to encourage some hoodlum to kill him on a dark, deserted street or in a lonely cell at Angola.

Our dependence on Cris further weakened our case against Sylvester. The transvestite's criminal record detracted from his believability, and the skilled Robert Glass would heap scorn on such a witness. How in the world can you believe this individual? the outraged Glass would sputter at the jury, dwelling for hours on Cris's past record and transvestism, which the veniremen couldn't possibly be expected to view with sympathy.

In Cris we leaned on a weak reed. His record showed aggravated battery (a shooting) and armed robbery. Glass's portrait of a violent heroin addict would be a true one. The jury would learn how Cris, dressed as a female prostitute, lured men into dark bedrooms so he could roll them.

Still, Glass would be wrong, in a sense, when he painted Cris as unbelievable. Who could be *more* believable? What nature of individual likely would know of the violent, evil events at Howard Johnson's? The really unbelievable witness would be the individual whose biography read like a cloistered nun's. Saintlike and ever the truth-teller she might be, but how could she know of the doings of Nelson Davis and David Sylvester?

The problem arises often. Many times the witnesses the police and prosecution rely upon possess a low credibility quotient. It has to be that way, though heavy emphasis needs to be placed on corroboration. Also on common sense. If the detective or prosecutor doesn't believe the witness, or if what the witness says doesn't coincide with other facts, then the testimony needs to be discarded.

Glass wouldn't like whatever plea bargain got worked out with Cris, and would make sure the jury knew it heard "purchased" testimony. Of course, Jessie Ford, or would

you rather I call you Cris, Glass would say, you're saving
your own life by talking against my client, aren't you?

The answer an obvious yes. And the prosecution would
need to persuade the jury of the desirability of applying a
lesser-evil theory: the "good guys" had to make a deal with
a "bad guy" to bring a monster to justice.

The more I thought about it, the weaker the case became.
It helped not at all that Clarence Davis put one of the guns in
Cris's hand. Plus, growing more depressed, I remembered
several instances when a judge told the jury that if they
disbelieved one part of a witness's testimony (and how could
they *not* believe Cris had given Sylvester the HoJo address?),
they could reasonably disbelieve everything he said.

Again, this wouldn't matter a great deal against the
Davises, because we had Samuel Williams corroborating
Cris. But against Sylvester . . . my stomach churned when I
thought of him loose on the street, preying in the Projects,
dealing degradation and death to citizens already among
society's weakest.

Disappointed, I realized the case against Sylvester
amounted to strictly circumstantial evidence. If Robert Glass
could provide reasonable alternative explanations for what
the prosecution alleged, we'd lose. Circumstantial evidence
only convicts when no other explanation for a defendant's
actions makes sense. I didn't doubt for a moment that the
dynamic Glass could, point-by-careful-point, provide alternatives.

POINT #1: Sylvester wanted Cris to go to Alexandria.
Of course he did, Glass might admit. Sylvester
wanted the witnesses located so his lawyers could
question Eddie Smith. Sylvester's intentions were
perfectly reasonable, in contrast to those of the
district attorney, who attempted to deny Sylvester's

legal counsel, namely Glass, access to Eddie Smith. And what better choice could Sylvester have made than Cris, a transvestite. Eddie Royal was also a transvestite, making Cris a likely person to know where he'd hang around. You simply wouldn't succeed by sending a straight-appearing private investigator to locate an individual belonging to such an unusual subculture.

POINT #2: Sylvester told Cris before the murders that Nelson Davis would pick him up. Aren't you simply lying? Glass would say. To save your own neck? You're an addict. This is a dope deal gone bad, and you're trying to save your skin by blaming my client. You mean to say you did this for my client for nothing? Glass would intone disbelievingly. You didn't get paid, did you? What, may I ask, are your other charitable activities? Clarence Davis, who's taking his medicine, says you were one of the shooters.

POINT #3: Sylvester returned a "safe" sign to Nelson Davis shortly after the killings. Nelson Davis denies this, Glass would say, or if we hadn't found Nelson yet, that Nelson isn't present to corroborate the lie. Clarence Davis didn't see this "safe" sign, the lawyer would emphasize. Even if there were a "safe" sign, is there any proof whatever it had to do with murder? Couldn't it mean any of a thousand other things? Of course it could, and the prosecution insults the intelligence of the jury by suggesting otherwise.

POINT #4: Cris heard Sylvester say at Two Jacks that he wanted Paulette and Eddie dead. You're lying again, Glass would contend, but even if you're not, couldn't that be normal conversational overstatement? What happened to the $20,000 Sylvester was supposed to pay? Not one penny has been accounted for. You say you didn't receive any money, and you admit you're not a charitable institution. You didn't hear Sylvester tell anybody to kill, did you? And you didn't see any money change hands, did you?

Emmett and the others came back about 6:30 A.M. looking dejected and absolutely worn out. Beard shadows, eyes dull and puffy, their demeanor misleadingly hyper, scarily alert from dozens of cups of coffee and countless cigarettes: sour, surly, not people to mess with this early June 23 morning. Emmett and Sam particularly, on their *second* dangerous assignment in the space of a few hours, looked worse than I did.

"No luck, huh, Emmett?" I asked as he put his shotgun and bulletproof vest away.

"Bad address. Nelson Davis could be anywhere in that Project. He could be anywhere, period."

Emmett walked to the coffeepot for a brew we took in doses that could kill. I was the last person to lecture him.

"How'd it go with you?" Emmett asked. "Did Clarence Davis cop?" He laughed cynically. He didn't for a moment believe Clarence Davis had talked.

"A verbal statement," I said. "Blames everybody but himself. If he says in court he was in Egypt when the murders came down, I can testify he told me he was at Howard Johnson's."

"He didn't pull the trigger," Emmett said, not asking a question.

"You got it."

"Sylvester?"

"Doesn't know him."

"Right. Well, what *did* he give you?"

"Claims to be the wheel man on a dope deal that went sour."

"He sure ditched Cris and Smitty fast enough. A great guy to have as a partner."

Emmett, Sam, and I went downstairs for a bite to eat, and they told me about the raid at 1114 South Johnson: shotguns front and back, the knock on the door, the agonized wait. But the sleepy woman they finally roused never heard of Nelson Davis. She had lived there a year, so he'd been gone at least that long.

A cold trail. Emmett apologized to her and left as gracefully as he could. I knew the feeling. Neither the police nor citizens need that show at six in the morning.

Duffy joined us. He'd been up as long as any of us but didn't show it. Maybe experience taught him how to look sharp when inwardly he neared collapse. Duffy agreed if we progressed no further than the deal with Cris, the D.A. could still go for an indictment of Sylvester. A slight chance of convicting the drug dealer beat none at all.

"But guys," Duffy said, "let's be realistic. You know the District Attorney's Office. They want sure winners. The testimony of this Cris . . . hellfire! A dangerous heroin addict in a dress isn't the best game plan for a sure victory."

Duffy knew of what he spoke, and maintained a cop's normal suspicion of prosecutors: sometimes too willing to make a deal, not eager enough to endanger their precious win-lose records. With some laudable exceptions, winning counts for everything to a prosecutor. The higher the winning percentage, the more glittering the record looks, no matter that the cases were so airtight a high school debater might have won them.

Of course, the prosecutor tells a different story, making sound points. The courts are clogged. Perhaps citizens shouldn't face jail unless the evidence overwhelms. Probably true, many police would concede, but exceptions such as Sylvester scream out for rolling the dice in court and letting the jury decide. I suspected that if Sylvester didn't have money to retain a lawyer of Glass's reputation, but rather had to rely on a public defender, the average prosecutor would be more willing to go to trial.

All this turmoil, back and forth, and we hadn't the slightest clue that the D.A. in this instance wouldn't do precisely what we wanted. We *anticipated*—a favorite pastime of detectives, often based on experience. We needed to keep in mind that this investigation might be different: The top man in the New Orleans judicial system, Harry Connick, had a personal stake in Sylvester. It took us all by surprise when we learned just how personal.

Somebody needed to get rest. Be able to work the case with a clear head. In the next few hours we might receive a tip and have to go back for Nelson Davis, *the* shooter. In our befogged state he might kill us all, or we might shoot each other or an innocent bystander. I told Sam to head home and grab some sleep. Emmett and I would handle the job at Morris's office.

Not five minutes after Sam left, Chief of Detectives Henry Morris himself sat down, pulled out a handkerchief approaching the size of a bedsheet, and blew his nose. Morris had been kept abreast of developments through the arrest of Clarence Davis, and we brought him up to date from there.

It felt special to sit with Duffy and Morris. Good old-fashioned cops who had seen almost everything, cared deeply about the Department and the city, and wanted more than anything to see David Sylvester serving a long jail term.

Duffy and Morris didn't hand the detective a case—be it a heater like HoJo or a murder in the Projects—and say "Let me know how it turns out." They followed the investigation, not interfering, but offering advice, encouragement, and assistance.

Morris listened to Emmett and me, grumbling now and then, his normal pattern of speech. "Goddamn," he said when we finished. "Looks like we're close to pulling everyone's ass out of the fire."

He turned to Emmett, holding out his hand. "Good job so far. You'll get written up for a commendation for this one, Thompson."

He turned to me, hand extended. "You, too. You should be proud of how you've handled this case. Good work, Dantagnan."

"It's Dillmann, Chief."

I didn't hear what he grumbled in reply.

CHAPTER
—11—

"I should kill you, Dillmann. Say one word and I *will* kill you. It'd be justifiable homicide."

Fred Dantagnan hissed these words sideways through tightly clenched teeth as we stood waiting in Chief Morris's office for the one late arrival, the assistant U.S. attorney, Daniel Bent.

"Be quiet, Fred," I whispered. "Do you want Cris to hear you?"

"That's it, Dillmann!" I felt him tense. The time had come to act.

"Step over here, Fred," I said, gently guiding him to a corner out of hearing range of the others. "What's bothering you, my friend?"

"Don't call me friend. I've been up all night baby-sitting your he/she. What *it* did was sit in front of a mirror primping itself and asking if I liked what I saw. You've got the nerve to ask me what's the matter?"

"It couldn't have been that bad."

"You ever had a he/she tell you you're cute?"

"You are cute. Sort of cuddly."

"Damn you, Dillmann . . ."

"Calm down, Fred. Cris is our star witness."

"It'll love that. Being in the limelight. It spent enough time getting ready at the motel last night."

"Were you an appreciative audience?" I knew I'd gone too far. "Listen, Fred," I said quickly. "Morris says he's going to write you up for this one. A commendation, good buddy."

Fred looked skeptical. "For baby-sitting a he/she?"

"I'm just reporting what he said."

"Count on this, Dillmann. The next big case I'm in charge of, you're going to be canvassing the world."

I believed him. Canvassing involves going door-to-door trying to locate witnesses who don't exist. Almost always a waste of time: If someone knows anything, he usually doesn't want to become involved; if he doesn't know anything, he often takes the opportunity to complain about poor city services to someone who deep in his heart probably agrees, but is just as helpless as the civilian to affect change.

At least Fred calmed down. "Did Cris say anything about the murders?" I asked. "Anything at all we can use?"

"Not that I heard. But I'd damn sure wager he's holding something back."

Like admitting he provided David Sylvester with the HoJo address, I thought.

At 9:30 A.M., virtually asleep on our feet, we learned hammering out the plea bargain agreement would have to wait until 1:00 P.M. Assistant U.S. Attorney Bent phoned to say he'd been detained on urgent business. Someone wisecracked that Bent's business would probably be less urgent if Paulette and Eddie had been killed while under *federal* protection.

It probably wasn't true, but rather an indication of how each of us had become testy under pressure. *All* witness protection programs would come under fire if someone decided to raise a ruckus over the Howard Johnson's murders.

I escorted Cris to the Homicide unit, which had plenty of day watch detectives to keep an eye on him. Then I debated whether to go home and catch a few hours of sleep, or tie up a last unpleasant loose end. Deciding two hours of sleep would be worse than none, I drove zombielike to Charity Hospital. The talk with ace witness Samuel Williams required no particular alertness on my part, though I dreaded the job.

Before heading for the hospital, however, I asked Lynn Schneider, Joe Miceli, and another detective, Jerry DeRose, to handle business at 1305 South Prieur Street, where Nelson Davis reportedly dropped off the guns. Schneider had to prepare an application for a search warrant, which listed probable cause, then type out the search warrant itself, with an accurate description of the residence (which I provided, having earlier gone out to look at the building), and then take the application to Judge Anthony Russo, who would review and likely sign it.

As before, I felt guilty asking others—in this case Schneider, Miceli, and DeRose—to handle a dangerous assignment (Nelson Davis might be at the residence), but I knew I'd been awake too long to perform the job professionally and safely.

At the hospital, Williams's head was still swathed in unnecessary bandages. I'd asked an intern to keep them on, if possible, to make the witness think he suffered a more serious injury than he actually had. He already itched to leave, which obviously we couldn't permit.

I found the door to the room open and Williams pacing the floor, complaining to the uniform guarding him that he should be allowed to return home to Alexandria. The uniform, acting under orders, didn't want to hear about it.

He had problems of his own. He made about $800 a month, and out of that he had to buy his service revolver, uniform, badge, and all accessories.

"You're going to be leaving soon, Mr. Williams," I said in the heartiest tone I could muster. I felt like a snake.

"Yeah? When?"

"Thirty minutes."

"All right! I'm going home! I've never been to this town before, I'm never coming back!"

"Mr. Williams, you won't be going home. You'll—"

"But you just said—"

"I said you'd be leaving, not that you'd be going home. I'd be happy if I could send you home, but I can't. Let me explain . . ."

"I want to go home!"

"I understand, but listen to me. Two vicious killers were hired by a drug dealer here in New Orleans to murder Paulette and Eddie. I was hoping that by the time you were ready to be released from the hospital we'd have all those people behind bars. But we don't.

"This drug dealer had planned to send people to Alexandria, your home, to find Paulette and Eddie—and this over a drug rap. Think what he'll do facing a murder charge. So listen. I've arranged for federal marshals to hold you in protective custody until we locate and arrest all the killers."

"You don't have them yet? Didn't I identify them?"

Williams wanted the same speed-of-light action the district attorney expected.

"No, we don't have all of them, not yet. We've got the one in the bandana. And the one who shot you."

"Just those two?"

"Yes."

"The two really bad ones—the drug dealer and the mean little guy—you ain't got?"

"The two we have are bad enough."

"What does this protective custody business mean?"

"I won't lie to you, Mr. Williams. It means jail. You'll have your own cell away from other people, and you'll only have to stay there until we're confident of your safety on the outside. We'll make every effort to see that you're as comfortable as possible. I'll personally try to get you a TV. You'll have phone and mail privileges. You'll—"

"Might be years before you arrest those guys," he interrupted.

He had a point.

"If it lasts any length of time, we'll make other arrangements."

"What arrangements?"

"The Federal Witness Protection Program. They'll send you out-of-state with a new identity. They'll pay your living expenses."

"I don't want to go out-of-state. I want to go home to Alexandria."

I couldn't help but feel compassion for Samuel Williams. He had to rank as one of history's unluckiest people. He came to New Orleans to find work and got shot in the head. He had to be detained in the hospital. Then, with the two main perpetrators still on the loose, and maybe gunning for him, *he* had to go to jail.

"I'm trying to make you understand, Mr. Williams, it's not safe for you to go home."

"Well, I'm not going to jail."

"I don't know a nice way to tell you this, Mr. Williams. Please believe me when I say you have my sympathy, and that what I'm doing is for your own good. If you don't go voluntarily, we'll hold you as a material witness."

"Can you do that?"

"Positively."

He hesitated. "I'm not going voluntarily."

I told Williams again I sympathized, and waited with him until the federal marshals arrived. They took him to the special federal tier on the top floor of central lockup.

Present at the meeting in Morris's office at 1:00 P.M. were Chief of Detectives Henry Morris, Homicide Commander Tom Duffy, U.S. attorneys Daniel Bent and Albert Winter, Assistant District Attorney Tim Cerniglia, private attorney Milton Masinter, Cris, Emmett, and me.

What evolved into a grueling session began slowly with Morris briefing Masinter on the investigation's progress, and then Masinter and Cris retiring to another room with Cris's signed statement. The rest of us lingered in Morris's office, filled with pictures and plaques, drinking coffee and recounting old cases. Morris amused us by recounting a smoking gun investigation he once handled at a bar. "Goddamn," he said. "The place was packed, but nobody saw anything. Thirty-five patrons in that saloon. To reconstruct the scene, as they said it was, I had to cram all thirty-five in the john."

I had the impression Cerniglia wanted Cris to plead guilty to manslaughter, penalty zero to twenty-one years, with the judge deciding: He'd probably hand down twenty-one. Al Winter, who'd been with the District Attorney's Office before becoming a U.S. attorney—a tall, broad, imposing man—wanted Cris for three counts of conspiracy to obstruct justice, carrying a maximum five-year term for each, plus a fine (the fine wouldn't be levied here, it's usually assessed for white-collar crimes to recoup loss of stolen property). Acting in concert, Cerniglia and Winter aimed for consecutive, not concurrent, sentences, a total of thirty-six years.

Leaning against a wall, my mind numb from lack of sleep, I felt out of my element amid this covey of legal eagles.

Emmett and I joined them because we had custody of Cris; regardless of the results of the negotiations, we would have to arrange for his safety.

Morris and Duffy sat in because of the import of the case—they had *nothing* more pressing than this—and intended to interject their ideas as they saw fit. The prosecutors seemed happy the cops were there, seeing it as insurance against any possible later complaints about deals being made behind the backs of the police. In reality, because of the extremely controversial nature of these killings, *everyone* wanted everyone else to know what went on. If something went wrong, blame could be spread collectively.

My own feelings: Short of the death penalty, Cris should be grateful for anything he received. His violent past rendered him dead meat against the murder charge. His age, twenty, worked in his favor, but when *does* the individual become responsible for his actions? My thoughts about Cris's imagined gratitude demonstrated in crystal clear fashion my unsuitability to practice law.

Milton Masinter, the Silver Fox, in his early forties, five feet ten, prematurely gray, stylishly dressed in expensive duds, waltzed back into Morris's office, leaving Cris outside.

Masinter's eyes twinkled as he asked what the prosecutors would offer, and he smiled and arched his eyebrows when he heard, an indication he'd accept when the temperature in New Orleans hit 30 degrees below.

The wily Silver Fox knew the score. He realized we really wanted to lock up Sylvester, and that Cris held the key. He also understood, though certainly no one dwelled on it, the potential time bomb of witnesses, *unprotected* witnesses, being killed. A nice, quick, quiet guilty plea by Cris would avoid at least one publicity-making trial, though if Sylvester ever came to court, Glass could be relied upon to be heard all the way to the offices of the *Times-Picayune* and the wire services.

Milton Masinter had defended Cris before, always being paid by the transvestite's long-suffering and, by all accounts, very religious, hard-working, and most decent mother. Once again Masinter had been called upon to represent Cris's— not society's—best interest, and he did his duty in praise-worthy fashion. He looked from one prosecutor to the other, allowing that he'd accept no deal without knowing how much time his client would receive.

"It's up to the judge," Cerniglia said. "You know that, Milton."

"C'mon, Tim, get off that. I didn't graduate law school yesterday. We both know the judge will follow your recommendations."

"Maybe. We've already told you what we'll recommend."

"It's too much."

"It's *not* too much. It's not enough. We've got your client for first-degree murder."

"What else do you have?"

The question hung in the air like a sword—a double-edged sword. It could slice Cris's neck off as surely as it could cause heads to roll in the District Attorney's Office.

One moment the negotiations appeared locked in stale-mate, the next the lawyers appeared close to agreement. I followed the jousting back and forth with almost a layman's fascination. One moment I believed Masinter held all the cards: We *needed* Cris. Then the prosecution rebutted: What kind of lawyer would Masinter be if he *didn't* cut a deal, and his client received life in prison without possibility of parole? Would Cris, locked in prison for all his days, really find adequate satisfaction in our chagrin over losing Sylvester? When Cerniglia and Winter talked, it seemed *we* held a fistful of aces. But that feeling only lasted until Masinter opened up again.

The machinations of the lawyers epitomized high drama for me, with the largest possible stake—a man's freedom. But more than one man's freedom. In the background always, seldom mentioned, hovered dope dealer David Sylvester.

They finally reached an understanding, with Masinter insisting it be put in writing—a shrewd, careful lawyer, leaving nothing to chance. He aimed to guarantee absolutely that his client wouldn't be popped twice: first in federal court, then all over again in state court. In fact, he didn't intend to have to trust a state court judge at all.

Everyone hears about plea bargain agreements, usually has strong opinions about them, but who ever sees one? I hadn't.

In retrospect, agreement became possible, almost mandatory, because both sides had major incentives to make the deal. The longest sentence Cris could receive came to fifteen years, which I didn't believe adequately fit the crime.

However, I'm not an attorney; my job description doesn't include working out plea bargains. Besides, I watched Winter, Bent, and Cerniglia go eyeball-to-eyeball with Masinter, and I'm not sure anyone else could have done better. Regardless, watching plea bargains always left me with a slightly sour taste in my mouth.

As older, wiser heads counseled, the detective, just as with his marriage, needs to keep his job separate from the wheeling and dealing of the law's prosecutorial arm. Although he wouldn't be a good detective if he didn't care how cases turned out, he'd spin off the track, be no good to anyone, if he became consumed by what others did.

Al Winter called in U.S. marshals to place Cris under federal protection. I suspected they'd keep him in a motel for a week until his indictment, then transfer him to the same federal tier—though far removed—where Samuel Williams resided, on the top floor of central lockup.

I must have resembled a creature from *Night of the Living Dead* when I arrived home at 5:00 P.M. this July 23. Diane hugged me lovingly but lightly, kissed my cheek, and stepped out of the way. I made a beeline for the bed.

I knew Diane wanted to talk, to hear what happened, to share my day, and that she didn't understand, even when refreshed and alert, why I kept much of my police business to myself. How could it be otherwise?

Would it help if she knew? Knew about elderly women, heads caved in by a brick, with sticks or knives shoved into their vaginas; or brain matter splattered onto a ceiling, dripping on me as I conduct a scene investigation; or running hands, searching for bullet holes, over a stinking, bloated, decomposed body, pulled from the water with crabs still gnawing on the flesh; or viewing the body of a child our son's age, a torture-murder victim lying on a mortuary slab as the coroner prepares to gut him throat to groin the way a fish gets cleaned; or pulling a hysterical, screaming, newly widowed woman off the body of her dismembered husband; or. . . .

Enough. I didn't want Diane to know, didn't believe her knowing would enrich her life one single bit.

"Keep your marriage and your job separate," old-timers tell recruits, the best advice a new cop can get, and the hardest to follow.

If police don't have the highest suicide and divorce rates in the nation, they're right behind whatever profession owns the dubious distinction. It may begin, at least in part, when the officer doesn't leave his job downtown, but brings it home and then feels he needs to explain *in detail* to loved ones why his mood often borders on the rotten.

CHAPTER
—12—

I talked with Joe Miceli at 11:45 P.M. on Friday, July 23, in the Homicide room. Miceli—age thirty-four, five feet eleven, medium build, and sandy hair—is a very handsome, mild-mannered man who always has a smile on his face and a good attitude for the job.

We relaxed, unwinding for a few minutes while chuckling about how Joe once wriggled his way out of a tight squeeze when, as a uniform, he answered a family disturbance call.

The wife met Joe outside her house, and frantically told him she wanted to leave her husband. "I need you to help me get my clothes and my child away from him," she told Joe. "Please make sure I'm all right. He's a wild man."

At the front door Miceli talked to the husband, who agreed to let his wife have her clothes, but not the child. Joe didn't need a hassle, so he tried playing peacemaker by running "tell her I said"/"you can tell him I said" messages between the feuding couple. It didn't work.

With the husband yelling obscenities, Joe led the wife inside, but stopped dead in his tracks when he turned to address the husband and found himself looking down the twin tunnels of a double-barrel shotgun. Caught completely off guard, Joe had no time to do anything but try to talk his way out of the house before the husband shot him. Joe pleaded with the man, at the same time telling the wife to collect her clothes, forget the kid for now, and get the hell out.

The wife moseyed into the bedroom, taking her time selecting her wardrobe, while the husband's hands trembled on the shotgun aimed at Joe's head. Finally she appeared, baggage in hand, in the living room, where the shotgun drama continued to run its course. "I want the baby, too," she announced.

"Lady, please," Joe said, sure she would get him killed.

"I'm not leaving without my baby."

"Lady, let's leave."

But the woman continued to argue, Joe sweated at gunpoint, and the husband grew more upset.

"Lady . . ."

"He's not a fit father, Officer."

Good God.

"She's not a fit mother, Officer."

I don't care right now, Joe thought.

"Please, lady, can't we discuss this later?"

"You want me to leave my baby with this horrible monster?"

"I'm certainly not letting *her* have the child."

"Lady . . ."

"I don't want to kill you, Officer, but you understand, with my child's future at stake, I may have to."

"Lady . . ."

"You can see he's a mean, violent man, Officer."

"Don't believe her, Officer. She's totally selfish. She's—"

"Selfish! Don't you call me selfish, you stingy son of a bitch!"

"Stingy? Hah! I work my fingers to the bone for you. Just who in hell do you think finances your marathon shopping campaign to move D.H. Holmes Department Store, piece by piece, into this house?''

"Now he's calling me a spendthrift, Officer. I only buy things to make our life easier.''

"Oh! Thanks a hell of a lot!'' the husband barked. ''I'm killing myself so you can make me more comfortable.''

"Lady . . .''

As the two continued to argue, distracting themselves, Joe managed to jump on and disarm the irate husband.

"I should have beat the shit out of him,'' Joe told me with a laugh. "But the wife would have testified against me if I had.''

When Joe Miceli joined the Homicide unit, we also handled rapes. In one such case he identified a multiple rapist, a seventeen-year-old with an extremely violent arrest record. The suspect's mother let Joe and other detectives into her home to search, and as Joe approached a closet door, the teenager burst out pointing a gun at him. Joe drew his weapon, lightning fast, and killed the youngster with a single shot into the heart.

Later, at the Homicide office, the mother approached Joe in front of a big crowd of brass. "Officer,'' she said, her heart breaking, "I know you did what you had to. My son had become uncontrollable. Everyone in our family was terrified of him.''

Police stories completed, Miceli told me about the raid for guns at 1305 South Prieur Street, Apartment C, in the Calliope Project. The apartment turned out not to be leased by Nelson Davis's girlfriend, but by one Henry Fisher, age forty-nine, a character whose name might have been "dirtbag,'' so often did I hear that moniker applied to him. The sheet containing Fisher's arrest record stretched a quarter of the width of the Homicide unit, a distance that would have challenged Jack Nicklaus's putting skills.

Fisher's latest method of earning a living involved rent-a-guns, which holdup artists obtained from him and returned when they completed the job. I guessed Nelson Davis rented the weapons used to kill Paulette and Eddie from Henry Fisher, though I doubted we'd ever prove it.

Miceli's raiding team didn't come up with the HoJo guns, but they did charge Fisher with possession of stolen property, namely a Luger automatic and a Stevens 16-gauge shotgun. They found four other guns they couldn't *prove* were stolen.

Fisher's lengthy record meant he faced a long prison sentence for the stolen weapons charges, thus he tried to be cooperative without linking himself to murder. He admitted he knew Nelson Davis, but not that he rented the guns to him. He agreed to help us find the killer.

Drugs and guns go together, and I believed Henry Fisher double-dipped: selling dope, which his clients paid for by renting his guns to obtain the necessary money. A sinister system that worked in a crazy, frighteningly logical way.

Among Henry Fisher's many arrests had been aggravated rape, armed robbery, and possession of heroin with intent to distribute. He'd accumulated three of the Big Four. Only murder was missing.

I suspected Henry Fisher probably threw the murder weapons in the Mississippi River when he learned what happened at Howard Johnson's. Still, I had a realistic hope he'd help us find Nelson Davis. If he did, we'd talk about the stolen gun charges, something he needed desperately in light of his multiple offender status.

So far the investigation had been one of steadily accumulating momentum, one surprising success following another, a tiny snowball starting with Sticks and growing to near-avalanche proportions. Now we'd drawn a goose egg on the guns. But more heartening news lay just ahead.

When I arrived at the Homicide office, three messages

awaited that I believed came from the same anonymous caller who tipped Emmett onto Clarence Davis. The last message said he would phone again at 1:00 A.M., and true to his word, he did. Unlike the time he talked to Emmett, he didn't appear high on drugs.

"Are you in charge of that murder case at Howard Johnson's?" The caller spoke with a deep, gruff voice.

"Yes. Who is this?"

"Never mind. I'm the guy who gave you Clarence. You want to know the name of the second one?"

I already knew. Nelson Davis.

"You know who it is?" I asked.

"Yeah, and I know who put out the contracts."

He had my total interest.

"You know a lot, don't you," I said.

"I know it all, man. I know the whole story."

"Why don't you meet me and run it down?"

"First, I need to know if you're going to help me if I help you."

"What kind of help do you need?"

"An armed robbery charge in High Court."

Street slang: High Court translates into Criminal Court.

"You've been around," I said. "You know I can't promise you anything. But I'll meet with you, if you really have something."

I meant Sylvester. We had serious need of corroboration for Cris.

"Who do you think put out the contracts?" I asked, getting right to the point.

"Think? I know, man. Does the name David Sylvester mean anything to you?"

"Where can we meet?"

"Bourbon Street. Corner of St. Ann. Be there in an hour."

Two A.M.

"What's your name?"

"Norwine."

"First name?"

"Norwine's enough for now."

"What do you look like?"

"Hey, don't pressure me! You'll know who I am."

"I'll be in a white Ford."

"No shit. White or blue. Supposed to be unmarked. I can spot them a mile away."

He wasn't as street smart as he thought. How many people named Norwine did he think would be in our computer?

One. John. Age thirty. It had to be him.

A career criminal, John Norwine served ten years in Angola for armed robbery. Since his release, he'd been arrested for possession of heroin and three counts of armed robbery; he currently faced an open armed robbery charge pending in Section B of Criminal Court.

He did indeed need help. He was looking at ninety-nine years, and had become a scared "jack artist," an individual who'd rob anyone, do anything, for dope. No price too high to pay.

Almost every other playground in the country is either winding down or closing down at 2:00 A.M., but not Bourbon Street. It's the shank of the night on Bourbon. Everybody is out: tourists, conventioneers, street people, night people, gamblers, prostitutes, hustlers, cops, couples on dates, musicians on a break, sidewalk entertainers—jugglers, singers, dancers, etc.—hot dog salesmen, a veritable carnival of humanity enjoying food, drink, and music galore.

I sat in the unmarked car on St. Ann next to blocked-off-for-vehicular-traffic Bourbon Street, listening to jazz coming from the open doors of several clubs. Cool music on a warm night in the middle of one of the French Quarter's best sections.

I saw Norwine approaching, six feet five and 230 pounds of him, walking with a confident strut as if he owned the streets. He knew better. That's why he wanted to talk to me.

Norwine stopped next to the driver's side, stomped out a cigarette, and said, "Pick me up on the next corner."

I gave him time to get there—Royal Street—and then cruised by at a snail's pace as he jumped into the front seat. Royal and St. Ann lay as dead to nightlife as Bourbon and St. Ann had been alive.

"Drive to Decatur. Hang a left. I'll tell you where to go from there."

What was this? Who ran this operation? I pulled the car to the curb. "Look, John," I said, intentionally using his first name.

"Where do you get that 'John' stuff?"

"Off your rap sheet. I guess you do want help, but you're going to have to operate my way. I'm not your chauffeur, and this isn't a game. I'll listen to what you've got to say, but no bullshit. *You* came to *me* because you've got serious problems and you're looking for a way out from under them. Just remember, I'm your ticket, you're not mine. You got that?"

"Hey, I just wanted to take you to a place where we could talk. This is dangerous. I can get killed. I don't want to be seen with you."

I looked at Norwine, a hulk. I'd known it from the rap sheet. My service revolver rested under my left thigh. I had no intention of fighting with this man. If push came to shove, I'd instantly jam the revolver into his face.

"*I'll* take you where we can talk," I said.

I drove out to eastern New Orleans to the L & N Railroad yards, ghosts of my great-grandfather and Harry Lester, and wound between parked boxcars and tankers. No one would see us here, except maybe a lone hobo catching sleep before riding the rails to another town. We sat silent for a moment in the deserted trainyard, the moon still full, just as it had been for Emmett, Sticks, and me on that Mississippi River wharf.

"Nelson Davis is your second shooter," Norwine said, having made up his mind to give a portion of what he knew. "And David Sylvester put out the contract."

"Do you know Nelson Davis and David Sylvester?"

"Do I know them? I'm into dope. Sylvester's the biggest dealer in the city. Nelson Davis is real bad. He's a bad dude. For a score he'd kill his own mother."

I looked at Norwine, almost a giant in size, and sensed how heartfelt was his fear of Nelson Davis. Size meant nothing. Not against a gun. Nelson Davis stood five feet six, but the strapping Norwine dreaded him.

"How do you know Nelson Davis took the contract?"

"Wait a minute, I know what I know. I can hand you Sylvester and Nelson Davis on a silver platter, but I want to walk on the armed robbery. That's my deal. Take it or leave it."

I felt like leaving it. The plea bargain arrangement with Cris remained a fresh, unpleasant memory. Regardless, rather than leaving and taking small, temporary satisfaction, I reminded myself what decisions my job *didn't* entail.

"Norwine," I said, "I can't even begin to talk to the district attorney until I know what you'll say. He doesn't want to hear speculation. Tell me what you know, or our conversation is over."

He didn't have a choice. He knew how plea bargains worked, and that I told him the truth. He had some chance, however slight—my talking to the D.A.—that beat no chance at all if he didn't tell me what he knew.

"Let me ask again," I said. "How do you know Nelson Davis took the contract?"

"He told me he did. He asked if I'd be the wheel man. He wanted me to make the score with him."

"When did this take place?" I permitted myself hope we'd get that critical corroboration for Cris.

"Tuesday, the day of the murders. About three in the afternoon."

"Where did your conversation with Nelson Davis take place?"

"Outside Two Jacks bar on South Liberty. Me and Davis were talking on the corner. David Sylvester walked up. When Davis saw Sylvester, he left me and huddled with him. After they talked for a few minutes, Davis asked me to give him a ride back into the Projects. He got in my car and told me he'd be taking care of some business. A big score. I asked him what kind of score, and he laughed and said he needed to get rid of some witnesses. Then he told me he needed wheels, and asked if I'd drive him on the hit. I told him no. I already had enough trouble of my own. I dropped him off on South Prieur."

The apartment building of Mr. Rent-a-Rod, Henry Fisher. I didn't doubt Norwine could point out the building. If he gave me the truth, and his information so far indicated he did, then Clarence Davis had not yet been chosen to accompany Nelson. Clarence had been a last-minute choice, an alternate selection.

"Did you actually hear Sylvester tell Nelson Davis to make the hit?"

"I could lie to you and say I did, but the answer's no. They stood only a few feet away from me, but they whispered, and I couldn't make out what they said."

I looked at an old, dented freight car, remembering as a boy how I'd wanted to travel on such a conveyance. Ride the rails. Live in perfect community with other hoboes. See the world.

"Look," Norwine said, aiming to please, "everybody in the Project knew Sylvester faced a bunch of trouble over those witnesses. As soon as Davis finished talking to Sylvester, he jumped right in my car and said he had to get rid of the witnesses. He didn't have to run down for me what Sylvester wanted. I knew."

And so would a jury, I thought.

"You called Homicide earlier with the name of Clarence. That was Clarence Davis. How did you know about him?"

"After the shootings, the word on the street said Clarence went along with Nelson. I know Clarence. He'd do a thing like this. Nelson Davis knew him, too. I figure Nelson used Clarence's wheels."

This part of Norwine's recital, completely speculative and inadmissible in court, didn't bother me, because Clarence Davis already had given a verbal statement, and Samuel Williams would identify him. On the other hand, Norwine's fingering of Sylvester, coming when it did (shortly before the murders), counted very strongly. The evidence still would be classed as circumstantial, but integrated into the whole it comprised an impressive set of coincidences. I suspected Glass might now have trouble explaining all of them away. It bordered on the preposterous that Sylvester, just by accident, met on the day of the killings—*before* they took place—with both Nelson Davis and Cris, and *afterward* flashed the "safe" sign to the main hitter.

"What do you know about a third person going with the two Davises to the motel?"

"I don't know anything about it. Was a third killer there?"

"Where can I find Nelson Davis?"

"I don't have any idea, but you'd better find him. And you'd better believe he won't come easy, like Clarence Davis did. He'll shoot you in a split second. Won't even think about it. You watch your ass close. I want you healthy to talk to the district attorney.''

I leaned back, listening to the quiet, the full moon the same as it had been sixty years ago, and let myself think about an old train robbery and a swamp at Honey Island. Then I looked Norwine in the eyes.

"I'm going to be upfront with you," I said. "The D.A. won't consider any type of reduced charge unless you're willing to testify."

"I'm dead if I testify."

I shrugged my shoulders.

Norwine thought it over, making the only sensible choice he could. "I'll testify," he said.

"I can't promise you anything," I repeated.

I started the engine, pulled out of the trainyard, with its ancestral memories, and drove along deserted streets to the French Quarter where I dropped off Cris's corroboration. I felt good about everything except the guns.

Later that morning, reviewing notes I'd taken at the Howard Johnson's crime scene, I was reminded of an incident I thought would never be far from my mind. The name of the motel suddenly triggered my memory of a terrible day in mid-January 1973; I was amazed that I hadn't remembered the awful incident before. I hoped the reason for the mental blackout stemmed from the all-out, intensely concentrated investigation into the murders of Paulette and Eddie, and not because I simply forgot such an event. To forget would be blasphemy.

The first police radio calls told of a small army of arsonists and snipers who had taken over the downtown Howard Johnson's high-rise. Smoke poured from half a dozen balconies—according to a witness, "light bulbs popping all over the place" from the heat—and shots rained down from several upper floors, not sporadic fire, but long, sustained bursts. Had crazed, brain-damaged Charles Whitman from the Texas Tower come back to life?

Hundreds of New Orleans policemen, myself among them, plus numerous officers from adjoining jurisdictions, and, unfortunately, citizens thirsting for action—who had to be kept away—responded to what seemed a war at Howard Johnson's. And like all wars, people died.

A fireman bravely investigating the flames, which he feared might consume the entire high-rise, perhaps even spread to other buildings, was shot and killed, blown off the ladder he'd been scaling. A young married couple were gunned down in a corridor, found later locked in each other's arms in a death embrace. Two uniforms died from gunfire. Also dead was the city's deputy police superintendent, Louis Sirgo.

The siege lasted *eleven hours*. Eleven hours of combat. An armor-plated marine helicopter made repeated passes over the building, but the shots kept coming. The assailant—it turned out to be *one* person—found refuge behind the concrete walls of the rooftop's boiler room, a virtually impregnable position. If he had food and water with him, he could hold out for a week or more. A long, suspenseful wait ensued, punctuated by gunfire from both sides.

At last, darkness having descended, he darted under the glare of a helicopter spotlight, raced zigzag fashion perhaps thirty feet, and fell dead, hit by more than a hundred bullets.

We waited through the night until morning, fearing the sniper had confederates, but he'd accomplished the bloodshed by himself: six dead, including three police officers; nine wounded, three of these police.

His name was James Robert Essex, age twenty-three. A teacher at the vocational school he attended called him "probably the best student in the class." Neighbors described Essex as "well liked" and "congenial," with "parents who are upstanding Christian people."

But the parents, contacted at their home in Emporia, Kansas, told a different story. He'd been "congenial," all right, until joining the U.S. Navy, where they said he encountered flagrant racism. Embittered, James Essex blamed all white people, and his hatred grew into an obsession.

Before the Essex case was closed, the NOPD came to believe he'd been responsible for the 1972 New Year's Eve killing of one policeman and the wounding of two others near police headquarters. Slugs recovered from two of the murder victims at the Howard Johnson's high-rise matched the .44-magnum bullets used in the New Year's Eve shootings.

Of course, along with almost every police officer in New Orleans, and with law enforcement representatives literally from all over the country, I attended the funerals of the slain policemen. The experience truly touched. A lump clogged every throat, and dry eyes were nowhere to be seen. As mentioned, it amazed me that it took three days after the murders of Paulette and Eddie to recall that other experience with violence at a Howard Johnson's.

Five and a half days after questioning John Norwine, on the morning of July 29, I presented our evidence to an Orleans Parish Grand Jury. At 2:00 P.M., The Grand Jury returned indictments against both Davises and David Sylvester, each of them charged with two counts of first-degree murder and one count of attempted murder.

By 2:30 P.M., Sam, Emmett, and I had the necessary paperwork prepared and headed over to Orleans Parish prison where David Sylvester currently resided. Out on bond for the drug charge (which would be dropped because of the murders of Paulette and Eddie), Sylvester, of his own free will, checked himself back into jail after the killings at HoJo. I didn't know why Sylvester chose incarceration over the freedom of the street, but I suspected it involved a mixup over paying Nelson Davis the $20,000. Perhaps the drug dealer planned on waiting for us to do his work for him—that is, kill Nelson Davis—because he suspected the extremely dangerous hitter would leave us no choice.

Guards brought Sylvester to a prison interrogation room. I'd never laid eyes on him before, and found myself surprised.

This pleasant-looking, thirty-two-year-old man might have been coming down to meet us for a cozy Sunday afternoon visit, so relaxed and laid-back did he appear. He stood five feet seven and weighed a plump 180 pounds; his clean-cut features and massive self-assurance more befitted a prosperous business executive than a sleazy drug dealer. Sylvester took a seat across from us, cool and unruffled, no sign whatever of fear, and fixed us with a stare of mild curiosity.

I introduced Sam, Emmett, and myself and told him he was under arrest for the murders of Paulette Royal and Eddie Smith and the attempted murder of Samuel Williams.

I counted that little speech a big moment in my life, though Sylvester's bland, benign expression didn't change. He leaned back slightly in his chair, whereupon Emmett read him his rights.

"Do you understand what I said?" Emmett asked.

The drug dealer didn't answer.

"Do you understand?" Emmett's voice, filled with distaste, rose an octave.

"Yes."

Emmett shoved the form upon which rights are written in front of the indicted murder suspect. "If you'll sign by the *X*, Sylvester, we'll be willing to listen to your confession."

"Talk to my attorney," said the drug dealer, and he said no more.

CHAPTER
–13–

Shop talk in the Homicide unit, indeed throughout the New Orleans Police Department, made the upcoming joint David Sylvester/Clarence Davis murder trial—they were to be prosecuted together—sound like nothing less than a war between good and evil, with the outcome dangerously in doubt.

On the "good" side stood the prosecution, police, and citizens concerned with a drug problem growing more out of control each day and the possibility that a murderous heroin purveyor might be set free; on the "evil" side sat Sylvester and a sizable contingent from the Projects who viewed him under a different light. This concept of good and evil, carried too far, could pose a serious threat to evenhanded, impartial justice. More than anyone else connected with the case, except perhaps Harry Connick, I needed to guard against a convict-at-any-cost mentality, because to my mind the evidence we'd gathered *proved* his guilt. The larger my stake in the trial's outcome—large indeed because my peers, superiors, and the jury would be grading my work—the more frequently I needed to remind myself that my job didn't include convicting.

To understand Sylvester and that light under which certain residents of the Projects viewed him, it helps to read the opening pages of *The Godfather*, where Don Corleone, Marlon Brando in the movie, dispenses favors to people with nowhere else to turn.

As we dug into Sylvester's past, we discovered he wore two hats. The one that far outweighed the other, in my opinion, was worn when he sold heroin to people who killed and were killed by it. Wearing the second hat, however, Sylvester starred in a ghetto Horatio Alger story, poor kid from the Projects makes good but never forgets his roots, and through luck and pluck scrambles to the top of the pile; a success story, patriarch, hero, even savior for those fortunate enough to know him.

Sylvester beat the odds and the system, rising from poverty—his first bust came as a hungry teenager for looting in the aftermath of a hurricane—to carry a fat bankroll and enjoy an extravagant life-style. *How* he succeeded didn't matter to admirers; the luster of his star blinded them to critical analysis. Besides, what other avenues lay open for him?

Sylvester didn't mug, rape, or burst through Project apartment windows to steal and terrorize, no matter that he created ogres who did. Subjects of his realm didn't view him as a mindless monster foraging at a beastly level while committing brutal crimes to feed an all-consuming drug addiction.

Quite the opposite. Like Don Corleone, Sylvester *helped* people. He helped them when others, including society, wouldn't.

The power company cut off your electricity? Sylvester might pay the bill for you. About to be evicted because you can't come up with the rent? See Sylvester—he's helped plenty of others. Need money to purchase milk for your hungry baby? Right: try Sylvester.

Often the assistance seemed to come without attached

strings. The drug dealer provided emergency aid when none other existed, and Project residents didn't care if he harbored concealed motives. Now these well-intentioned citizens would show support in *his* hour of need.

One attorney with whom I chatted compared David Sylvester to Robin Hood, a description accurate to a degree, I suppose, since the drug pusher did on occasion help the poor. But how did he take from the rich I wanted to know. The vast preponderance of his victims lived in the Projects. I doubted David Sylvester really provided lasting help for anyone, or that his donations amounted to much more than insurance premiums, or IOUs collected in any manner he thought needed.

Unfortunately, in the minds of some who opposed Sylvester, the impending court battle also featured "good" and "evil" in the persons of the antagonists, Harry Connick and Robert Glass. Connick, the University of Tulane graduate, symbolized safe streets, clean living, law and order. Glass, simply because he defended a major drug dealer, someone absolutely entitled to a first-rate defense, found himself stigmatized—happily not by the majority—merely by association.

Whatever, Connick versus Glass, the top law enforcement official in New Orleans pitted against a defense practitioner with perhaps the city's most astounding success record, promised the sort of sensational legal battle that was apt to jolt the walls of the normally staid Criminal Courts building.

Glass, whom I consider an idealist, attended the University of Pennsylvania Law School, migrating after graduation to New Orleans in 1968 as part of a federally funded program to provide poor people with needed legal representation. A man of strong principles, Glass later lost his job when he expanded the program into areas where Washington, D.C., officials didn't believe it belonged—namely, representing unpopular defendants in criminal cases. The activist Glass, who demonstrated against America's involvement in the Vietnam War, called himself an "egalitarian. I enjoy taking the hard side, when the odds are against me. How do I describe myself? Sympathetic to oppressed people."

Glass also proved himself almost unbeatable in court. Three times he represented Black Panthers, and three times he won—this in the Deep South! One of the Panther cases involved a shoot-out in the Desire Project, with twelve defendants accused of attempting to murder five policemen. Glass won acquittals for all twelve.

Another time he represented occupants of a car caravan, organized by Jane Fonda, who were arrested as they headed for the Black Panther Constitutional Convention in Philadelphia. Again Glass emerged 100 percent victorious.

Glass had courage. He never took a backward step when, during a Panther trial, he received threats against his personal safety. Later, in a trial garnering enormous national media attention, he represented a former official of the National Organization for Women (NOW), Ginny Foat, and won acquittal against a murder charge.

In 1976, at age thirty-four, a veteran of ACLU battles, Glass already had earned a reputation as one of the Crescent City's most able cross-examiners, and as a spellbinder during closing arguments. Especially in the area of cross-examination, we had reason to fear him. Prosecution witnesses in *State of Louisiana* vs. *David Sylvester/Clarence Davis* hardly qualified as high moral types. Glass surely would cut them to ribbons, quite possibly in the process adding another glittering win to his shining victory record.

Acquittal, if it occurred, wouldn't come easy. Harry Connick, some ten years Glass's senior, might have been born to handle this case: His main strength came from being able to explain a complex series of events in a way average citizens could understand. I believed Connick could weave all the threads of Sylvester's complicated involvement into a coherent whole. Once he accomplished this task, I firmly believed, any interpretation of Sylvester's actions, other than what we offered, would strike jurors as farfetched and absurd.

Harry Connick had a great deal at stake. He'd decided to prosecute the case himself, an almost unprecedented action, before or since (and he is still district attorney in New Orleans), for an individual holding his high position. The only other major example springing to mind occurred when Jim Garrison prosecuted Clay Shaw on conspiracy charges in the JFK assassination. An equivalent situation to Connick's would be if the U.S. attorney general personally appeared in federal court to handle a prosecution, a rare occurrence. Connick's assuming the reins demonstrated his deep concern for the HoJo case, and the critical importance he attached to it.

I admired Connick for his "buck stops here" position on the murders of Paulette and Eddie. If the office he headed bore responsibility for the killings, he at least intended personally to seek punishment for those responsible.

By taking a case no one believed airtight, Connick exposed himself to double jeopardy. If he lost, his office—he himself if you subscribe to theories of executive responsibility—would not only have lost the witnesses, but also the murderers who eliminated the witnesses.

Thus Connick operated under extreme pressure. He needed a victory. A defeat would be devastating. If he lost it would be remembered as a big negative in his career. This alone, in my eyes at least, transported the gutsy district attorney into a most favorable light.

Glass versus Connick. In charge of the HoJo murder investigation, I'd be the chief police witness at the trial. But even if I hadn't been involved, I would have stood in line to see this battle.

Life for me assumed a sort of grisly normalcy after the incredible three-and-a-half-day adventure of the HoJo investigation. Shortly after David Sylvester's arrest I drew a case in which I came to suspect the son of wealthy uptown New Orleans parents, afraid of being cut out of their will, of hiring a hit man to murder his parents in order to inherit the sizable estate. This investigation and others were piled on me at the rate of perhaps one every dozen days. Their accompanying ever-present paperwork, always mountainlike, kept me busy and tested the tensile strength of my desk as well as my personal endurance. Despite this avalanche of work, thoughts of the impending trial were never far from my mind.

The real meat of my participation in the case, not including the Grand Jury appearance and Sylvester's arrest, stretched only over those three and a half days. Then Harry Connick and his own investigative staff took over, and they didn't want me pestering them with calls about the latest developments. But I couldn't curb my curiosity.

I got a taste of how concerned figures close to my own investigations felt and why they constantly called to learn what was going on. The most recent example being the city's brass continually trying to reach us on the car radio while Emmett and I combed the Quarter for Sticks.

Jane Belton, Paulette's friend from the Project, who'd called me early in the case, phoned one day for an update. "Are you going to put that slime Sylvester away?" she asked.

"We're giving it everything we have," I told her. "It will be up to a jury now. The district attorney himself is handling the case."

"Sylvester's got money," Janet Belton said. "Money talks loud in a courtroom."

"I promise you, this case is very important to all of us, Mrs. Belton."

"I hope so. Paulette was trying hard to straighten her life out. I think about her at the oddest times. I used to talk to her often, and knowing I'll never be able to again makes me sad. I miss Paulette, Detective Dillmann. It's not right that the people who killed her get away with it."

"I agree."

And, I thought, it said something good about Paulette that she had such a friend.

During the wait for the trial, I did everything in my power to find Nelson Davis, who seemed to have vanished off the face of the earth. John Norwine and Henry Fisher kept eyes peeled and ears open in the Projects, and I continued to hope one of these would come through. They fit comfortably in the same tough environment in which Nelson Davis moved, and they possessed the highest motivation to help: Each hoped to avoid having prison doors slam shut behind him for possibly the remainder of his life.

Other detectives throughout the Department, recognizing Nelson Davis as an enemy shared by every police unit, cooperated with Homicide by asking their confidential informants to keep ears to the ground concerning the suspect's whereabouts. Again, a blank. Wanted posters plastered the murderer's picture, along with reward information, all over New Orleans and surrounding parishes:

NEW ORLEANS POLICE DEPT.
REWARD
WANTED FOR MURDER

A reward will be paid by this department for information leading to the arrest of the following named and described subject:

* * *

Nelson Davis, alias Smitty, alias Knucklehead, Negro
male, age 24, height 5'6", weight 125 lbs., gold tooth
in front of mouth. Formerly resided 1114 South Johnson St.

Wanted subject is a drug addict and should be considered armed and dangerous. Nelson Davis and two other
subjects shot and killed two subjects on July 20, 1976,
and wounded a third subject.

Any and all information furnished on Nelson Davis or
his whereabouts will be kept in the strictest confidence.

Direct all information to the Criminal Investigation
Division, Detectives John Dillmann, Emmett Thompson, and Sam Gebbia. Telephone 822-2813, and 822-
2708.

> Major Henry M. Morris
> Chief of Detectives
> New Orleans Police Dept.

In addition, I notified the FBI, and inserted Nelson
Davis's name in the National Crime Information Center
computer. If he got stopped for any reason, anywhere in the
country, local authorities would hold him and contact us.

Our fear of Nelson Davis proved justified when we
received the first notice of his whereabouts. Store workers
positively identified Davis as the perpetrator of an armed
robbery at a New Orleans grocery. Wisely, no one resisted
the holdup.

The fact that the armed robbery took place in New Orleans
didn't convince me Nelson Davis spent his time principally
in the Crescent City. More likely, I believed, he moved from

state to state, and the New Orleans robbery occurred during a brief stopover. We had too many lines out not to net this dangerous fish if he swam regularly in our waters.

On the other hand, Nelson Davis beat that September 1974 first-degree murder charge when witnesses against him became too frightened to testify. Perhaps the same fear factor still applied, silencing any leads on him.

Murder trials always encounter at least one postponement. When it happened in the Sylvester/Davis case, I took pity on Samuel Williams and pulled every string necessary to have him transferred into the Federal Witness Protection Program. Continuing to detain him ranked as a major injustice. He could rot on the upper level of city lockup in the event of numerous postponements, continuances, and, heaven forbid, a hung jury or mistrial. After all, he had been extremely cooperative and I thought we owed him the benefits of the Witness Protection Program, and more.

As the November 11, 1976, trial date approached, employees in the District Attorney's Office could almost reach out and touch the pressure they worked under. I could sense it even in secretaries, a reflection of the feelings of their bosses—investigators, assistant district attorneys, right up to the top—as they closed ranks behind and felt a terrific responsibility for Harry Connick, the man in the hot seat.

Then a bombshell dropped on the very eve of the trial. Clarence Davis decided to cop a plea and turn state's evidence against Sylvester, which immediately separated his trial from that of the drug dealer. I assumed this development heralded good news in the prosecution's case against the main man. Why else make a deal? Convicting Clarence Davis, whom both Cris and Samuel Williams stood ready to identify, had never seemed a problem to me.

I worried increasingly this last night before the showdown. Unless Clarence Davis gave the D.A. more than he told me, I figured he might turn out to be a liability. Did we need still another prosecution witness plea bargaining a lesser sentence? Another witness Glass could paint as unworthy of belief?

Still, in an ascetic sense, it seemed right. From almost the beginning, I felt we'd have to score ourselves as losers if we didn't convict Sylvester. Trying someone else with him would only muddle the whole issue.

Late on the evening of the trial, I drank coffee with Fred Dantagnan at a Shoney's. I confessed to him how much I feared the circumstantial nature of our case.

"You'll find out starting tomorrow," Dantagnan said. "We'll win or we'll lose. You did your best and it's out of your hands now, so cheer hard—silently—and don't let it mess your mind, no matter how it turns out."

CHAPTER
—14—

The crowd that filled Judge Charles Ward's courtroom this November 11, 1976, was both for and against the defendants, and the aisle down the center of the huge, high-ceilinged room served as a don't-cross line. The emotionally charged air crackled with distrust and hostility.

Spectators on Judge Ward's right, behind Sylvester and Robert Glass, had come to support a man who helped them in their hours of need. They'd ridden buses, even taken time off from work, to get here, but they'd have sacrificed even more for David Sylvester.

On Judge Ward's left, behind Harry Connick and First Assistant District Attorney William Wessel (the city had rolled out its two biggest guns), sat numerous policemen, drug agents, and prosecutors. The officers and the narcs hoped to witness Sylvester's comeuppance, each could tell drug horror stories to sicken and sadden the hardest heart. The assistant district attorneys—coming in and out of the courtroom throughout the trial, running over during breaks in their own cases—were here to grab a few moments of the drama, to see their boss in action, to observe firsthand a top lawyer operating under heavy personal and professional pressure.

Judge Ward, a big, nice-looking man in his late forties, with a reputation for fairness, warned the tense assemblage that he'd tolerate no outbursts in his courtroom. Stern as he looked and sounded, he had to know, merely by gazing at the gallery he faced, feeling the electricity shooting back and forth across the aisle, that warnings likely wouldn't suffice.

The situation cried out for a mediator, a teacher, a peacemaker, *someone,* to explain to the opposing factions they needn't be enemies. Those rooting for Connick needed to realize that the people supporting Sylvester were good, law-abiding citizens with an understandable, long-standing skepticism of the established power structure.

Sylvester hadn't packed the courtroom with runners, pushers, junkies, and degenerates. He was too cunning for that. Those backing Sylvester would benefit from hearing the evidence, keeping their minds open till it got presented. They needed to see the other face of Sylvester, the one selling heroin and ordering murder. So far only Sylvester's version had reached their ears. What I considered an astounding set of circumstances, leading to only one possible conclusion, had not yet been aired, as it would in the courtroom.

Actually, the tension manifested itself before the spectators ever sat down. Glass, in the hallway on his way toward the courtroom doors, walked by a group of police officers who bristled with hostility, eyes turning hard as stone as the lawyer passed. Perhaps they remembered the Black Panther acquittals, and here came Glass again, representing a man they considered to be Public Enemy Number One.

Again, a conciliator would have been useful. These officers, if forced to think about it, wouldn't want anyone denied the right to expert counsel. What they reacted to was a city threatened by violence and drugs—they lived with it every day, seeing the wasted bodies civilians only encounter as statistics—and a lawyer whose sworn duty obligated him to attempt with all his being to let a monster loose on the street.

Not that Glass thought Sylvester was guilty. He didn't. Glass says he'll go to his grave believing his client innocent, and I have to believe him. His absolutely convincing performance in court, the fascinating alternate explanations he expounded to the jury, couldn't have been delivered with such passion and conviction by a man simply complying with his constitutional duty to provide a vigorous, competent defense.

Harry Connick, perfect for the case, as I've explained, addressed the jurors in the hushed courtroom the way a schoolteacher might talk to his class. Explaining in a quiet voice; just wanting them to understand. If they understood, he was confident they'd convict.

First, speaking slowly, voice conversational, he gave the definition of first-degree murder:

> First-degree murder is the killing of a human being: when the offender has a specific intent to kill or to inflict great bodily harm; or, when the offender has a specific intent to commit murder and has been offered or has received anything of value for committing the murder.

Next, the district attorney—what inner battles he must have fought to remain calm, to save any emotion and histrionics for later—explained the Louisiana first-degree murder law that applied to principals:

> All persons concerned in the commission of a crime, whether present or absent, and whether they directly commit the act constituting the offense, aid and abet in

its commission, or directly or indirectly counsel or procure another to commit the crime, are principals.

Harry Connick proceeded with a bare-bones sketch of what the state intended to prove. He kept his voice inflections to a minimum. This expert advocate didn't need to call up fire and brimstone to hold an audience in thrall. Later, to drive home the calculating, cold-blooded nature of the murders, to show his own outrage at their commission, he would summon appropriate emotion, but now he just wanted the jury to hear facts:

The State of Louisiana is asking you, as jurors, to find David Joseph Sylvester guilty of the crime of first-degree murder. Before you can do that, though, we are going to have to prove, and we will prove, certain things to you.

First, that the killers, and that includes Sylvester, had a specific intent to kill or inflict great bodily harm upon Paulette Royal and Eddie Smith. Or, that David Joseph Sylvester offered something of value, money or narcotics, or whatever, to Jessie Ford or Nelson Grant Davis and/or Clarence Davis to commit the murders. And, also, that Paulette Royal and Eddie Smith were, in fact, murdered by Clarence Davis and Nelson Grant Davis, acting together but under the direction of Sylvester.

The State is prepared to prove those allegations beyond a reasonable doubt.

An appropriate starting point for the State is David Joseph Sylvester himself, the defendant. Who is he? Why is he here? And why would he conspire with other people to cause these murders?

The State is going to prove there is one, and only one,

reason for these killings. And that Sylvester is the one who caused them.

We are going to prove Sylvester had everything to gain and not one thing to lose from the murders of Paulette Royal and Eddie Smith.

It is a fact that on May 1, 1975, Sylvester was indicted by the Grand Jury in Orleans Parish for possession with intent to distribute heroin. The penalty for this crime, upon conviction, is a mandatory life sentence in the State Penitentiary at Angola, Louisiana.

We will show that during the Court hearing, and before the trial of the narcotics case, Sylvester learned the identity of at least two of the witnesses the State planned to use against him. Those two witnesses were Paulette Royal and Eddie Smith.

Sylvester also learned that the testimony of these two witnesses, especially the testimony of Paulette Royal, would be damaging to his case.

The Court records are going to show that on April 26, 1976, during the pretrial hearing, Paulette Royal, in the presence of Sylvester, actually testified against him concerning his participation in certain narcotics transactions.

The case was ultimately set for trial on July 22, 1976. But before that, on July 12, Sylvester, through his attorneys, filed a motion to produce Eddie Smith for a defense interview. The motion was granted, and Eddie Smith was ordered produced on July 20, just two days before he and Paulette Royal were to testify against Sylvester.

On July 20, the same day of the murders, Eddie Smith was brought to Court. The State is going to show you how on that night, just two days before the narcotics trial, Paulette Royal and Eddie Smith were executed in gangland fashion.

The State will show that because they were going to testify against him, Sylvester ordered them murdered.

Now, you know it's not necessary for the State to prove motive in a criminal case. All the State has to prove is that one person did in fact commit a crime against another person, and this is sufficient for any jury to convict. But in this case, we're not only going to prove the motive, but prove beyond a reasonable doubt that Sylvester caused the murders. That's *why* it happened.

How it happened: Sylvester needed two things, a killer or killers; and he needed someone who knew Paulette Royal and Eddie Smith. Someone who could get close enough to these people to allow the killers to act.

About a week before the narcotics trial, Sylvester saw Jessie Ford and told him Paulette and Eddie were coming to town. He knew that. We're going to show you he knew that. Sylvester also said to Ford, and Ford's going to be a State witness, that Paulette Royal and Eddie Smith were in Alexandria, Louisiana, and he wanted them located. He even offered to rent a car for Ford to go up there and find them.

We're going to show you that on July 19, one day before the murders, in a bar called Two Jacks, Sylvester and one of the defendants, who's not here, Nelson Davis, also known as Knucklehead, discussed the contract. Jessie Ford was present and overheard this discussion about the contract. On the following day, the day of the murders, it's going to be proved that Sylvester, again, saw Ford both before and after the killings.

Now, Jessie Ford is going to testify, and he's going to describe the details of the murder-for-hire, and he'll identify the mastermind of the plan. Jessie Ford was actually present when these murders occurred.

We are going to show you that Jessie Ford knew Eddie Smith and Paulette Royal. Because of his association with them, he gained entrance into that room at the Howard Johnson's motel. And once there, he will tell how the killers took over and executed these people.

We are going to show you, once inside that room, Knucklehead—Nelson Davis—killed Paulette Royal and Eddie Smith by placing pillows over their heads and firing the gun point-blank three times into the head of one, and then three times point-blank into the head of the other.

While Nelson Davis did that, Clarence Davis did the same thing to Samuel Williams. For some miraculous reason we don't know, the gun jammed, and Samuel Williams, while shot in the head, survived. And he is going to tell you in detail what happened in the motel that day.

You are going to hear, also, from detectives of the New Orleans Police Department, who went to the scene of these brutal murders and gathered the evidence relating to the crimes; you will hear a doctor, Dr. Monroe Samuels, from the coroner's office, testify as to the cause of death.

This and other evidence is going to be presented to you. And we're asking, when all the evidence is in, that you return a verdict of guilty as charged against David Joseph Sylvester.

I thought Connick's opening statement short and sweet. Just the way the murder investigation had been. I didn't expect the rest of the case to proceed with anything approaching Connick's opening dispatch. From the lengthy list of proposed prosecution and defense witnesses, experienced courtroom hands expected the trial to be a long and difficult one.

Everyone would be surprised. The trial, like the investigation, moved with lightning speed.

Connick took the early lead in the contest, planting the seeds of reason into the jury's mind. I didn't delude myself we'd stay in front for long. When the opening statements end, the advantage, most of the time, belongs to the defense. Theoretically, what jurors hear last they remember best, and the defense speaks last.

But that advantage would get canceled in final arguments. Here the prosecution speaks first, the defense second, and the prosecution closes the proceedings. The reasoning behind permitting the prosecution to get in the last word is that it operates at a disadvantage: It needs to *prove its case beyond reasonable doubt,* while the defense, if it chooses, needs to do nothing.

I wondered how badly Glass would hurt us in his opening statement:

Ladies and gentlemen of the jury, the opening statement by the prosecution, just as the opening statement by the defense, is not evidence. It is merely a statement of expectation of what will be proved. The prosecution has a blueprint in advance of the trial, in advance of the hearing of evidence, to put things into a reasonable framework.

When the prosecution suggests what it expects to prove, it is making promises to you. And I ask you, listen to the case and hold the prosecution to its promises. I ask you, further, to listen closely to my cross-examination of prosecution witnesses. Listen closely to evaluate their believability, their worthiness of belief, before you make any judgment.

A large part of the defense case will come directly from the mouths of prosecution witnesses on cross-examination. When the prosecution concludes, the defense will make a decision, as is its right, whether to rest fully on the presumption of innocence, or offer additional evidence for your consideration.

But, for the time being, let me state my expectations on what will be proven from the mouths of the witnesses the prosecution calls.

At the hearing where Miss Paulette Royal testified prior to the trial, you will learn Miss Royal's testimony was severely impeached. She was made to appear, and in fact was, an almost totally incredible witness by reason of her admissions under oath on the witness stand.

You will learn Paulette Royal admitted that Eddie Smith was a female impersonator, known as Miss Edie. That Miss Edie had a modus operandi for making money, mainly going into the French Quarter and hustling tricks on the corner of St. Louis and Burgundy streets. That her preference, Miss Edie's preference, involved picking up men in the French Quarter, and rolling them—that is, robbing them.

Miss Edie disguised himself as a woman, and if he couldn't roll the man in the French Quarter, he tricked him into coming to his place on Philip Street.

At the house on Philip Street, if the man was satisfied with oral sex, then Miss Edie would take care of that. If not, Miss Edie would give him Paulette Royal. And while Paulette Royal had oral or genital sex with the trick, Miss Edie robbed him by going into his wallet.

Miss Royal further admitted, under oath, that Miss Edie became an informer for the Federal Drug Enforcement Administration as a result of Miss Edie's getting caught in the sale of heroin to an agent.

Miss Edie convinced Paulette to go to the Federal Drug-Enforcement Administration, putting the fear of God in Paulette by saying he, Eddie, could do life for a heroin charge if Paulette didn't become an informer.

That is the level of this so-called essential witness, who was told by Miss Edie, the informer, that the federal government people were interested in Sylvester. So Paulette gave them Sylvester.

From the mouths of State's witnesses, you will learn there was a pending federal indictment involving the same charge, and various substantive and conspiracy counts, against Mr. Sylvester, and also some *eight or ten* other individuals, when these murders occurred.

I give you the names of these individuals: Larry Whatley, Larry Benoit, Roy Sawyer, Herbert Lee, Sam Smith, Andrew Wilson, Harold Richardson, and an individual identified only as John Doe, aka Blue. All of these, at the time of the murders, were on the street either on bond or as fugitives.

Thus, the defense, through the mouths of the prosecution's witnesses, will establish there was motive to eliminate Paulette Royal and Eddie Smith by a number of individuals in addition to Sylvester. These individuals were in position to arrange for that elimination, since they were on the street at the time.

In addition, from the mouths of the State's witnesses, the defense will suggest to you there was motive totally independent of Paulette Royal and Eddie Smith's functions as witnesses.

You will learn from the mouths of the State's

witnesses that the individuals, Clarence Davis, Nelson Grant Davis, and Jessie Ford, who went to Room 215 of the Howard Johnson's motel, went with a purpose of either robbing for money, or robbing for dope.

You will conclude, after listening to the State's witnesses, not the police officers necessarily, but these other witnesses, that they're not credible.

Directing your attention to the one witness mentioned by the prosecution in its opening statement, Jessie Ford, you will learn from the mouth of Jessie Ford that he is a dope addict, a homosexual, and a female impersonator.

You will learn Jessie Ford was under the effect of narcotics on the day of his detention by the New Orleans police officer, some two days after the killings.

You will learn Jessie Ford understood the seriousness of the situation. He understood he could get out of it. He could get out of a life-without-benefit-of-parole-for-forty-years sentence.

Or, perhaps at that time, he thought he faced a death case.

You will find the facts, the alleged facts, which Jessie Ford tells you are improbable, impossible, or just clearly untrue.

You will find Jessie Ford received total immunity for his agreement to put David Joseph Sylvester into this case.

You will learn the police suggested to him they wanted Sylvester, and would give him a deal for his testimony.

And you will conclude at the end of the case, Jessie Ford is testifying because he's getting his life for it, not because David Joseph Sylvester, beyond a reasonable doubt, had anything whatever to do with a crime.

I suggest to you, and I will suggest at the conclusion

of the case, there was in fact a conspiracy, and that conspiracy had as its object to rob and ultimately murder Paulette Royal and Eddie Smith. But the members of the conspiracy were Clarence Davis, Nelson Grant Davis, and the State's own immunized, totally-free-from-State-fear witness, Jessie Ford.

At the conclusion of the case, I will ask you to uphold your sacred duty and decide, without partiality, the true facts of this case, what has been proven clearly and beyond a reasonable doubt. And I will ask you to enter a verdict of not guilty.

My feelings counted among the least significant of the players involved, but I sighed when I heard several of Glass's remarks. I needed to develop a thicker skin. Experience would help, I suspected. But why, *always,* in every homicide I worked that went to trial, did innuendos get bandied about regarding my improper behavior? *I'd* believe I was a constitution-trampling extremist maniac if I accepted just 5 percent of what defense lawyers said about me.

I would have complained to wise old head Pascal Saladino, but I knew what he'd say: First, he'd quote Harry Truman on hot kitchens, then he'd run down a nearly infinite number of murder trials to prove I wasn't unique, it happened to every detective. Still, being called a liar and a brute so consistently led to bouts of depression.

Do defense attorneys really believe what they say? It goes like this: "Here's my innocent, naive client, Sid Cesspool [Sid has forty priors, knows the law better than Blackstone] who didn't have his rights read to him [they were, of course, four times] and he was starved and beaten to obtain his confession [hogwash, he insisted on talking, hoping to draw a lighter sentence by ratting on a friend, and we hardly had him long enough to beat him, much less starve him, since his bondsman had him out in just a few hours]."

Glass said Cris had been under the influence of narcotics when I questioned him. Jesus. Was the defense lawyer going to claim I preyed on a helpless junkie? Glass also wondered if maybe Cris thought he faced the death penalty. If Cris received the death-penalty impression from me, I indeed ranked as a rascal and a rogue who deserved to be drummed off the force.

I suspected Glass's remarks merely served as preview, and knew when my turn came I'd be in for rough cross-examination. Fine and good. I just hoped I wouldn't have to defend myself against something totally imagined, gross, or bizarre.

The opening trial remarks, I'd learned, intriguing as they might be for clues suggesting the direction each side intended to take, could prove a very inaccurate gauge for anyone trying to predict an outcome.

Glass himself had said it: "The opening statement by the prosecution, just as the opening statement by the defense, is not evidence."

I thought Glass had the jury leaning in Sylvester's favor at this point. Glass's allegations had by far been the more sensational.

But now the real battle commenced.

CHAPTER
–15–

It turned out that the voir dire—the selection of the jury—lasted longer than the trial itself. Each side thought the case might be decided before the first witness ever testified, that the composition and mentality of the jury might override everything else, so potential panel members endured lengthier and much deeper-than-usual questioning.

Both Connick and Glass, in the main, wanted jurors of above-average intelligence: Connick because he needed people who could see the utter implausibility of Sylvester's actions, unless connected to the murders; Glass because he sincerely believed in Sylvester's innocence, and reasoned that an intelligent jury would agree with him.

Glass had an additional problem. Intelligence in the jury wasn't enough. He needed people willing to follow the law. There was no way he could keep word of Sylvester's unsavory heroin dealing from being brought out in open court. But since Sylvester *wasn't charged with selling drugs* in this case, Glass's greatest fear was that the jury would hear *heroin heroin heroin* and convict because of that.

Jessie Ford—Cris—took the stand first, our ace witness (it was chiefly Cris who connected David Sylvester to the murders) and our most vulnerable. Cris wore a tan jacket, sports shirt open at the neck, and men's slacks, a far cry from the blue dress in which I'd come to identify him.

Except for admitting *he'd* knocked on the door of Room 215, Cris's testimony, with William Wessel asking the questions, dovetailed neatly with what he told me. But this didn't constitute the test: a prosecutor questioning a prosecution witness. Glass might have been a hungry lion licking its lips and anticipating a quick, easy kill, so eager did he appear for his turn to come. That Glass would chew Cris to pieces I didn't doubt. But would he destroy the transvestite's testimony?

He didn't waste any time trying:

GLASS: Mr. Ford, you said you're also known as "Cris"?
FORD: Yes, sir.
GLASS: Are you sometimes called "Miss Cris"?
FORD: Yes, sir.
GLASS: Is that part of your given name, or a name you adopted?
FORD: A name I adopted.
GLASS: And you adopted it in your role as a female impersonator, did you not?

William Wessel came flying out of his chair: "I object! The question is inadmissible under Title 15, Section 491. I would like the Court to review that, 491 and 490."

Judge Ward didn't want to hear picayune legal points in a trial that might turn into a circus: "I deny the objection. The objection is overruled. Answer the question."

FORD: Yes, sir.
GLASS: Would you tell us, please, what a female impersonator is?

FORD: It's a boy that dresses in drag, wears women's clothes.

GLASS: Does that include women's undergarments?

WESSEL: I object!

WARD: Sustained.

GLASS: Your Honor, please, it has to do with credibility, with fooling other people, with a pattern of misrepresentation to the public.

WESSEL: Your Honor . . .

WARD: I sustain the objection.

GLASS: In your role as a female impersonator, you put yourself out to men as though you were a woman?

FORD: Yes, sir.

GLASS: How long have you been a female impersonator?

FORD: Eight, maybe nine years.

GLASS: How old are you?

FORD: Twenty.

GLASS: Since you were eleven years old?

FORD: Yes, sir.

GLASS: When did you meet Eddie Smith?

FORD: In 1971.

GLASS: When did Paulette Royal come on the scene?

FORD: Some time in 1974.

GLASS: Didn't you and Eddie Smith often stand on the corner of St. Louis and Burgundy?

FORD: Yes, sir.

GLASS: Why did you and Eddie stand on the corner of St. Louis and Burgundy?

FORD: Prostitution.

GLASS: In other words, you and Eddie and other female impersonators would stand on the corner and pick up men?

FORD: Yes, sir.

GLASS: Did you ever roll a man in your role as a female impersonator?

FORD: Yes.

GLASS: So the purpose sometimes was robbery?

WESSEL: I object. Section 491 of Title 15 says, "Can't go into particular acts, vices, or portions of conduct."

WARD: That's the general rule as to impeachment. I feel you have explored it enough, Mr. Glass.

GLASS: You lived with Eddie Smith on Philip Street, didn't you?

FORD: Yes, sir.

GLASS: In one of Miss Mary Henderson's apartments on Philip Street?

FORD: Yes, sir.

GLASS: Now, Eddie Smith was paying the rent?

FORD: Yes, sir.

GLASS: But you were sharing in the food?

FORD: Yes, sir.

GLASS: And other expenses for the apartment?

FORD: Yes, sir.

GLASS: And shared meals, didn't you?

FORD: Yes, sir.

GLASS: And you went together, didn't you?

FORD: Yes, sir.

GLASS: You were friends, weren't you?

FORD: Yes, sir.

GLASS: And did you meet Paulette Royal at Eddie Smith's apartment on Philip Street?

FORD: Yes, sir.

GLASS: And you knew then, after that first meeting, she was staying with Eddie Smith on Philip Street?

FORD: Yes, sir.

GLASS: My question is: From that point on, isn't it true
that you did not stay with Eddie Smith on Philip
Street?

FORD: Yes, sir.

Although he couldn't get Jessie Ford (Cris) to admit it,
Glass tried to plant in the minds of jurors that a sexual
relationship existed between Cris and Eddie Smith, which
Paulette Royal had broken up. Thus, perhaps, Cris had a
motive to kill the two, irrespective of Sylvester.

Glass then went on to show Cris wasn't tied to the Philip
Street address. When Sylvester allegedly told Cris to wait for
Nelson Davis to pick him up, Glass made it clear Cris, if
he'd really been an unwilling participant, had plenty of
alternatives: mainly the homes of a dozen or so relatives
scattered throughout the city.

GLASS: After Sylvester told you to wait, you didn't leave
and try to avoid Nelson Davis?

FORD: No, sir.

GLASS: And when Smitty came, you entered the car?

FORD: No, sir.

GLASS: You never entered the car?

FORD: No, sir.

GLASS: How did you get up to the Howard Johnson's?

FORD: After he pulled his gun on me, I entered the car,
sir.

GLASS: Oh, he pulled a gun on you?

FORD: Yes.

I groaned when I heard this answer, and hoped Cris didn't
embellish to paint his role more innocent than it was. He
hadn't told me anything about Nelson Davis pulling a gun on

him. It didn't seem something that would slip his mind. I prayed that early on he'd told the prosecutor's investigators about the gun. They didn't need this sort of surprise.

GLASS: Now, of course, you had, according to your story, only gone with Smitty and Clarence Davis because Smitty thought he had something over you, and you say he had a gun?

FORD: Yes, sir.

GLASS: And so you want it understood by these ladies and gentlemen that you were an unwilling accomplice going down to the Howard Johnson's?

FORD: Yes.

GLASS: And after you returned from Howard Johnson's that night, you did, of course, immediately contact the police, didn't you, to tell them what happened to your good friend, Eddie Smith?

FORD: No, sir.

GLASS: Well, you didn't know what those crazy fools, Clarence Davis and Nelson Davis, would do knowing you were a witness, did you?

FORD: No, sir.

GLASS: And they knew since they had picked you up there, that you were staying on Philip Street, didn't they?

FORD: Yes, sir.

GLASS: And so, of course, you ran, you went to some other apartment in the city so you couldn't be located?

FORD: No, sir.

GLASS: You continued to stay on Philip Street, sir?

FORD: Yes, sir.

GLASS: In the Mae West apartment?

FORD: Yes, sir.

GLASS: Well, the next day, Wednesday, you called the police, didn't you?

FORD: No, sir.

GLASS: You left the area, didn't you?

FORD: No, sir.

GLASS: You didn't try to make yourself scarce?

FORD: No, sir.

Glass next attacked Cris's testimony about overhearing Sylvester and Nelson Davis discuss the contract on July 19, in Two Jacks bar.

GLASS: So, according to your story, Mr. Sylvester was in the back room gambling on Monday night?

FORD: Yes, sir.

GLASS: Was anybody else in the back room with him?

FORD: Other people were there.

GLASS: Who?

FORD: I don't know their names, sir.

GLASS: None of them, sir?

FORD: None of them.

GLASS: You went to that bar regularly over a course of four or five months?

FORD: Just weekends.

GLASS: And Wednesday nights, isn't that right?

FORD: Yes, sir.

GLASS: Don't forget Wednesday night. That's show night, isn't it?

FORD: Yes.

GLASS: Who was on duty that night? Who was manager?

WARD: Mr. Glass, I feel you have gone into that enough.

GLASS: Your Honor, please, we are trying to establish

who else was there and who else might give a
contrary version of this story. And I have the right to
find out the names of potential witnesses.

WARD: Ask the question directly. But I feel going into
other things surrounding Two Jacks is too much
detail.

GLASS: On Monday night, was there a manager on duty?

FORD: If there was, sir, I wouldn't know.

GLASS: Do you know the owner of the bar, Oliver
Jackson, also known as "Sonny"?

FORD: No, sir.

GLASS: Do you know the assistant manager?

FORD: No.

GLASS: I'm . . .

WARD: I'm curtailing examination.

GLASS: That's sufficient, Your Honor, please, for my
purpose.

I wondered if it were sufficient. Cris hardly qualified as a
witness of sterling character, but we knew that long before he
took the stand. I didn't think Glass destroyed the primary
elements of the case, those five key meetings with Sylvester.
The defense attorney did point out that Cris didn't know how
to drive a car, so why would Sylvester want to rent him one to
travel to Alexandria? But the fact remained, the drug dealer
might have intended someone to drive him.

Both defense and prosecution attempted to locate those
witnesses reportedly gambling in Two Jacks when Sylvester
and Nelson Davis talked about the contract, but neither side
succeeded. This came as no surprise to me. Two Jacks
ranked as a rough place. I'd have been surprised if someone
had admitted being present. The clientele of Two Jacks didn't
have a get-involved, be-a-good-neighbor reputation.

Sylvester supporters in the courtroom, surprisingly, drew only one warning from Judge Ward to keep absolutely quiet. Mumbles of disbelief and outrage at Cris's testimony dotted the examinations by both prosecution and defense. The people on Sylvester's side couldn't stomach that an individual with the transvestite's background should be afforded any believability whatever. Of course, there were those on the aisle's other side who considered Sylvester as the real heavy.

Janet Belton sat with the police and prosecutors—alongside them, anyway. Her friend Paulette had been murdered, and she personally wanted to see the man whom she knew in her heart did it get punished.

Sylvester himself played Mr. Cool. Looking properly conservative in a dark suit, he managed just the right blend of confidence and concern. I could only judge by how I'd feel if our roles were reversed, and believed he had to be putting on an act. What else could it be? His stomach had to churn and his mind recoil in horror whenever he thought about what was at stake: how he'd spend the rest of his life.

It was only shortly after 11:00 A.M. this first day of the trial when Harry Connick called Samuel Williams to the stand. I figured the ultrasympathetic Williams could only help our case and hurt the defense's.

And so it happened. With Connick himself doing the questioning, Samuel Williams glided smoothly through the recount of that terrible evening at Howard Johnson's. The story he told counted important for a reason not immediately obvious: It corroborated almost exactly what Cris said. If jurors wondered, and they should, whether the transvestite told the truth in other matters, they could at least *know* he didn't lie about the events in Room 215, because Samuel Williams, with no reason to make up a story, related an identical version.

Even Robert Glass treaded carefully with Samuel Williams. A jury likely wouldn't appreciate this unlucky man being treated harshly. Wisely, Glass didn't even ask Samuel Williams his address. That might have opened up a whole new can of worms: letting the jury know we considered Sylvester so dangerous that we had to place Samuel Williams under federal protection.

The shrewd Glass minimized the damage:

GLASS: Mr. Williams, this gentleman, Mr. Sylvester, my client, did you see him at any time on Tuesday, July 20, 1976?

WILLIAMS: No.

GLASS: Or Monday, July 19?

WILLIAMS: No.

GLASS: He was not one of the men in Room 215?

WILLIAMS: No.

GLASS: And when those three fellows were in your room the night of the murders, did you hear anyone mention the name David Sylvester?

WILLIAMS: No, I didn't.

My turn to testify had come, and I'd learned from the past not to look forward to the experience. I counted myself grateful my son, Todd, didn't have to listen: If he believed just one of the accusations I expected to have thrown at me, he'd wonder what kind of father he had.

For three days I'd prepared myself for this appearance. I had to be ready or else Glass would eat me alive. I didn't dread that prospect nearly as much as the possibility of making an error and being responsible for Sylvester's getting back on the street. If that occurred, he might consider himself invulnerable, and he might be right: Should a prosecutor charge him for another, later offense, that prosecutor better have a can't-lose-unless-the-sky-falls case, or be prepared to endure serious charges of harassing a citizen.

I spent those three intense days of study even though I felt I thoroughly remembered everything I'd done on the case. Detectives don't forget the heaters. Rightly or wrongly, they follow the heaters to a conclusion.

The Connick part of the questioning was easy. I recounted the investigation for the jury.

Then came Glass.

GLASS: You found heroin paraphernalia, did you not, in Jessie Ford's room at the time of his arrest?

DILLMANN: Yes, sir, I believe we did.

GLASS: Did you advise Mr. Ford he was being arrested for possession of heroin?

DILLMANN: No, sir, I did not advise him of that.

GLASS: Before you left the house where you made the arrest, didn't you mention the name of David Joseph Sylvester to Jessie Ford?

DILLMANN: No, sir, I didn't.

GLASS: When you got to the detective bureau, did you mention Sylvester's name?

DILLMANN: At one point I did.

But Glass didn't get on to what point. He would have been happy to portray me as shouting David Sylvester's name before the handcuffs even got slapped on Cris, thus alerting the transvestite that if he gave me what I wanted, he could make a deal.

Well, Glass was just doing his job. Tossing out innuendos he hoped the jury caught. I knew it would get worse, and it did.

GLASS: My question is: Were you made familiar with the fact that the two dead persons were witnesses in the case against Mr. Sylvester coming up for trial two days later?

DILLMANN: Correct.

GLASS: That raised a suspicion in your mind concerning Mr. Sylvester, did it not?

DILLMANN: Of course.

GLASS: He was a focus of your investigation from that point onward?

DILLMANN: Correct.

GLASS: At the time of Jessie Ford's arrest, Mr. Sylvester was the subject of a focused inquiry in connection with a possible involvement in the murders, wasn't he?

DILLMANN: Yes, sir, that's correct.

GLASS: You were very interested, weren't you, in obtaining from Jessie Ford any information you could about Sylvester?

DILLMANN: Any information at all pertinent to the murders.

GLASS: Including information about Mr. Sylvester?

DILLMANN: Of course.

The preceding attempted to show I'd been blindered by an obsession with David Sylvester, a very bad thing to happen to a detective. He must keep his mind open for all evidence absolving or pointing guilt at any suspect. But in this investigation, speeded up like a movie film, I'd started with Sylvester and nothing led away from him. An even greater mistake would have been *inventing* leads, and diligently pursuing them merely to convey open-mindedness. Meanwhile, the killers could have been covering their tracks.

GLASS: You are a detective of some ten years' experience?

DILLMANN: Nine years.

GLASS: And for how much of that time have you been in Homicide?

DILLMANN: Five years.

GLASS: Over the course of that five years, you have had occasion to interview lots of witnesses and defendants, have you not?

DILLMANN: That's correct, sir.

GLASS: And you have become experienced asking questions and giving answers you need to further your investigation, you hope?

DILLMANN: I hope to think so.

GLASS: I take it you wouldn't hesitate to ask Mr. Ford questions about Mr. Sylvester?

DILLMANN: Correct.

GLASS: Are you sure you didn't ask him any questions about Mr. Sylvester at 2812 Philip Street before you took him outside?

DILLMANN: Yes, sir, I'm positive.

GLASS: Jessie Ford was advised of his rights immediately, wasn't he?

DILLMANN: Correct.

Glass had tried to draw out that my cleverness as an interrogator, rather than a crude bribe—"Cris, give me Sylvester and I'll make a deal"—imparted to the transvestite what I really wanted.

The days, which I'm sure once existed, when detectives used every underhanded trick imaginable are largely over, especially in New Orleans—I can attest to that. And I wonder if defense attorneys score points with the jury by asking these questions. They surely think they do, or why else continue? On the other side of the coin, jurors hear that nothing illegal was done, and thus points may be scored for the other side.

Perhaps the object is to plant suspicion. Why would the defense attorney ask the question if he didn't have reason to believe illegal tactics had been used?

GLASS: Now, after the arrest of Clarence Davis, did you have occasion to bring him down to the Homicide Division?

DILLMANN: That's correct.

GLASS: And in connection with your investigation, did you advise him of his rights, his constitutional rights against self-incrimination, his right to have counsel and so on?

DILLMANN: Yes, sir.

GLASS: And after advising him of those rights, did you have occasion to speak with him about his knowledge of the crime?

DILLMANN: Yes, sir, I did.

GLASS: Now, did you in any way use any kind of physical force on him in order to induce him to speak with you?

DILLMANN: No, sir.

GLASS: Did you threaten him in any way?

DILLMANN: No, sir.

GLASS: Did you use anything, such as plastic bags, or telephone books, or kicks with a foot, or slaps with a hand, that might intimidate him or hurt him or suggest he better cooperate or else?

DILLMANN: No, sir.

I'd known from the beginning it would happen! Maybe the danger wasn't my son Todd hearing *one* case. He could dismiss one case. But what if he heard dozens? A hundred? I'd be asked the same questions if he watched a thousand cases. He'd have to believe fire raged amid all that lawyer smoke.

Plastic bags?

Answering questions of this sort (how would the average citizen respond to queries about plastic bags?), while not rivaling attendance at autopsies, or notifying a wife her husband has been murdered, or seeing a young child mutilated, qualifies as one of the detective's least pleasant duties.

Nevertheless, Glass finished the Sylvester tune on an upbeat note, just as he'd done with Samuel Williams.

GLASS: When you spoke with Clarence Davis, you wanted to know if he could provide information about Mr. Sylvester, didn't you?

DILLMANN: Yes, sir.

GLASS: And you asked him, did you not, whether he knew Mr. Sylvester?

DILLMANN: Yes, sir, I did.

GLASS: What was his answer?

DILLMANN: "No," he did not.

My testimony had inched the clock toward 1:00 P.M., and when Glass dismissed me, Judge Ward called for a lunch break. He'd made it clear, because of the always-packed-to-bursting court docket, he intended the proceedings to stretch into the evening.

CHAPTER

–16–

I had the chance to exchange a few words with Harry Connick during the break, and like any interested spectator at a contest he didn't fully understand—a nonchess player, for instance, observing a match between two grandmasters—I asked him how we stood.

"Glass may be laying back," Connick said. "But he hasn't broken our basic story yet."

Yet?

"I don't know what he plans to do," Connick said. "It's not good when you can't see which way the defense is going. Glass *knows* what we've got, and it doesn't seem to scare him."

Connick was in a hurry to get somewhere, but except for that he didn't show any of the pressure I knew he operated under.

Still, I wondered if Connick would ever handle another case more personally important to him than this one. Besides the natural fear of losing, he had to remember those miracles Glass pulled in the Panther cases.

Talking with assistant prosecutors over sandwiches in a diner across the street from the courthouse, I learned Connick had finally decided not to use John Norwine as a witness against Sylvester. Norwine, who'd seen Nelson Davis talking to Sylvester outside Two Jacks bar the afternoon of the murders, and then been propositioned by Nelson Davis to serve as wheel man, would have provided valuable testimony further linking the drug dealer to the HoJo killings.

Still, I thought Connick's decision deserved applause. I imagined he, just as I did, had grown tired of seeing deals made, and dangerous criminals being released early due to our zeal to remove David Sylvester from the scene. At some point it had to stop, and the present seemed perfect.

In fact, Connick's decision qualified as doubly admirable, because the district attorney stood to be the biggest loser of all if Sylvester won acquittal. It would have been easy to rationalize the use of every weapon in the war against Sylvester. And who would remember, when Norwine committed another violent crime, as he surely would, that Connick set him free to commit the deed? No one except the D.A. himself.

Connick, during the lunch break, told me he had no surprises for Robert Glass. Maybe so, but he had a few for me among the remaining eleven witnesses he called:

1. Philip Aviles: Employed by the NOPD, criminalist Aviles testified about the pillows and bullets recovered from Room 215. Technical testimony, boring to everyone except Aviles, it nonetheless had to be introduced into the trial record. Glass didn't bother to cross-examine, undoubtedly earning the jury's goodwill.

2. Albert Winter: This was something I'd never seen before: an assistant U.S. attorney summoned to testify in a state murder case. But the prosecution needed to deal with Glass's opening statement, in which he indicated individuals other than Sylvester had strong motives to kill Paulette and Eddie.

Winter pointed out that a *federal* conspiracy case against David Sylvester *and others* was not prosecutable because an important witness had fled after receiving threats on her life. Thus, went the implication, since the others were in no immediate danger of being prosecuted, their motives for eliminating Paulette and Eddie were slight at best. But the missing witness wasn't needed in the *state* case against Sylvester: The evidence Paulette and Eddie would provide was deemed sufficient.

It was the state trial, carrying possible life imprisonment for Sylvester, that we contended he tried to continue forever by having the witnesses killed. Still, in the battle over motive, Glass didn't come unarmed. He brought out that the threats which caused the missing witness to flee had been made while Sylvester was in jail. Thus, Glass demonstrated, with Sylvester incarcerated and not likely responsible for them, threats had been made previously in a drug case in which he was involved.

In addition, Glass showed that Paulette and Eddie would have testified against eight other defendants in the federal case.

True enough: Others stood to lose if Paulette and Eddie testified. I found myself hoping, however, right along with Connick and Glass, that they indeed had picked an intelligent jury. The motives, if any, of the other defendants in that infinitely delayed federal case hardly ranked up there with Sylvester's, who on July 20, 1976, found himself under the gun. The other defendants were home free if the missing witness didn't get located. Would one of them really order executions when not even a trial date had been set?

Nonetheless, I feared the issue might easily be muddled and misunderstood. The jury might acquit over just such a question: Did *eight* other individuals really have strong, immediate reasons to kill?

3. Frank Catalano: U.S. Marshal Catalano testified that he turned over a spent bullet he found in Room 215 to NOPD officer Robert Laviolette. Glass asked no questions.

4. Robert Laviolette: Officer Laviolette testified that he'd handed the same bullet to me. I, of course, had earlier sworn to having given the bullet to Dr. Monroe Samuels of the coroner's office. All this was necessary to preserve what is known as the "chain of evidence." Glass asked no questions.

5. Monroe Samuels: Despite speaking in doctor-ese, Samuels couldn't avoid giving jurors a clear picture of the horrid nature of the wounds. Good, I thought. The crime *had been* horrible, and the jury should know it.

Again, Glass didn't cross-examine. Nothing could be gained by grilling the respected Dr. Samuels, but I suspected the defense attorney might become worried about the "rhythm" of the trial. The prosecution piled witness upon witness, and some of these Glass had no cause to question: like Laviolette and Catalano, and now Samuels (the quicker he could be gotten off the stand, with his talk about bullets in the brain, the better). But the very number of these witnesses, no matter how minor their testimony, might begin to carry great weight in the minds of the jurors.

What to do? Bore the jury with meaningless questions, or risk that they might believe the only side with anything to say was the prosecution?

6. Sam Miles: This witness, tears in his eyes, obviously grieving, gave testimony that was brief and to the point: He identified pictures of his murdered brother-in-law, Eddie Smith.

I wanted to shout hooray for Sam Miles. Too often, I'd felt—and I was the worst offender of all—we'd overlooked the individuality and humanity of the victims. Paulette and Eddie might have been a dance team for all the compassion we showed them, or one person, PauletteandEddie, we could use in order to get Sylvester. But they'd been living, breathing beings, maybe on their way to productive lives, and Sam Miles's grief showed us they had loved ones, friends and relatives who cared.

Glass had no questions.

But he had plenty to say a moment later when Connick addressed the judge: "Your Honor, in connection with this witness's testimony, I'd like to offer and file into evidence S-17."

"Your Honor!" Glass was on his feet. "I have no objection to Mr. Miles identifying Eddie Smith from that photograph. But I think it's unnecessarily gruesome. If there's a question of identity, of who the person was, I will be glad to stipulate."

Connick wanted the jury to see the victim: "Your Honor," he said, "I feel the Supreme Court of the State of Louisiana has held that although photographs are sometimes gruesome, the jury is entitled to look at them if they wish. This photograph is in keeping with what the State has to prove, and we feel it's admissible."

"Mr. Glass," said Judge Ward, "just offered to stipulate that Eddie Smith has been identified. Isn't that true, Mr. Glass?"

"Yes, sir," said Glass.

"I'm going to sustain the objection as to S-17."

It didn't seem to me a major defeat. A jury, hearing a picture described as gruesome, might fantasize an even worse horror. Certainly I'd seen many bodies that looked worse than Eddie Smith's.

7. *Richard Royal:* A witness even more grief-stricken than Sam Miles was Richard Royal, a dignified-looking man with the big callused hands of a worker. Though I didn't know Royal's story, I imagined it filled with nightmares as his

daughter slipped away from him, tempered by hope when she appeared to choose another road, then ground into despair when Nelson Davis squeezed the trigger.

Harry Connick tendered Richard Royal after he identified Paulette's picture, but Glass had no questions.

"For the purposes of clarification," Connick asked, "is there an objection to this photograph?" The D.A. hadn't given up on the jury seeing a dead body.

"There certainly is," said Glass.

"I didn't have a chance to look at the picture," said Judge Ward. A brief glimpse was all he needed. "I'll sustain the objection."

Connick, a normally mild-mannered man, turned into a bundle of aggression wanting to know why the objection was sustained.

"The gruesomeness of the photograph," Judge Ward ruled, "outweighs the evidentiary value, which in light of the stipulation is very little."

Connick's calling Sam Miles and Richard Royal to the stand demonstrated the sort of hardball he'd been determined all along to play. Other methods existed to identify the victims, but none quite so heartrending.

I think Sylvester sensed it, too. The man pursuing him, and he indeed qualified as the hunted, possessed no mercy. Sylvester seemed more alert, more tense, more aware of the deadly seriousness of the drama being played out in Judge Ward's courtroom.

I thought I could read the drug dealer's mind: This prosecutor really hates me. Why should he hate me? I can understand him doing his job, his duty, but he's gone way beyond that.

I think it had. And not because Connick lost witnesses, but rather because Connick, personally involved in a case, not supervising someone else, had come to know Sylvester the way a detective from Narcotics would, and he despised what he'd learned.

8. *Martin Alonzo:* Alonzo, a New Orleans policeman assigned to the crime lab as a firearms examiner, testified he could identify the types of guns used to fire five of the bullets found in HoJo Room 215. Because Alonzo used words like "broached," "hooked," "rifling," "twists," "lands," "grooves," "striation," and "spirals," even Connick had trouble following him.

It was almost amusing to watch Connick struggle with Alonzo. Connick knew what he wanted to prove—that the ballistics evidence bore out the prosecution's version of events (specifically, two guns being fired)—but if *he* didn't understand what Alonzo said, how could he be sure the jury did? Alonzo, on the other hand, had little patience with a man unable to grasp the "fundamentals" of a field he considered critical to civilization's survival.

Spectators could hear the sense of relief in the district attorney's voice when he dismissed Martin Alonzo. Though Glass's defense didn't hinge on anything the crime lab officer said, he didn't seem sorry to let the witness go either.

It was after 5:00 P.M. this November evening, and the skies outside were quickly darkening. Many of us thought Judge Ward would order a break until morning, but instead he called a ten-minute recess. The judge talked briefly about "a crowded docket," "moving things along," and allowing "the defense to start fresh in the morning," which meant he expected the prosecution to finish on the same day it started.

Fine, I thought. Just three witnesses, albeit major ones, remained of the prosecution's case, and I doubted any of us could have rested with the end so near in sight.

CHAPTER
–17–

I might have been working for the Gallup organization, taking a poll, so many people did I garner opinions from during the ten-minute recess. What spectators thought depended on which side of the aisle they sat. The cops, district attorneys, and Janet Belton believed Connick securing a conviction involved only the amount of time needed to get the case to the jury. The district attorney had built an overwhelming lead against which Glass could never rally. Verdict: conviction on two counts of first-degree murder and one count of attempted murder.

A night-and-day difference contrasted the feelings of those who backed Sylvester. The witnesses Connick presented— "crooks, cops, people who work for the district attorney, and a dude who never even heard of Sylvester" (Samuel Williams)—were absolutely unbelievable, and the jury would see it. "I'd acquit him right now," said a gentleman dressed like he'd come straight from church. "Who'd believe that transvestite, rolling people and shooting dope like he did? The rest of it was just fluff."

My job as a detective required keeping my mind open— though Glass questioned whether I did—and I thought the issue far from decided. The prosecution was ahead (better than being behind), but the defense hadn't even presented its case yet. In baseball terms, we'd had a big top of the first inning, but soon the other team would come to bat, and they might have heavy hitters.

What everyone looked forward to was seeing if Connick could throw fastballs, strikeout pitches, past Sylvester. The icy drug dealer had plenty of smarts, and his life was in the balance, but Connick's stake in the confrontation's outcome perhaps weighed just as heavily.

As the normal hour for dinner approached—we'd eat very late this night—and Judge Ward gaveled the assemblage to order, one side of the courtroom looked as if Connick had called a meeting of his entire office legal staff and attendance was mandatory.

But no one needed to be forced to attend this show. Other courts had adjourned for the day, and all manner of prosecutors gathered in Judge Ward's bailiwick, a kind of busman's holiday, to see how the district attorney, the boss, drove his own bus.

"We've saved our best for last," an assistant prosecutor told me, as he headed inside.

9. *Clarence Davis:* At the last minute, Clarence Davis had pled guilty to attempted murder, carrying a maximum sentence of fifty years with parole possible after serving a third of the sentence. In exchange, he agreed to testify truthfully in *State of Louisiana* vs. *David Sylvester*.

DAVIS: Knucklehead said we were going to meet a sissy named Cris about five o'clock. So about five o'clock we went by his house on Philip Street and got him. Cris came over and got in the car. He carried a brown paper bag with two guns in it. And we were going out

to the Howard Johnson's. Cris said, "Y'all going to
make money," just like that. I said, "I don't care."
Cris said, "They got two State witnesses to testify
against David Sylvester." So we went out there.

CONNICK: Who mentioned State witnesses?

DAVIS: Cris. Jessie Ford.

This testimony simply amazed. Had Connick lost his
mind? Along with everyone rooting for justice, which meant
rooting against Sylvester, I felt the first pangs of sickness
starting deep in my stomach.

Clarence Davis seemed the best and worst of worlds, but I
only saw the worst: *Cris* had brought the guns to the car?

I didn't think it possible. I knew Nelson Davis dropped the
guns off at the apartment of weapons dealer Henry Fisher.
Clarence Davis probably lied, or was mistaken. Maybe he
thought saying Cris brought the guns to the car lessened his
own involvement, even though he'd already made his own
plea bargain.

The best of worlds centered on the testimony: "They got
two State witnesses to testify against David Sylvester."
Clarence Davis heard the words said! This corroborated
everything we'd been contending. Those three hadn't traveled to Howard Johnson's for a dope score or a robbery, but
to eliminate witnesses against Sylvester.

DAVIS: Jessie Ford knocked on the door. Somebody
opened it and Knucklehead rushed in. Knucklehead
shot two of them, and I shot one. Cris put pillows
over the heads and we just shot them.

Clarence Davis, *the state's own witness,* impeached the
testimony of the state's ace witness, Cris. Davis said *Cris* put

the pillows over the heads of the victims. Davis's story shed a less glaring light on his own role. Of course, the same held true for Cris. But regardless of how it happened, Glass now had openings to explore that might turn into gaping holes through which the prosecution's entire case could fall.

Whatever Connick had in mind when he called Clarence Davis to the stand—and I suspected it involved the mention of Sylvester as the killers drove toward Howard Johnson's— it deserved admiration. Although looking for every advantage—for example, calling Sam Miles and Richard Royal to the stand—he had decided to take the evidence as he found it, present it to the jury, and let them decide. There'd be no cover-up to secure an easy conviction.

CONNICK: What kind of gun did you use?

DAVIS: A .32.

CONNICK: What kind of gun did Nelson Davis use?

DAVIS: A .38.

CONNICK: Who did you shoot?

DAVIS: The one who lived, Samuel Williams.

CONNICK: Who did Nelson Davis shoot?

DAVIS: The other two. Paulette Royal and Eddie Smith.

CONNICK: Did you know any of the people in Howard Johnson's Room 215?

DAVIS: No, sir.

CONNICK: Did Knucklehead know any of the people in that room?

GLASS: Objection! Unless he can testify from his own knowledge, it's hearsay.

WARD: Sustained.

CONNICK: Did Jessie Ford know any of the people in the room?

DAVIS: He must have known somebody, they opened the door for him.

CONNICK: Who went in first?

DAVIS: Jessie Ford.

CONNICK: Who went after Ford?

DAVIS: Nelson Davis.

CONNICK: And you were then third into the room?

DAVIS: Yes, sir.

CONNICK: Did you commit a robbery in that room? Did you take anything from those people?

DAVIS: No, sir.

CONNICK: Did Jessie Ford or Knucklehead take anything?

DAVIS: No, sir.

CONNICK: Did anyone look around to try to take anything before you left?

DAVIS: No, sir.

CONNICK: When you left the room, you went back to this black automobile?

DAVIS: Yes, sir.

CONNICK: Who was driving?

DAVIS: I was driving.

CONNICK: Where did you go?

DAVIS: To the Calliope Project.

All this testimony, given before by Cris, was important precisely because it *had been* presented before. Clarence Davis's recollections of what happened in Room 215, except for the placing of the pillows, corroborated what Cris said. But Connick was about to face more trouble.

CONNICK: Did you take anything at all out of Room 215?

DAVIS: I didn't take anything, but they had a pillow-case.

CONNICK: What was in the pillowcase?

DAVIS: They had the guns wrapped up in it.

CONNICK: How many guns did you leave with?

DAVIS: Two.

CONNICK: The same two guns you went in with?

DAVIS: Yes, sir.

CONNICK: What happened in the Calliope Project?

DAVIS: We came to get rid of the guns. Jessie Ford, he wanted to get rid of them. I said, "No," just like that. And Nelson Davis said, "No, I don't want to get rid of them." I said, "No." Then Knucklehead decided he wanted to get rid of them, so we gave them to him.

CONNICK: What did Knucklehead do with the guns?

DAVIS: I don't know where he dropped them off.

CONNICK: Then what happened?

DAVIS: Knucklehead got back in the car with us.

CONNICK: On the way back from the motel, but before reaching the Project, did anyone in the car talk about David Sylvester?

DAVIS: No, sir. The only thing they said, they were going to get some money.

CONNICK: When Knucklehead got back in the car, where did you go?

DAVIS: Knucklehead told me to drop him off at Two Jacks.

CONNICK: Did you do that?

DAVIS: Yes, sir.

CONNICK: Whom did you drop off at Two Jacks?

DAVIS: Knucklehead and Jessie Ford.

Holy Moley. Jesse Ford said Clarence Davis drove him to

the house on Philip Street. Just speculating about Glass's cross-examination made me cringe.

> CONNICK: Now, Mr. Davis, I'm going to ask if you know the defendant, David Sylvester?
> DAVIS: I don't know him. I've seen him.
> CONNICK: When did you first see him?
> DAVIS: I've seen him around the Project.
> CONNICK: Did you see him on the day of the killings?
> DAVIS: I saw him one time.
> CONNICK: Where and when?
> DAVIS: On the corner near Two Jacks, when I dropped off Knucklehead and Jessie Ford.
> CONNICK: Did you see either of them talk to Sylvester?
> DAVIS: No, sir.

Valuable testimony even though Clarence Davis hadn't seen the hand signal between Nelson Davis and Sylvester about which Cris testified. I hoped the corroboration of Sylvester being at Two Jacks when Nelson Davis (and Jessie Ford?) got dropped off outweighed somewhat the two different versions the jury heard.

> CONNICK: Were you to get any money for what you did?
> DAVIS: They told me I was going to get some. They told me to wait in the Project for him.
> CONNICK: For whom?
> DAVIS: Knucklehead. Nelson Davis and Jessie Ford told me to wait in the Project.

Robert Glass, fighting hard to keep a smile off his face so as not to appear *too* eager, approached the witness. I moaned, not wanting to witness the slaughter.

* * *

GLASS: Mr. Davis, up until yesterday you were a
    defendant in this case?

DAVIS: Yes, sir.

GLASS: You had alibi witnesses?

DAVIS: Yes, sir.

GLASS: And you were going to call Miss Leona Davis?

DAVIS: For what?

GLASS: As an alibi witness.

DAVIS: No, sir.

GLASS: Samuel Karr?

DAVIS: Yes, sir.

GLASS: Jerry Carter?

DAVIS: Yes, sir.

GLASS: Brenda Johnkeer?

DAVIS: Yes, sir.

GLASS: Miss Marcileen Johnkeer?

DAVIS: Yes, sir.

GLASS: And Mr. Oscar Peters?

DAVIS: Yes, sir.

The courtroom tittered as Glass ran down the names of
Clarence Davis's alibi witnesses. Alibi witnesses? He had
just admitted he took part in the killings!

Disastrous as Clarence Davis's testimony was to his own
credibility, I wondered if there might be a beneficial side
effect for the prosecution. Did David Sylvester have alibi
witnesses? If he did, could jurors really believe them?

GLASS: Didn't your attorney say you were a principal to
    the murder of Eddie Smith and the murder of Paulette
    Royal?

DAVIS: No, sir.

GLASS: He didn't say you were as guilty as the man who
    pulled the trigger?

DAVIS: Yes, he told me that.

GLASS: You know that charge gets you life without benefit of parole for forty years? He told you that, didn't he?

DAVIS: Yes, sir.

GLASS: And by pleading guilty, you would get an attempted murder charge, is that right?

DAVIS: Yes, sir.

GLASS: And the maximum is fifty years?

DAVIS: Yes, sir.

GLASS: And you can be paroled after one third of that time?

DAVIS: Yes, sir.

Glass wanted, through these questions, to reemphasize that Clarence Davis saved a good portion of his own life by testifying. Finally, making clear his disbelief was aimed at Cris, Glass had Clarence Davis repeat that Cris brought the guns to the car, Cris placed the pillows on the heads of the victims, and Cris was dropped off at Two Jacks.

I thought Clarence Davis's testimony had been a big negative for us. Either he told the truth or Cris did, but we couldn't have it both ways. Harry Connick, interestingly enough, never wavered in his belief that Clarence Davis was a positive. Connick said the real time to worry came when no difference existed between witness versions.

But differences this large?

If I wondered about the value of Clarence Davis's testimony, I had no similar misgivings about the next-to-last witness Harry Connick called to the stand. His testimony came as a complete and very pleasant surprise to me. I'd like to believe I would have uncovered this witness's testimony had arrests not been made so quickly, but the credit goes to the district attorney's own investigators.

10. Wilfred Kinn:

* * *

CONNICK: Mr. Kinn, would you tell us where you live?

KINN: At 2808 Philip.

CONNICK: Where do you work, and what do you do?

KINN: I work at Pete's, part-time. I'm a female impersonator.

CONNICK: Pete's?

KINN: It's a gay bar.

CONNICK: Do you know Jessie Ford?

KINN: Yes, I do.

CONNICK: Do you know David Sylvester?

KINN: Yes.

CONNICK: Do you see him in court today?

KINN: Yes, sir.

CONNICK: Would you point him out?

KINN: Over there.

CONNICK: Where were you during the late afternoon of July 20, 1976?

KINN: I was on Miss Henderson's steps.

CONNICK: Who is Miss Henderson?

KINN: She's my landlord.

CONNICK: That's where you live, 2808 Philip?

KINN: Yes, sir.

CONNICK: Around this time, did you see Jessie Ford?

KINN: Yes, sir.

CONNICK: Did you see David Sylvester at about this time?

KINN: Yes, sir.

CONNICK: What did Jessie Ford do?

KINN: Two guys came along in a car and picked him up.

CONNICK: Where did the automobile go after the two guys picked Jessie Ford up?

KINN: It went toward Dupree's, this barroom on the corner.

CONNICK: Was anyone at Dupree's?

KINN: Well, there were people standing outside, and Mr. Sylvester.

CONNICK: Mr. Sylvester was outside?

KINN: Yes, sir.

CONNICK: Did Sylvester do anything?

KINN: They stopped, and he went over to them and laughed. That's all I could see.

CONNICK: Sylvester went over where and laughed?

KINN: By the car.

CONNICK: The same car?

KINN: Yes, the one Mr. Ford and them was in.

CONNICK: What did they do after that?

KINN: They just drove off.

Kinn's testimony belonged in the bombshell category. It furnished still another, and this time independent, account of a suspicious meeting between Sylvester and one or more of the perpetrators, most of them right before or right after the killings.

The killers hadn't traveled a single block on their deadly mission before encountering their master. Had Sylvester simply been checking to make sure they were on their way? Did he, like a careful teacher or coach, have last-minute advice to offer.

No matter. His presence in front of Dupree's as the killers headed for Howard Johnson's added to his presence at so many other places at key times, made a mockery of any claim the set of circumstances could be coincidental.

Kinn's testimony did raise an ugly question: Why hadn't either Clarence Davis or Jessie Ford told us of the meeting in front of Dupree's? Could it have slipped their minds? It didn't seem possible, even granting the extreme pressure of the moment. Perhaps the fact that neither would have sparkled on an intelligence test—Glass said Clarence Davis had a mentality more befitting a seventh-grader—caused some of the mix-ups in their testimony.

I don't know. I have seen virtually incredible variations in stories told by different people witnessing, and participating in, the same event.

Glass asked several perfunctory questions about where Sylvester stood when Wilfred Kinn saw him, and then dismissed the witness. Whether the defense attorney didn't feel he could shake Kinn's story, whether he thought it merely unworthy of belief, whether . . . I didn't know. I'd have to wait for the closing arguments when he addressed the issue himself.

11. Tim Cerniglia: If the jury possessed the intelligence each side hoped for, it realized this case was anything but an ordinary murder trial. First, the courtroom was filled. Most murder trials play out with three or four onlookers, at most. But more indicative, the prosecution doesn't often call a U.S. attorney to testify, and then come back with an assistant district attorney.

Al Winter testified that the federal case against Sylvester and the others had been put on indefinite hold, and now Cerniglia appeared to say the testimony of Paulette and Eddie in the state's case, the one in Judge Winsberg's court, involved only Sylvester. No one connected with this trial, Cerniglia tried to indicate, except Sylvester, possessed a motive to do away with Paulette and Eddie.

On cross-examination, Glass cleverly adopted a different tack, claiming Paulette and Eddie *weren't* key witnesses, that because of information uncovered in pretrial maneuvering, their testimony had been rendered virtually useless. I was fascinated watching the two lawyers, one accustomed to asking the questions now having to answer them, and the other digging deep into his bag of tricks, knowing he faced a tough adversary.

During the Glass/Cerniglia battle, what had been a dirty set of circumstances for the jury to consider became downright filthy, X-rated.

GLASS: Didn't Paulette Royal, in pretrial hearings, admit Eddie Smith was a female impersonator?

CERNIGLIA: Yes.

GLASS: Didn't she admit that Eddie made his living by going down to the French Quarter dressed as a woman, picked up men, and tried to roll them?

CERNIGLIA: That's correct.

GLASS: Didn't Paulette Royal further say that Eddie Smith, if he couldn't succeed in rolling them in the French Quarter, would bring them back to Philip Street?

CERNIGLIA: What you say is true.

GLASS: And Eddie would bring the man home, and if the man wanted oral sex, Eddie would take care of him. Isn't that true?

CERNIGLIA: Paulette testified to that.

GLASS: The man, on discovering that Eddie was a male, might decide he didn't want Eddie to give oral sex, then Paulette would have regular sex with the man. Isn't that true?

CERNIGLIA: Yes, she testified to that.

GLASS: Didn't Paulette also say that while she gave sex to the trick, Eddie would roll, that is rob, from the man's wallet?

CERNIGLIA: I believe the testimony was more along the line that once the pants were down, Eddie would steal the wallet. No force was used. Not from those two.

GLASS: Mr. Cerniglia, in your opinion, wasn't Paulette Royal's testimony substantially impeached?

CERNIGLIA: Not for this type of case.
GLASS: Your answer is "No"?
CERNIGLIA: That's correct.

That Glass wondered if Paulette's testimony had been "substantially impeached" because of an unsavory background may have been his way of imparting the same idea to the jury in this case. Were Cris and Clarence Davis really believable? Without an immediately identifiable overwhelming motive to commit crime, they'd gone ahead. Now, with strong motives—saving their own necks—did anyone truly believe they'd hesitate to lie?

The problem crops up so often. In my opinion, with corroboration, the *best* type of testimony in cases such as these comes from the Paulette Royals, Eddie Smiths, and Jessie Fords of the world.

Tim Cerniglia was dismissed.

Harry Connick rose from his chair. "Your Honor," he said, "the State rests."

Judge Ward coughed, rubbed his eyes, and prepared to tell the jury it would be sequestered for the night in the Warwick Hotel. The defense would begin presenting its case in the morning.

But no. Robert Glass shocked everyone. "Your Honor, please," he said, "the State has rested and, with respect, the Defense rests."

CHAPTER
–18–

Court convened at 8:30 A.M., but I arrived a half hour early, eager to listen to even the most ill-informed scuttlebutt. A murder trial, like a good soap opera, grips by the throat; but unlike a soap opera, except for the rather rare instance of a hung jury, it provides an answer, a solution.

I understand why people become murder trial junkies. So much of life is gray, not black or white, right or wrong, good or evil. When a murder trial gets decided—and it's impossible to have more riding on the outcome—what occurs, depending on your point of view, is a terrifying or celebratory finale.

My reading in the hallway outside the courtroom told me the Sylvester supporters were more disappointed than the law-and-order advocates over Glass's decision not to present a defense. Those wanting acquittal had suffered through the testimony of a long list of witnesses hostile to their man, drawing succor because his version, sure to blow the prosecution from the water, hadn't been heard yet. Now it would never be heard.

But these were below-the-surface readings. What people *said* didn't bear them out.

"I wish Glass *had* presented a defense," an assistant D.A.

told me. "Put that scumbag Sylvester on the stand. To know him is to hate him."

"Why *should* Glass bother answering that scurvy testimony we heard?" a woman in Sylvester's corner wanted to know. "This is still America. State's gotta prove a man's guilty, not the other way around, and that fancy D.A. didn't prove shit."

I thought Connick had proved a lot more than that, but as I drifted from person to person in the hallway, I wondered if I hadn't heard what I wanted, not what actually occurred. After all, I had a considerable stake in the outcome: What would that investigation amount to if Sylvester got acquitted?

Harry Connick, tense and grim, opted for logic and reason, not histrionics, in perhaps the most important closing statement he'd ever give:

> I think we all agree Paulette Royal got shot in the head three times on the floor of the Howard Johnson's motel room. And Eddie Smith was shot and killed. You heard Jessie Ford, Clarence Davis, and Samuel Williams testify about these murders.
>
> We said we would prove they were murdered, and why they were murdered, and when they were murdered. I don't think anybody can test that, not even the defense lawyer.
>
> We also said we would show you how they were killed. And you heard testimony to that effect from a number of people.
>
> That's been proved. So I'm not going to spend a lot of time on it.
>
> The question becomes: Is that the man responsible? Is David Sylvester the one who masterminded those murders?
>
> First, you have to answer two questions: Did David

Sylvester have a reason for doing what he did? And second, did he do anything to further the activity? Did he contribute in any way? Was he responsible for the idea? And did he convey the idea to Knucklehead?

We say he did. If you find he had a reason, and if you find he did anything to further that conspiracy, that particular crime, then you have to find him guilty. There's no other answer. You've got to find him guilty.

Let's examine question number one, which goes to motive. Did Sylvester want Paulette Royal and Eddie Smith dead? We say, "yes."

Sylvester was charged with possession with intent to distribute 353 caps of heroin. The penalty is life in prison at Angola. And the trial date—keep this in mind—was July 22, 1976. The date of these killings was July 20, two days before.

So what did Paulette Royal and Eddie Smith mean to the State's case? You heard the person best qualified to answer that question, Assistant District Attorney Tim Cerniglia, testify they were *essential* witnesses, *critical* witnesses.

Now, what about question number two? Did this defendant do anything or have anything to do with the murders? Did he cause them?

What did Jessie Ford say? He said he had *five different meetings* with this defendant.

The first was on Clara and Philip Street, a week or so before the killings occurred. Sylvester talked to Jessie Ford. Now, believe me, I wish I could put an FBI agent on the stand to testify about these murders. But I don't have one. I have to take the man who actually killed these people.

At this first meeting, Sylvester wanted Ford to locate the witnesses in Alexandria, Louisiana. Sylvester said the witnesses would soon be coming to New Orleans. He wanted Ford to go to Alexandria and point them out to his men up there, and Sylvester was willing to provide a car, private transportation.

True or false? True! You know why? Because it's corroborated. Samuel Williams testified they were in Alexandria. They came to New Orleans from there. That corroborated what Jessie Ford said.

The second meeting occurred on Monday, the day before the killings, July 19, in the rear room of Two Jacks Bar when the defendant and Knucklehead, Nelson Davis, discussed the contract. And Knucklehead wanted to make sure he would get his $20,000. Sylvester said, "No trouble. I already have it."

What corroborated this particular meeting? A discussion about killing people with the man who was there—Sylvester—materialized into fact!

What more corroboration do you want? And was any of it rebutted? I didn't hear it.

The third meeting occurred shortly before the killings, when Clarence Davis and Knucklehead picked up Jessie Ford. Jessie Ford testified that he was told Knucklehead would come by to pick him up. Is that corroborated? Another witness took the stand, Wilfred Kinn. He was on his steps and saw Jessie Ford and Sylvester together.

Number four: On Tuesday, at Two Jacks Bar after the killings occurred, when Ford, Knucklehead, and Clarence Davis came back, you need to remember the testimony about hand movements. And it's corroborated by another witness, Clarence Davis, who drove the car and testified about the incident.

Finally, number five: The last meeting on Philip and Clara, on Wednesday, the day after the killings. This is when Sylvester told Jessie Ford to stand on the corner, that Knucklehead would bring him something. And he left. He didn't want to wait for Knucklehead. I think he had some reservations about what Knucklehead was going to bring him.

And you recall Jessie Ford said the defendant, Sylvester, turned himself in on that date. And he did. All of this was corroborated.

Is Jessie Ford a bad guy? Yes. Is he a female impersonator? Yes. Is he a dope addict? Yes. Sure he is. He said that. But none of the essential elements of his testimony was contradicted or rebutted.

What did he get for the murders? What's the best thing you can give an addict? A fix. Give him a bunch of heroin. He'll do anything for it. He'll point the finger at someone to have him killed. In reality, Jessie Ford received nothing. But what he expected to receive was heroin.

Why did the defendant, Sylvester, want Jessie Ford? Because Ford knew the two who were going to be killed.

Why did we call Clarence Davis? It was an eleventh-hour decision, incidentally.

We called Clarence Davis because he said certain things that rebutted what the defense said they would prove.

Remember what the defense lawyer said: They went out there to commit a robbery or get dope. First of all, Clarence Davis's testimony is extremely important testimony because it connects the defendant, David Sylvester, further with this conspiracy. Jessie Ford did it. But Clarence Davis also did it.

Clarence Davis corroborates [that] Sylvester, the defendant, contracted to have these people killed. And here is a man, Clarence Davis, who was part of it. "The reason we were going there," said Clarence Davis, "was to kill two State witnesses in the case of David Sylvester."

The second thing Clarence Davis said: They didn't go to the Howard Johnson's Motor Hotel to rob anybody or to get dope. Corroborated? Yes. Samuel Williams testified nobody went there to stick them up. They went there to fulfill the contract Sylvester had put out on two people.

What it boils down to, very simply, is a case proven beyond a reasonable doubt, that the defendant conspired to and participated in the murders of Paulette Royal and Eddie Smith. We have proven it beyond a reasonable doubt, and based on that, we ask you to return a verdict of guilty as charged against David Joseph Sylvester.

When Connick finished, I had to face the fact that if the prosecution lost, it likely would be my fault, not the district attorney's.

I couldn't have asked for a better summation. If it wasn't enough, I hadn't done enough, simply hadn't gathered evidence sufficient to convict.

Glass had one last chance. I leaned forward to listen, fearing what I might hear.

CHAPTER
–19–

Robert Glass, son of a good Pennsylvania schoolteacher, champion of the underdog, genuinely believed what he said. Unlike many lawyers, Glass didn't blow smoke or put on an act. Moreover, he firmly believed in the law of the land, and that law said the burden of proof rested with the state.

The state hadn't met its burden: It was as simple as that. Why should Glass pretend otherwise by presenting a defense? Defense against what?

I think it seemed utterly preposterous to Glass that the type of testimony offered against his client should be believed by anyone. The witnesses were lowlifes, incredible. They contradicted one another. Liars and criminals most of their lives, they now owned the highest motivation to lie again. And that's what they'd done.

The state stood on feet of clay: One foot rested unsteadily on an entirely circumstantial case, the weakest kind; the other wobbled on the backs of despicable witnesses, perverts and murderers, whose paid-for testimony (through plea-bargains) smacked of perjury.

Glass, as eloquent as Connick but more outwardly emotional, gave the speech he hoped would save his client from a lifetime in prison:

* * *

The questions *not* asked, says Mr. Connick, are important for you. So I ask you to step back and see what questions were not asked at the very beginning of this case.

The police found Jessie Ford after these horrible murders. And Jessie Ford was known to the police immediately as a narcotics addict with a large habit, arrested in what Officer Dillmann called a "shooting gallery."

Jessie Ford has lied all his life, not in the ordinary manner of a homosexual who does what he does in private, not as a homosexual who is also a female impersonator.

Jessie Ford is a female impersonator who lies to the public, and tries to convince them he is a woman, so he can have sex with them for money or rob them.

Jessie Ford did this since *age eleven*. So when the police first approached him, he was, if you step back from the case, an inherently questionable truthteller.

So the story is, on the day of the murders, Sylvester came by and said, "Smitty's going to come a little later on, and you're going for a ride to take care of those witnesses."

Jessie Ford says this happened around two or two-thirty. And Smitty came by around five-thirty, six o'clock.

If the police weren't overcome by this huge thing, motive, and therefore, suspicion, they would stand back and ask easy questions: Well, Mr. Ford, you knew Eddie Smith over a period of five years? You lived with him? You shared expenses with him? You broke bread with him? He's your friend? You say you didn't want to do this, it was against your will, you were just a pawn out of control?

Well, my God, Mr. Ford, if Sylvester came by your house at two, two-thirty, and told you this other man was going to come by a little later, why did you wait around?

Why did you sit on the front steps and wait, and go back and forth and wait, and wait, and wait until the man came? Why, Mr. Ford? Didn't you have a mother on Galvez Street? Didn't you have nine, ten, or eleven relatives with separate pieces of property in the city, out of the central city area? Why didn't you go there? Why didn't you leave, not be available as the pawn for the murders at Howard Johnson's?

But the police didn't ask those questions. They are important, easy questions. It doesn't take a genius. It doesn't take a brilliant defense attorney. It doesn't take a brilliant prosecutor. It takes common sense. It takes merely a desire to inquire.

Officer Dillmann told you he suspected my client from the very beginning, almost immediately after the killings, when he learned Paulette Royal and Eddie Smith were to be witnesses in the case against Sylvester. Essentially, the only thing on Dillmann's mind was Sylvester must have done it; so let's go out and prove it.

Dillmann wasn't concerned when he found Jessie Ford to learn if Jessie Ford told the truth. He was only concerned to prove out his theory, based on suspicion, based on the overwhelming motive they could ascribe to my client.

Now, aside from not asking the questions about the friendship, why would Jessie Ford wait around to do it? They didn't even ask the questions about whether or not Jessie Ford had prior contact with Eddie Smith and Paulette Royal. The prosecutor didn't ask it on direct examination.

Yes, there was prior contact. In the dark hours before that bloody Tuesday there was contact. Eddie Smith came down to Philip Street. Jessie Ford came out and spoke with Eddie Smith. The police were concerned about proving a theory they had fixed in their minds and were not making an openminded inquiry for the truth. They were out to prove Mr. Sylvester guilty.

And even Mr. Connick, in closing arguments today, said, "Why did we do all of these things? Why did we give all of these benefits to all these bad people? So we could prosecute David Sylvester."

That's a wrong attitude. That's not the way to approach the truth. What is Jessie Ford's motive for lying? Well, he faced a life sentence with forty years before he could even be eligible for parole.

That's a lot hanging over a man's head, and a lot of folks would have no trouble lying even a little bit to get out from under it. And Jessie Ford did it magnificently, didn't he?

Since he was eleven years old, he has been fooling men, and when he made twenty, he fooled the police, and he fooled the prosecutors. He convinced them and he got total immunity. He wasn't facing death. He wasn't facing life without benefit of parole for forty years. He wasn't facing a manslaughter charge with a maximum of twenty, or aggravated battery with a miximum of ten. He wasn't facing even a simple battery charge carrying six months, or a simple trespassing, which carries a fifty-dollar fine. Nothing! Absolutely nothing!

Is that a motive to distort the truth?

The police knew Jessie Ford had been to the motel. The police knew Jessie Ford was the instrument for entry into that motel room.

Throughout this trial, we have heard argument on what a principal is. Someone who aids, abets, encourages, enables, helps. Jessie Ford was a principal to first-degree murder. No penalties.

Well, the prosecution says we can't pick and choose our people. That's true. They can't pick and choose who are witnesses. But they should have perspective. They should have judgment. Instead, when they bought Jessie Ford at face value on the first day, they committed themselves. They could no longer prosecute Jessie Ford if it turned out Jessie Ford was a moving force in this thing.

Jessie Ford was in Room 215 of the Howard Johnson's motel. A man survived; Samuel Williams was alive after the killings. If Jessie Ford were to tell a story, he could not vary from the truth about what happened. So anything that corroborates his story at the Howard Johnson's motel room is irrelevant to whether the rest of it is truth.

If you will, Officer Dillmann told you he was concerned about Sylvester. Don't you think that wasn't communicated to Jessie Ford right off?

One thing Jessie Ford had going for him with that living witness, he didn't have one of the guns whose barrel was pressed against the head of Eddie Smith, Paulette Royal, or Samuel Williams. And so this live witness could say Jessie Ford didn't have a gun in his hand. And Jessie Ford could parlay that into his role as an unwilling participant. You want David Sylvester? Okay.

Did anyone corroborate Sylvester's supposed proposal that Jessie Ford make the trip to Alexandria? Only Jessie Ford.

Now, I don't understand why I have to go further to

show that Jessie Ford, who did not drive, was a most
unlikely candidate for anyone to solicit to rent a car. The
prosecution may suggest, since Jessie Ford was to point
out these people to somebody, that maybe somebody
else was going to drive. You didn't hear that from Jessie
Ford.

How about the incident at Two Jacks Bar? I asked,
"Mr. Ford, who else was in that back room?"

"Four or five dudes. They were gambling."

"In addition to Mr. Sylvester and Smitty?"

"Yes, in addition to them, five were gambling."

"Mr. Ford, are you familiar with Two Jacks? You
have been going there four, five, or six months regularly?"

"Yes, on weekends."

"Not Wednesday nights for the female impersonator
shows?"

"Oh, yes, Wednesday nights, too."

"You know a lot of people there?"

"Yes."

"Well, who were the other four or five people in the
back room gambling? Did you tell the police? Are they
here to corroborate? Who were they?"

"Oh, gee, I can't remember any of them. I don't
know who they were. I can't say anything about them."

The inherent incredibility of such a story! What are
we talking about? A $20,000 contract? Twenty thou-
sand dollars buys a New York Mafia–level operation
with hit men from Chicago or L.A. Isn't that what the
movies say? L.A. or Chicago or maybe Boston? *Who*
are we talking about? Are we talking about Jessie Ford,
who is vulnerable? A dope addict, a female impersonator, who would fold if you touched him on the head. Is
that the kind of person you choose to perform a $20,000

hit? Or, this guy Knucklehead? Or Clarence Davis? But $20,000 mentioned in front of four or five people gambling in a bar, it's incredible. And no corroboration of it is equally incredible.

There were witnesses around, says Jessie Ford. But where are the witnesses? The prosecution is not concerned about that because they say they have motive. And since the motive is so overriding, it overrode a good detective like Detective Dillmann. And it overrode the prosecutors in their desire to get Sylvester.

And Wilfred Kinn. Mr. Connick admits Kinn diverges in several particulars from other witnesses. Is that supposed to make Kinn honest, honorable, and believable?

The defense didn't cross-examine.

I mean, I'm far from the perfect defense attorney, but I heard the prior testimony. I heard Jessie Ford and Clarence Davis. And I heard no mention of meeting with Sylvester on the corner.

I mean, these are witnesses they gave the world to. Jessie Ford, did he say anything about running into Sylvester on the way to Howard Johnson's?

Wilfred Kinn testified because the way this case has been presented, ladies and gentlemen, the prosecution accumulated for you any snatch of anything from any witness—no matter how weak, unbelievable, or crazy —if it mentions Sylvester's name.

If this evil genius, Sylvester, this mastermind, just stepped back a minute, he'd see these killings were a bad idea.

If you were a clever, evil-minded, masterminding genius, would you arrange for the killing of two witnesses to testify in a trial against you that's *two days* away? Wouldn't you automatically think like the prosecutors want you to think? ''My God, the police will point the finger at me. I'm the one they'll nab.''

Isn't that what you would think if you were just *reasonably* intelligent? Not superiorly intelligent or clever?

When you heard Clarence Davis testify, did your blood rise against my client, Sylvester? Who made your blood boil? Jessie Ford! Jessie Ford!

Jessie Ford had a plan. He had prior contact with Eddie Smith. He brought a brown paper bag with the guns into the car. He went to the motel, and when they got there, he gave one gun to Nelson Grant Davis— Smitty—and one to Clarence Davis. And he went in, but before he went in, Jessie Ford knocked. And Eddie said, ''Who is it?'' Jessie Ford said, ''It's Cris.'' Nothing more, because he was expected.

That's what Clarence Davis told you, ''expected,'' and they went in. There was no pushing aside, as Jessie Ford said, by Nelson Grant Davis. No pushing aside. Jessie Ford was no pawn.

And so you wonder at that point, doesn't the prosecution realize Jessie Ford is the person who should have been prosecuted as the ''brains'' in the murder?

The only mention of Sylvester is Jessie Ford saying— these are his words, not what Mr. Connick said—these two witnesses were against Sylvester. That was the extent of it. Not they were going to eliminate witnesses against Sylvester; not that that was their plan; nothing like that.

In an automobile, the entire time, going to the motel and back, the only mention is Jessie Ford saying something about these two people who were witnesses against Sylvester. No witnesses to any money passing in advance for this horrible thing, no evidence.

Jessie Ford said he never received any money. Clarence Davis said he never received any money.

Why Sylvester? Why did the State make a deal with this sociopath, with Clarence Davis, this danger to society, this conscienceless man? Why? So he could say Jessie Ford mumbled something about the two witnesses involved in the Sylvester case! That's all he could say for the deal they gave him!

If you believe Jessie Ford, you can't believe Clarence Davis. If you believe Clarence Davis, you can't believe Jessie Ford.

If you believe Jessie Ford, he was forced under gunpoint to go to the Howard Johnson's motel. If you believe Clarence Davis, Jessie Ford provided the two guns.

If you believe Jessie Ford, he knocked on the door as a pawn in the hands of these ruthless killers. And if you believe Clarence Davis, Jessie Ford had prior knowledge and an arrangement to get in the door.

If you believe Jessie Ford, he had nothing to do with what went on in the room. He stood there because he was captive. And if you believe Clarence Davis, Jessie Ford gave him the pillow.

If you believe Jessie Ford, Knucklehead said something in the car about keeping the weapons in case Sylvester got out of hand. And if you believe Clarence Davis, there was no mention of Sylvester in the car going back to the Calliope Project, ultimately to drop off the other two.

If you believe Jessie Ford, this poor, poor captive of circumstance, he was dropped off at his house on Philip Street. If you believe Clarence Davis, Jessie Ford was dropped off with Knucklehead in front of Two Jacks.

If you believe Jessie Ford, there were hand signals

with Sylvester in front of Two Jacks as they were getting out. If you believe Clarence Davis, there was no communication between Sylvester and Nelson Davis.

There is a reasonable question each of you must ask: What are the prosecutorial functions in bringing a case to trial?

I think if you walk along with me through the plea-bargaining arrangements with Jessie Ford, the question becomes: Are we interested in justice, or are we interested in hooking somebody we think in our guts *might be* guilty? Somebody we think might be a bad man? Making an example to the citizenry, that witnesses can't be killed; therefore, put Sylvester away!

What are the proper prosecutorial functions? Well, you heard Mr. Cerniglia say, "We, in the office, prosecute borderline cases." That was his testimony from the witness stand.

Maybe Mr. Connick, when he stands up again, will tell you what he meant by that. We believe he is guilty, but the evidence is borderline? Therefore, we'll present it in Court, even though we lose?

Borderline case. Hard-line office. No plea-bargaining with guilty people. But we'll give Jessie Ford total immunity.

It all comes down to very simple things. Very simple things. If the police don't have any obligations before they arrest to prove guilt beyond a reasonable doubt, they have to act on reasonable suspicion. And even if it's distorted, like a blinkered horse walking down the street unable to see right or left, it can be reasonable.

Guilt beyond a reasonable doubt is a standard sacred in our system of justice.

Your liberty is at stake in the case, your life. So the prosecution doesn't only have to show you there's a probability the defendant did it, doesn't even have to show you it's clearly more likely than not that the defendant did it. He has to show you beyond a *reasonable doubt*.

Now, when we act in our daily lives and make important decisions, often the information on each side is closely weighed. And you're not sure how to tip the scale, whether or not to make that investment, to buy that car, or increase your monthly money burden. You don't know. But you don't act on information beyond a reasonable doubt in those cases. You make a decision based on the best information available.

But in a Court of criminal law, you can only act against a defendant if the defendant has been proven guilty beyond a reasonable doubt, if every reasonable doubt has been eliminated.

On voir dire, you were all asked, would the idea that Mr. Sylvester might be a bad person prevent you from giving him every benefit of a reasonable doubt. You said, "No."

On voir dire, you were asked whether the possibility or probability that Mr. Sylvester was a bad man, a dope dealer, what have you, would that make it easier for the prosecution to prove him guilty? Your answers were, "No."

In a criminal case, when you enter a verdict of not guilty, you do not find the defendant innocent. You find only that the proof was not sufficient beyond a reasonable doubt, to say to a moral satisfaction, that he is guilty.

I think the evidence in this case, for the first time tested by someone who does not have a policeman's attitude of suspicion, or a prosecutor's action motivated by whatever they're motivated by, someone testing from

the other side, the first time, any of this evidence—
Jessie Ford, Clarence Davis, Wilfred Kinn, Officer
Dillmann—the first time their information was ever
tested by someone whose objective was to get to the
truth occurred in this courtroom yesterday.

Anything that went before yesterday was intent solely
on prosecuting this man.

In the courtroom yesterday they were over here. I was
over there. The judge was in the middle. The rules of
evidence were followed and the rules created to give
fairness and truth were followed. They have been tested.
The evidence has been tested. The prosecution's evidence out of the mouths of their own witnesses has been
tested. By the trial, by fire of cross-examination.

Your duty is sacred. You have had a terribly fascinating view of another world, of promises and motivation.
You have determinations of credibility and believability
to make.

I can only ask you to uphold your oath and follow
your sacred duty, as neutral jurors, as a cross-section of
the community, as the conscience of the community, in
determining the road between prosecutorial overreach-
ing and the liberty of a citizen. And I ask you to do that.
Thank you.

Seldom have I heard a defense attorney not close his case
with, "And I ask you to return a verdict of not guilty against
my client."

Glass didn't do it, and I think the omission was deliberate.
He didn't feel he had to ask. To him, the state's case didn't
measure up.

Nor did Glass hammer on his client's innocence, though
surely he believed in it. According to the law, the state had to
prove its case, and it failed. Glass expected his and

Connick's intelligent jury to see that, do its duty—guilt or innocence didn't matter, a higher principle applied here: the constitutionally critical presumption of innocence—and set Sylvester free.

William Wessel addressed the jurors last, but I believe they knew they'd already heard all that counted. Generally, Wessel low-keyed the jury through what amounted to a rerun of Connick's statement, event after event, too many ever for them to be coincidences, pointing the finger of guilt at David Sylvester. He, too, aimed at the jury's intelligence.

The prosecution played hardball right to the finish. Just as he approached the conclusion of his statement, Wessel wheeled, and dramatically pointed at Sylvester: "That man is a killer in more ways than one!"

Glass came out of his chair, livid. "Your Honor, please!"

"He killed two people," said Wessel innocently.

But hadn't Wessel really meant more than that? Hadn't he meant people dead on the streets from heroin? What did he mean?

"I sustain the objection," ruled Judge Ward. "Disregard that remark."

But could it be disregarded?

The jury stayed out three hours. I was drinking coffee in the middle of the afternoon with Dantagnan when we learned a verdict had been reached. Fred hurried with me to the courtroom.

I sat on the prosecution side, thinking *three hours doesn't tell anything*. Three hours meant the jury had reviewed the evidence and hadn't quarreled over the verdict.

What verdict?

The inclusion or exclusion of one word—the word *not*—would affect several lives for many years to come. I looked at

Connick, his face a deathly white. And at Sylvester, fingers intertwined beneath his chin, head bowed, as if in prayer.

One word. *Please,* I thought, *not* a *"not."*

"We the jury find the defendant, David Joseph Sylvester" —here it comes, always preceded by a pause, the pause always seeming longer than in reality it is—"guilty of . . ."

I clutched Fred's hand and squeezed it.

"They nailed the son of a bitch," he said.

AFTERWORD

Sergeant Paul Melancon, testifying during the murder trial of Nelson Grant Davis, described the February 2, 1978, arrest in New Orleans of the man who pulled the trigger on Paulette Royal and Eddie Smith. At the time, Melancon and his partner were investigating an unconnected case.

I was standing up and talking to the male and the female, standing right by the kitchen looking down the hall, as Detective Reed searched the hall closet, which is located on the left-hand side. At this time, Officer Reed screamed. I saw this subject come out of the closet and start fighting with Officer Reed. I went to Officer Reed's assistance. The fight continued down a hall and into a bedroom located at the rear of the residence. The struggle went on for a few minutes.

It was, in fact, a ferocious battle, won by the police, which left all three bruised and battered. If Nelson Davis had kept a gun within reach, I didn't doubt he'd have kept his promise not to be taken alive. As it was, I testified at the trial, prosecuted ably by Nick Noriea, that found Davis guilty of two counts of murder. He and David Sylvester occupy cells in the same prison, Angola.

Harry Connick is still the district attorney in New Orleans. To this day he doesn't handle many cases personally. Anyone wondering about his competence to do so, however, well, I wish that individual could have seen him up against Sylvester during two glorious days in November 1976.

I talked with Robert Glass recently. He still steadfastly holds to David Sylvester's innocence. With more than a decade to think it over, and numerous glittering victories in between, he now thinks the jury didn't lack in intelligence, but in respect for the law as written. The jury heard the word *heroin* so often, Glass believes, it didn't matter to them what charge Sylvester faced; he deserved punishment, and they gave it to him.

I respect Glass very much but disagree with him 100 percent on the Sylvester trial. Perhaps the great poet Ralph Waldo Emerson said it best:

> Finish every day and be done with it. You have done what you could; some blunders and absurdities crept in; forget them as soon as you can. Tomorrow is a new day; you shall begin it well and serenely and with too high a spirit to be encumbered with your old nonsense.

BLOOD
WARNING

The True Story of the New Orleans Slasher
by JOHN DILLMANN

The shocking true story of a ruthless killer, told by the detective who tracked him down.

On the day before Thanksgiving, 1980, Detective John Dillmann was summoned to the scene of a homicide in New Orleans. What he found that day was the most savage and bizarre killing he had ever seen. And it was not to be the last…

Coming soon in hardcover to bookstores everywhere.

G. P. PUTNAM'S SONS